From the foreword:

"... When I realized where he was going with this story, my first reaction was, 'He isn't going to be able to pull this one off.' Not without getting trite, or cute, or moralistic—or falling into any number of the many pitfalls I foresaw with regard to this material. I was wrong. He not only avoided them all, he told a fantastically engaging story with consummate grace and genuine artistry."

—Roger Zelazny

TO REIGN IN HELL

STEVEN BRUST

WITH A FOREWORD BY ROGER ZELAZNY

ACE FANTASY BOOKS
NEW YORK

Lines from the song "November Song" copyright © 1984 by Mark Henley. Used by permission of Mark Henley.

Lines from the song "Friend of the Devil" copyright © 1970 by Ice Nine Publishing Company, Inc. Music by Jerry Garcia and John Dawson; words by Robert Hunter. Used by permission of Ice Nine Publishing Company, Inc.

TO REIGN IN HELL

An Ace Fantasy Book/published by arrangement with
the author

PRINTING HISTORY
SteelDragon Press edition published 1984
Ace edition/May 1985

ISBN: 0-441-81496-4

Ace Fantasy Books are published by The Berkley Publishing Group,
200 Madison Avenue, New York, New York 10016.
PRINTED IN THE UNITED STATES OF AMERICA

This book was written for my wife, Reen, whom I love and cherish.

"Wheresoever she was, *there* was Eden."
—Mark Twain

Acknowledgments

My thanks to my first readers and critics, Martin Schafer and John Robey, and to Pat Wrede, Kara Dalkey, Pamela Dean, and the rest of our writers' group for much helpful criticism. Special thanks to Emma Bull and Will Shetterly for angelic patience and persistence in tweaking the final drafts. Also, thanks to Joel Halpern for technical assistance, to my agent, Valerie Smith, for her encouragement, and to editor Terri Windling and proofreeders Nate Bucklin and Jon Singer for very fine jobs. Last, thanks to Pamela Dean for corrections on the Elizabethan English.

Foreword

It was almost by accident that I read the MS of Steven Brust's *To Reign in Hell*. Actually, it was because of a courtesy on the part of the author, the story of which is not terribly material here. But that's why I said "almost." I can't really consider a character trait an accident.

I read the beginning to see what he was doing. I don't know him personally. I know little about him, save what I can tell from his writing. When I realized where he was going with this story, my first reaction was, "He isn't going to be able to pull this one off." Not without getting trite, or cute, or moralistic—or falling into any number of the many pitfalls I foresaw with regard to this material. I was wrong. He not only avoided them all, he told a fantastically engaging story with consummate grace and genuine artistry. I had not seen anything really new done with this subject since Anatole France's *Revolt of the Angels*, with the possible exception of Taylor Caldwell's *Dialogues with the Devil*. And frankly, Brust's book is a more ambitious and successful work than *Dialogues*.

My immediate reaction was to provide one of those brief dust jacket comments containing a few loaded adjectives and to hope that this would help call some attention to the book and sell a few extra copies. "A hell of a good book" or "A damned fine story" sprang to mind, because I am what I am—and they're both true, despite the flippancy. But on reflection I knew that that would not be enough, because I am not always so fortunate as to encounter a writer as good as Steven Brust this early in his career. This is because there is so much science fiction and fantasy being published these days—and some of it very good—that it would be a full-time job just trying to keep up with the best as it appears. I have to be selective in my reading and I miss a lot. But this time I was lucky, and I owe it to this kind of talent to remark upon it when I see it.

(I should add, here, that I have also read his other two books—*Jhereg* and *Yendi*—and that they are a part of the reason I am hitting these typewriter keys.)

A dust jacket blurb only gives an opinion without reasons, and I need a little more room because I feel obliged to tell you why I like Steven Brust's stories: Most good writers have one or two strong points for which they are known, and upon which they rely to carry a tale to its successful conclusion. Excellent plotting, say, can carry a story even if the writing itself is undistinguished. One can live with this. Good plotting is a virtue. Fine writing is a pleasure. A graceful prose stylist is a treat to read—even if the author is shaky when it comes to plotting or characterization. And then there are the specialists in people, who can entertain and delight with their development of character, their revelations—even if they are not strong plotters or powerful descriptive writers. And there are masters and mistresses of dialogue who can make you feel as if you are witnessing an engaging play, and you can almost forget the setting and the story while trying to anticipate what one of the characters will say next. And so on and so on.

Yes.

Yes, I feel that Steven Brust has this whole catalog of virtues—solid plotting, good prose, insightful characterizations and fine dialogue.

Going further, he has those little tricks of ironic wordplay which appeal. —"'Milord,' called Beelzebub, 'get thee behind me.'" It tickles.

And there is his use of the fabulous. Pure science fiction is, ultimately, cut-and-dried, explaining everything in the end.

Pure fantasy generally does not explain enough. A writer who respects the rational yet pays homage to the dark areas where all is not known also has my respect, as herein lies a higher level of verisimilitude, mirroring life, which really is that way. It is that mixture of light and darkness which fascinates me, personally. It is a special kind of *mimesis*, cutting across the categories—and here, too, Mr. Brust wields a finely honed blade.

A rare, resourceful writer, who has distinguished himself in my mind this early in his career, Steven Brust: I feel he is worth noting now, for what he will achieve eventually, as well as for what he has already done.

—Roger Zelazny

Angels and mortals
    Fight for the right
To have a little pleasure
    And enjoy an easy flight.

Angels and mortals
    Sometimes get their way. . . .

                    —Mark Henley,
                    "November Song"

FLUX

FLUX

NORTHERN
Regency

Western
Regency

Eastern
Regency

Southern
Regency

FLUX

© 1983
MORSCHALL

W   E

S

SOUTHERN HOLD

HEAVEN

Prologue

I was set up everlasting, from the
beginning, or ever the earth was.

Before the mountains were settled,
before the hills, was I brought forth.

—Proverbs, 8:23-24

Snow, tenderly caught by eddying breezes, swirled and spun
in to and out of bright, lustrous shapes that gleamed against
the emerald-blazoned black drape of sky and sparkled there for
a moment, hanging, before settling gently to the soft, green-
tufted plain with all the sickly sweetness of an over-written
sentence.

The Regent of the South looked upon this white-on-black-
over-green perfection and he saw that it was revolting. His
eyes, a green that was positively startling, narrowed, and his
nostrils flared.

The being next to him took the shape of an animal that would someday be called a golden retriever. It shook its head and snorted, since barking was yet a few millennia away.

"My gorge rises to think on't," said the dog.

The Regent nodded without speaking.

The other continued, "I mind a time when thou didst delight to see decadence."

"I mind a time when there were things other than decadence to compare it to."

"Verily," the dog admitted. "But think'st thou this can last forever?"

The Regent shrugged. "No, I know it won't. The Wave is still recent; its effects linger. Soon enough, form will be form again, and jokes like this will be too difficult to be worth the bother. But it sickens me."

"Whose working is this then, milord?" the dog asked.

"It doesn't matter," said the Regent. "One of our archbrethren, certainly. Maybe it was whoever put Marfiel into a six-day sleep so she missed the harvest. It's the same stupid sense of humor."

"Certes thou art aware of that thou hast earned: to relax thy vigilance and enjoy this time, as thy archbrethren do."

The Regent shook his head. "Perhaps," he said, "that is my own form of decadence."

The smaller one laughed and wagged his tail.

It had hard green scales, fiery red eyes, and a long forked tongue, and was several times what would become known as man-high someday. You may as well call it a dragon and have done with it. It was the Regent of the North.

It—he? He, then. He lived far in the north of Heaven, beneath mountains known for vulcanism. He had carved places out of the rock at the heart of the mountain, where he could feel warm and safe.

His former shape had been lost near the end of the Third Wave, and he had taken this one. It was very resistant to the effects of the flux. His breath could break any material down to its basic components, or turn a wave of cacoastrum into living illiaster.

None of the new angels entered the Northern Regency, and no one at all lived there, save the Regent. All feared him, for it was said that he was mad, that he had been wounded deeply, and it was unsafe to be near him.

Alone, unchanging, nursing his rage and his fear, the Regent of the North turned in his sleep. The Third Wave was over now, but when the next came, he would wake.

League upon league upon league of sea rose in temperature by exactly one and a half degrees, and she basked in it. The tip of her tail broke the water and waved snake-like (had there been snakes) for a bit and then a bit. The water was a blue that an artist would despair of capturing. Above, the air smelled of the sea.

Her sea! Here she was the master. As the last effects of the raw cacoastrum vanished, she found she could command this water by an effort of will, for it was hers.

The Second Wave had driven her to create and enter the sea, forsaking her form in order to live. She could have used the free illiaster from the Third Wave to recreate her old form, but she would not leave the protection the waters gave her. And she had come to love the flowing, breathing sensuality of the currents, caressing and soothing her.

The green coiled length of her body straightened, and she closed her eyes as she accepted the warmth into herself. She sent forth a laugh that reverberated through the waters, which picked it up and carried it, as fresh currents, to every shore.

The Regent of the West was at peace, for a while. Let us leave her there.

The Youth With Golden Locks looked to the west. He rested his left hand upon the golden hilt of the shaft of scarlet light that hung from his waist and reached down to his knees. He was dressed in a tunic of light brown that called attention to his remote blue eyes. He, the Regent of the East, was a proper half-a-head taller than the black-haired, dark woman who stood at his side and caressed his arm.

She scrutinized him for a moment, then shook her head.

"Too much," she remarked.

He shrugged, and darkened his complexion a shade or two.

"Better," she said. "But the hair is still overdoing it a bit, don't you think?"

"If you say so," said the youth, and eased the curls somewhat, darkened the tone. As the woman studied this version, impatience crossed the Regent's face.

"Forget it," he snapped. "It just isn't me."

She shrugged. "As you wish."

His hair grew lighter again, his form taller and thinner, and his skin took on an aspect of transparency. "We're not going to be able to do this much longer," he said. "The effects of the Wave have nearly worn off."

"It doesn't matter," she said, soothingly.

"I don't understand this concern everyone suddenly has with appearance, anyway."

"What else is there to be concerned with? I expect things will occur soon enough, but for now—"

"I suppose. But is there any reason for *me* to spend all this time working on a form that I never look at anyway?"

"Maybe not. But as a Regent, I should think—"

"That's another thing. There was a time when it actually meant something to be a Regent."

"I remember."

"When we first created this place," he gestured vaguely around them, "it meant that I was responsible for a quarter of the terrain of Heaven. And it was needed then. Our brethren from the Second and Third Waves needed guidance and leadership. But we're secure now. There hasn't been an influx in thousands of days. And if there *is* another, Yaweh will call us—"

"You certainly are in a foul mood today, aren't you?"

He stopped. "You're right," he said after a moment. "Sorry."

"It's all right. Is there something I can do?"

She said it with no special emphasis, but he suddenly felt the grass beneath his bare feet grow thicker and longer.

"Yes," he said. "I think so."

The healer was tall, full-bodied, and pale of complexion. She wore a gold cloak over white garments. A silver chain around her waist held a six-pointed star. She faced the sword-bearer, who was large, well-muscled, and brown haired. He, also, wore a cloak of gold.

"Yaweh," he said, "wants to put it in his throne room, in a case, next to his sceptre."

"Fitting," she said. "I suppose it is cumbersome—and you don't need it now."

"Not for a while, at any rate. And I'm near to the Palace, so I can easily fetch it when I need it."

The healer studied the massive sword which the other carried over his right shoulder. Then she looked away.

"I hope," she said, "that you don't need it for a long time."

He nodded without speaking.

He stood in the center of Heaven and looked about it, having chosen to have four eyes today. He noticed that with less than two looking in any one direction, he couldn't see as well as he ought. He resolved to set someone to discover the reason for this.

Outside of Heaven, cacoastrum still did its mindless, eternal dance of destruction. One day, he knew, he and his brethren would face it again, for that was the way of the universe. When that happened, he would again feel the sorrow of losing his brothers, perhaps one of those who had been with him from the beginning. He would know the joy of seeing new ones created from illiaster, and the pleasure of watching them become aware of themselves and the others around them, but nothing could heal the pain of loss.

Again, as he had so many times before, he wondered if there couldn't be a way to end the conflict forever.

He sighed, and, with his four eyes, looked about the ways of Heaven. He saw that it was good. But not quite good enough.

Second Prologue

"There's plenty of pain here—but it
    don't kill.
There's plenty of suffering here, but it
don't last. You see, happiness ain't a
thing in itself—it's only a *contrast* with
something that ain't pleasant."

—Mark Twain, "Extract from
Captain Stormfield's Visit to Heaven"

"There seems to be a lot of work left to do on it," said the
Regent of the South. "All you have is the barest outline."

"I know," said Yaweh, "but what do you think of it so far?"

The Regent licked his lips. "I . . . to be honest, I'm afraid
of it—afraid to hope for it. It seems like a dream. Of course,
it's what we've always wanted, but—I don't know, Yaweh.
Can it be done?"

"I think so. The one who'd be best at it is working on the
details; he thinks so."

The Regent raised a brow over a bright green eye. "Lucifer?"

Yaweh smiled. "Who else? He and Lilith are—" He stopped, as a look of pain crossed the Regent's face. "What is it, old friend?"

The other shook his head, then smiled, ruefully. "Lilith."

"I'm sorry I—"

"Don't, Yaweh. If everyone had to apologize for all the hearts Lilith's broken, we could hardly speak to each other."

Yaweh studied him closely. "Does she know how much hurt she causes?"

"She didn't do any hurting. I did it to myself. It was stupid, really. I wanted her to move into the Hold with me. She wasn't sure, and I tried to push her, without thinking, and—" He punctuated the sentence with a shrug.

Yaweh studied him somberly for a moment, then sighed. "I wish there was something I could do for you."

The Regent shook his head. "It doesn't matter. I'll get over it. Maybe it'll teach me something. But enough. What do you want me to do?"

Yaweh cleared his throat. "In order to accomplish this, we need the cooperation of every angel in Heaven. But when I mentioned the plan to one of the angels who dwells here, he had a strange reaction. Rather than being excited by the idea, he was frightened by it."

The Regent's eyes widened. "Why?"

"There will be some danger associated with it. I don't know how much yet, but certainly some. He understood that, and was more frightened by the plan than happy with the idea of the safety that would follow." He shrugged. "It's natural, now that I think of it. Most angels remember little or nothing of their first Wave—the one that created them. Our hatred of the flux comes later."

"I don't believe that any angel could fail to see what we gain with this, Yaweh. We may have to explain it to them, but certainly not more than that."

Yaweh sighed. "I hope you're right."

"I am," said the other. "It may take a little time, that's all."

"I hope you're right," he repeated. "In any case, Lucifer will be coming this evening, and we'll go over the general plans then, and discuss things in more detail. There is an archangel named Uriel who can help you—"

"Help me *what*, Yaweh? You still haven't told me."

"Let me save it for tonight."

The Regent looked at him closely. "Whatever it is, you don't like it, do you?" Yaweh shook his head. The Regent changed the subject. "I'll want to go back to the Hold soon. It's quite a walk."

"All right. But can you wait until tomorrow? It's been a long time since you've slept under my roof. We'll be having some pin-dancing. I would be pleased," he added.

"All right, old friend," said the other. "I'll stay the night. Have you brandy?"

Yaweh nodded. They both stood at once, as if a hidden message had come to them, and embraced. "I don't see you often enough," said Yaweh.

"Heaven has grown too large," said Satan.

One

Descend, then! I could also say: Ascend!
'Twere all the same. Escape from the
      Created
To shapeless forms in liberated spaces!
Enjoy what long ere this was dissipated!

—Goethe, *Faust*

Primordial ooze. Flux. Chaos. Cacoastrum.

The essential of the universe, in all its myriad forms and shapes. Essence.

Any and all combinations of form and shape exist within this essence. Eventually, of course, cacoastrum may deny itself. Order within chaos.

How many times is order created? The question has no meaning. A tree falls in the forest, and the universe hears it. Order doesn't last; cacoastrum will out.

The flux creates the essence of order, which is illiaster, which was the staff of life long before bread had the privilege.

11

It can't last, however. Conscious? Sentient? Self-aware? Perhaps these things exist for a timeless instant, only to be lost again before they can begin to understand. They may have shape; they may have the seeds of thoughts—none of this matters. One of them may be a unicorn, another a greyish stone of unknown properties, still another a girl-child with big brown eyes who vanishes before she really appears. It doesn't matter.

But let us give to one of these forms something new. Let us give it, for the sake of argument, an instinct to survive. Ah! Now the game is different, you see.

So this form resists, and strives to hold itself together. And as it strives, cacoastrum and illiaster produce more illiaster, and consciousness produces more consciousness, and now there are two.

The two of them strive; and then they find that they can communicate, and time means something now. And space, as well.

As they work together, to hold onto themselves, a third one appears. They find that they can bend the cacoastrum to their will, and force shape upon it, and command it to hold, for a while. They build walls at this place where the three of them are, and a top and a bottom.

Cacoastrum howls, almost as a living thing itself, and seeks entry. The three resist, and then there are four, then five, then six, then seven.

And the seven finish the walls, and the top, and the bottom and for a moment, at last, there is peace from the storm.

The Southern Wall of Heaven stretched long and stark. It spanned six hundred leagues and more, fading out of sight above, where it met with the azure ceiling. Its length was unmarked; its width unmeasured; its touch cool; its look foreboding and ageless.

The Regent had built it in the days of the Second Wave, and expanded it in the days of the Third. He had built his home into it, and out from it.

The foundations of the Southern Hold were deep into the bedrock of Heaven, carved and scorched with the fires of Belial, made immutable by the sceptre of Yaweh. Plain and grey like the Wall, the Hold rose over grassland and stoney plain, even and unbroken until its northern wall ended abruptly and became a roof that sloped sharply up to the top. There it blended into the Wall, giving the impression that the entire affair was an accidental blister from the Wall and would soon sink back into it.

The only entrance was built into the northern wall of the Hold. Here were placed a pair of massive oak doors, with finely carved wooden handles.

A visitor to the Hold, no matter how often he had been there, would be moved by the stature of the hard grey edifice—lonely, cold, distant, and proud. Like the Regent of the South himself, some said. But once inside, the illusion was shattered.

The visitor, a medium-sized golden haired dog, padded through the hallway. Being a dog, and therefore colorblind, he didn't see the cheerful blue of the walls. But he noticed the brightness of the lamps of iron and glass, one every twenty dogpaces. The oil for the lamps, pressed from local vegetation and refined in the basement of the Hold, had been scented with lilac.

The dog continued until he came to an archway. There was a small chamber, with large green couches and overstuffed chairs. The north wall held a burgundy-colored buffet, with cups and bottles of cut glass and stoneware. The lamps were always low in this room, but the dog heard the sounds of breathing, and smelled a friend.

He leapt onto a couch, facing this friend across a table of glass. Neither spoke; the dog moved slightly toward the Regent, who was seated with one leg on the table, his left arm across the back of the couch, his right hand loosely holding a glass into which he was staring. The dog caught a strong, sweet smell from the glass.

"'Tis but cheap wine, milord," he said.

"It fits my mood, friend Beelzebub. I'm feeling cheap today."

"Hath thy mood a cause, Lord?"

"All things have a cause, my friend."

"Would'st care to speak on't?"

His answer was silence. Beelzebub studied his friend as best he could in the dim light. The Regent was smooth shaven and somewhat dark of complexion. His hair was dark brown, almost black, perhaps a bit wavy, and curled over the ears. His brows were thick, his eyes narrow, yet wide-set, with shocking green irises and lines of humor or anger around the edges. His jaw was strong, his nose straight and pronounced; and he wore colors matching his eyes beneath a cloak that was full and gold. Brown boots covered his feet, and upon his chest was an emerald, as large as his fist, on a chain of gold.

Beelzebub studied him for a moment longer. "Perchance 'twould do thee good to speak, Lord Satan."

The Regent set down his wine glass, found a small bowl, and poured into it.

"Maybe. Drink."

The dog moved forward on the couch, sniffed, but kept his opinion to himself. He lapped up a bit and managed not to shudder.

"What do you, friend Beelzebub, think of Yaweh's plans regarding the Fourth Wave?"

"Milord? Then it draweth nigh?"

"Who can say? It'll come eventually."

"Soon?"

"Not that we know. But Yaweh wants to be ready this time. He wants to build a place that will be safe from the flux."

"Verily, have we not that now?"

"Not permanently. What he has in mind is a place that's complete by itself, and won't be subject to Waves at all."

"Hmmm. Ambitious, nay?"

Satan glanced at him sharply. "You sound skeptical."

"Thy pardon, milord—who is't shall build this place? They must deal with the outside, so they must needs risk the ultimate end. Who is't shall do this? Thyself and thy brethren? You are strong, but only seven. Those of us from the Second Wave? We're less than a score of scores; the task is beyond us. Those of the Third Wave? Aye, they can do't, milord. Will they? For they know naught of such things save the fear of them. They must needs see the danger ere they fight it, I fear."

"You have a way," said Satan, "of getting right to the heart of things."

"It cannot last," says the first.

"We will make it last," says the second.

"We will build walls that are yet stronger," says the third.

"They must be larger," says the fourth, "for there will be more of us."

"That is good," says the second.

"Aye," says the first. "Let us begin, then, for I see the walls crumble before me."

And the evening and the morning are the Second Wave.

"Milord?"

"Hmmm—yes?"

"Thou seem'd befuddled."

"I was thinking. Sorry." He shook his head. "Maybe they do need a Wave before they can understand—that's what Yaweh was afraid of—but I don't think so. We, the Firstborn, didn't, and we are all of the illiaster. No, I think our brethren will aid us."

"Perchance, milord. An they do not?"

"Have more wine."

Beelzebub felt the hair above his eyebrows twitch, and he bent his ears forward. "I have not yet finished the dregs of this bowl thou hast poured. An they do not aid us, Lord Satan?"

"Perhaps some brandy, then. I've some as a gift from—"

Beelzebub felt his ears lie back against his head. "Milord," he barked, "I crave an answer! Suppose our younger brethren aid us not? What then wilt thou do?"

Satan sighed and sat back. This time Beelzebub remained silent.

"All right," said the Regent at last, "what if they don't? What if we do nothing? I've been thinking about this for the last twenty days, Beelzebub. I haven't been able to find an answer I like. What if they don't help us, and we do nothing? What then?"

"The task will not see its end."

"And eventually another Wave will come. We'll lose more friends."

"Aye."

"If the angels from the Third Wave help with the plan, we can save tens of thousands—millions—of our future brethren."

"Aye."

"So it is in everyone's interest that they help, even if they don't know it."

"Aye."

"So we have the right to coerce them."

"Nay."

"I agree."

"But—"

"Or rather, I'm unsure. Yaweh isn't sure. Michael isn't sure. Lucifer is sure and Raphael is sure. We haven't spoken to Belial or Leviathan."

Beelzebub absent-mindedly lapped up wine from his bowl and then rested his head on his forepaws. "Meseemeth," he said at last, "that thou and thy friends have taken much upon you e'en to think on't."

"I agree," said Satan. He shrugged. "Nothing like this has come up before." He drained his glass. "I admit it, Beelzebub: I have doubts. I reassured Yaweh, but his questions have worn off on me."

Beelzebub looked up as Satan's voice rose.

"You think we can sit here asking ourselves if what we do is right, while the Storm rages out there? Do *I* think so? By what right do I argue the right and wrong of saving millions of lives? Answer me that!" Satan gave a short laugh. "Coercion? We are the ones being coerced. By *that*." He gestured vaguely southward.

"How so, milord?"

He shook his head. "Lucifer is right, as usual. We know that we risk all of Heaven, if we do nothing. Each Wave has come nearer to destroying us completely—Lucifer proved it with numbers, somehow. Sooner or later, we'll have to do something." He laughed again, bitterly. "No, I shouldn't say that the flux outside is coercing us; what is coercing us is our own understanding. We can't know what the problem is, and know what to do about it, without acting. That is our curse."

Beelzebub watched him, his mind unclear but his heart filled with pity. "Thinkest thou to have no choice at all, then?"

"The greater one's understanding, Beelzebub, the less choice one has. For the love of Heaven itself, my friend—if you can, remain ignorant!"

The dog lowered his head and his voice. "Then thou hast chosen, milord? An the hosts wish not to help thy plan?"

Satan stood. His eyes flashed green fires; his cloak shone gold in the flickering light. Two paces brought him to the buffet, where he grasped a brown stoneware bottle. He brought it back to the table, throwing the cork impatiently to the floor. He sloshed red-hued liquid into his glass, unmindful of the spillage. He slammed the bottle down, then lifted and drained the glass. He fixed Beelzebub with his gaze.

"Then," he said icily, "it is my task to make them."

Yaweh stood by the Sword of Michael, regarding it in its glass case. He stood in a spacious chamber of white curtains, tiled floor, and silvery walls. Toward the back was a throne—huge and gold. Opposite the case was another case, this one holding a large sceptre, also of gold. A great arched doorway opposed the throne.

The room had been designed by Yaweh, who wished it to be bare and unimposing. Those who entered, by dress and attitude, set its mood; it had none of its own. Here, Yaweh could address the archangels, all three hundred, if needed. He blended in so well that he nearly wasn't there.

Next to him, regarding the case, was an archangel. He was of the Second Wave, and small, thin, and black-bearded. A brief glance would lead one to think his frame slight; a closer look would reveal chest and shoulder muscles confined within the frame as though trapped and held in place with iron bands.

Yaweh turned from the case to him.

"You build well, Asmodai."

"Thank you, Lord. I am pleased. It served well in the Third Wave."

"Yes, it did. As did my sceptre, and Satan's emerald, and—but why go on? I am pleased with with your work. Now I want more."

"Anything I can do, Lord."

Yaweh smiled at him and placed a hand on his shoulder. "Thank you, Asmodai. This means a great deal to me, and to all of us. Come, I'll show you what I want. It isn't small, I'm afraid."

Yaweh was overcome with a great fondness for the little craftsman, but that wasn't unusual. He had never felt anything but fondness for anyone, and the occasional enmity between angels left him sad and puzzled.

They turned from the Sword and left the room.

A wide, sweeping stairway of white marble brought them up and around amid paintings and sculpture in a large hallway of bone-white walls. Some of the art wasn't very good—but Yaweh took delight in the joy of an artist whose work was placed here, so he rarely had the heart to say that a piece wasn't good enough.

They walked, arm in arm, until they came to a small chamber containing a long table covered with papers.

"Here, Asmodai. This is what we plan to make."

Asmodai spread the parchment and began studying it. By increments, wonder and amazement spread over his features. "My Lord," he cried, "but this is. . . ."

"Large?" suggested Yaweh, gentle amusement on his face.

"Aye, large! It's bigger than Heaven itself!"

"Many times bigger."

"My Lord—where will we *put* it?"

"Outside, of course. It will exist amid the flux, just as heaven does."

"How can that be?"

"It will be your task to discover this, my friend. It will require nearly everyone working together, and many days at that. And the longer we're out there, the more of us will be maimed or destroyed. So we must decide exactly how this is to be put together, what each angel is to do, so that we can spend the shortest amount of time at it. This is your task, if you are willing to undertake it."

"Lord! I cannot—"

"If you cannot, there is no one who can. You know what it takes to build from raw cacoastrum, and that is what we need. Your name is tied to the Sword, the Sceptre, the Throne, the Star, and many more things. You are trusted—and deservedly so. If you cannot, who can?"

Asmodai was silent for a long time. Yaweh knew what he was thinking—he was thinking of the greatness of the triumph if he succeeded, and the magnitude of the failure if he didn't. But Yaweh himself had asked him to—and that would make a difference.

"I'll do it, Lord," said Asmodai. "I'll try."

It rages, it cries, it tears and bites and burns. The first one is nearly overcome, but holds himself together despite the violence of the flux. The second is filled with rage, and it falls back before him. He causes a wall to be, and envisions his home extending from the wall. He doesn't see the scores of beings that come into existence as he rages and shapes, nor do the others see the results of their actions, except as their area becomes larger.

The third one goes to the aid of the first, but his help is no longer needed. They stand near each other, and cacoastrum flares yellow and red and blue, and dies, turning into illiaster, which shapes itself.

Some of the new ones are destroyed even as they come into existence. The first one, alone of the Seven, notices this and is saddened by it.

The sixth one is suddenly overborne. She cries in pain as her shape begins to slip away, but the fourth one comes to her aid. She remains alive, but her form is changed now, into something long and powerful. She creates water around herself, and it soothes her. She feels she should rejoin the battle, but as her head clears the water, she sees peace around her, and four walls, and more than three hundred angels who hadn't been there before. She realizes that, for now, it is over again. She dives to the bottom so that none can hear her cries of anguish.

The first one hears anyway, and sends to her aid the fifth one, who heals her wounds and soothes her, though her shape cannot be restored to her.

But she has the capacity to be happy with what is. She learns to enjoy the water, and life goes on.

Thrumb thrumb thrumb.

The Regent of the West heard it, distantly, through leagues of water, and recognized it at once.

Thrumb thrumb thrumb.

She rolled over, dived, and headed for it, her tail flipping and her enormous eyes alight.

Thrumb thrumb thrumb.

She broke the water and he was there—very dark, small, stooped, seated on a rock along the southeastern shore of her Regency. His head was covered with a small hat, narrow brimmed and of dark grey. His eyes were covered by a brown bandage, almost matching his skin. In his lap was a device made of mahogany from the forests of Lucifer. It was strung with silk wrapped over fine steel.

He heard her approach, and he began humming along with his playing. His fingers moved as fast as the Emerald of Satan, as his lips emitted a string of nonsense sounds that took her back to the brief moments before the Second Wave, when she had been whole and healthy, yet not aware of it.

She waited, perfectly still, and let voice and instrument transport her to places she'd wished to be—the Southern Hold, Yaweh's palace, the meadows of Lucifer. Slowly, his voice faded, and his hands were still.

She sighed. "Welcome, Harut."

"Thank you, Leviathan. Been a long while."

It was strange, she reflected, but when he wasn't singing, his voice sounded harsh and raspy. "Yes, it has. Have you been happy, Harut?"

"Hard to say. Been making music. People seem pleased to see me. I think I'm gettin' better. Yeah, I guess that makes me happy. You?"

"I'm at peace with myself. It took me a long time, but I'm not bitter anymore."

"I'm glad," he said.

"Have you heard news?"

"Yeah. I visited with Yaweh himself a while ago, and with Michael, and an archangel named Asmodai, and an angel named Abdiel. They're planning something big, honey."

She was instantly alert. "Is another Wave coming?"

"I don't think so. It sounded more as if they were gonna start one themselves—well, not exactly, but something like it. All I heard were bits and pieces of the talk."

Leviathan was silent for a moment, then she said, "Harut, will you be seeing Ariel?"

"I see him from time to time. Pretty often, I guess."

"When you see him next, would you send him here?"

"Sure, honey."

"Thank you." She relaxed. "Play me something, Harut. I think I'm going to need it."

His answer was not with words.

Thrumb thrumb thrumb.

An owl circled over the vast expanse of water, hooting loudly, and then flew back to the shore. Soon Leviathan's head broke the water. She looked around and quickly spotted the bird on the rock that Harut had occupied a few days before. A lash of her tail brought her close.

The owl spoke. "O mighty one of salty sea, word has come you've need of me."

"Hello, Ariel. Yes, I'd like a favor. And your scansion is off, by the by."

"This life would be both hard and droll, took everyone the critic's role."

"I suppose. Well, I've heard strange things are happening in the center. I'd like you to find out what you can and, in particular, why no one mentioned it to me."

Ariel snorted at this last. "If your time were spent upon dry ground, perhaps you'd be more easily found!"

She shrugged with her eyes and lashed her tail a bit. "I'd suggest you get help."

"Your every wish and whim to please, I'll speak to Mephistopheles."

"And you might want to consider some form other than rhyming couplets. They do get dull, after a while."

Ariel ruffled his feathers with displeasure, and cleared his throat.

"The judgments that you tend to pass,
On poets you wish to harass,
Would give me to swear,
Were I unaware,
That you are naught but an asset to the Heavenly throne, wherefore I leave you alone."

And, having gotten in the last word, he spread his wings and departed, just too late to miss a deluge of sea water.

After the Second Wave there is a pause, and a naming of names. It is a time of creation. The Seven Firstborn, called Yaweh, Satan, Michael, Lucifer, Raphael, Leviathan, and Belial, fear another Wave, but can only wait and watch.

They are given tasks, by each other and for each other.

Yaweh takes the center of Heaven, where he can look out at everything during the Waves and influence the illiaster everywhere.

Michael stays nearby, ready to protect Yaweh with his strength and power.

Raphael also stays near the center, for it is her task to heal those who are injured by the flux and save those she can.

Leviathan is given a Regency in the West, most of which is her sea.

Belial—indrawn and quiet, yet nearly as powerful as

Michael—takes the North to watch, and finds pleasure in the barren rocks and crags there.

Lucifer, during the Second Wave, found himself in the East, and had accidentally discovered how to make the soil of Heaven produce things that grew. Now the eastern lands are covered with grasses and shrubs, which are spreading to the rest of Heaven. So Lucifer takes the East, and he is content.

Satan was in the South, where the battle was thickest. It is the most populous area of Heaven save for the very center, because so much was done there that many were created.

It is a time of learning, and the beginning of art. It is found that those who came from the Second Wave are weaker than those who came from the First, and have less control of their own illiaster. It is also found that as time passes, all use of illiaster is limited. It is, at least in part, due to this that the angels stop varying their forms, unless there is some need to change.

Lucifer discovers that many of the growing things of Heaven, when eaten, bring sustenance to angels—restoring illiaster to those who are tired. Eventually, farming becomes a major occupation in Heaven.

Raphael discovers that those damaged by the flux cannot be fully healed, or resume their old shapes. She travels among them, healing as best she can, but the maimed remain maimed.

Asmodai, who came into being during this Wave, discovers how to shape the textures of Heaven. He envisions Michael, who has more raw power than any other of the Firstborn, cutting through the cacoastrum and leaving a wake of illiaster behind him. He creates a tool for this.

Others see and admire it, so Asmodai makes more, and is still making tools when the Third Wave begins, with no warning, as the southeastern side of Heaven begins to yield.

The Sword of Michael does as it was intended. Yaweh holds a sceptre, which forces shape and order upon chaos. Satan bears an emerald, which turns cacoastrum in upon itself, burning until it is consumed. And other tools are used, as well.

The Seven Firstborn lead the hosts into battle.

Mephistopheles strode up to the doors of Yaweh's palace, an almost-smile upon his lips. Inside, he found a page and asked said page to announce him to Uriel, who dwelt within.

The page scurried off, pagelike; Mephistopheles placed his hands behind his back and studied the huge entry-way of the palace.

The archangel Mephistopheles wore only black. After Bethor had invented whiskers he had adopted the custom. He sported a thin mustache that curled just a little around his lips. His face was high and angular; his eyes slanted upward a bit beneath thick black brows that nearly met over his nose. As he waited, he began whistling tunelessly between his teeth.

Uriel appeared behind the page, saw the dark angel in his usual carefree attitude, and didn't quite gnash his teeth. Mephistopheles saw big, somber Uriel in his purple and silver, and didn't quite laugh. Nor did he quite hide his desire to do so.

Uriel dismissed the page with a nod, and led the way to a small sitting room with a pair of comfortably padded beige chairs against walls of mushroom. He offered wine because it was expected; Mephistopheles accepted to be difficult.

"Cool," he announced, as he tasted the wine, "and yet it warms the heart. Sweet, and yet an almost bitter aftertaste."

Uriel was stubbornly silent.

"It reminds one of Heaven, nearly."

Uriel opened his mouth a couple of times, but didn't say anything. Mephistopheles decided that he was trying to find a way to say, "What do you want?" that didn't sound quite so rude. He took another drink, closing his eyes to further enjoy the coolness and the sweetness.

"This place is a bit degenerate, you know," he remarked. "I mean, not to cast aspersions on anyone in particular, but one would think that a few things worth doing would get done from time to time, rather than this continuous revelry—"

"You don't consider our studies worthwhile?" interrupted Uriel.

"Ah! So you can speak after all! I'd started to wonder."

Uriel's lips compressed. Mephistopheles continued. "As to studies, I don't know. It depends. What are you studying? For what purpose? To satisfy idle curiosity?"

Uriel scowled. "Who are you to belittle the efforts of any-one? So far as I know, you haven't done anything of any benefit to anyone since the Third Wave."

"As opposed to whom?"

Uriel shrugged and looked away. "I doubt any of this was what brought you here."

"Why shouldn't it be? I just thought I'd stop by and find out how you and my other friends are." Uriel opened his mouth as if to say, *"What* other friends?" but didn't. "I thought," continued Mephistopheles, "that I might give you news from other parts of Heaven. Did you know, for example, that Lilith had been seeing Lucifer since—"

"Enough!" cried Uriel, the shadow of pain crossing his features. "If all you came to do is distribute and collect petty gossip, you may leave again. I have no wish to hear such things."

Mephistopheles's face softened, and he bit his lip. His voice was lower as he said, "I'm sorry, Uriel. I'd forgotten that perhaps you wouldn't wish to know how Lilith fares just now; after all—"

"Please!"

"Certainly, my friend. I have no wish to torment you."

Uriel scowled.

"No, I mean it. I enjoy bantering, but I don't want to hurt anyone." He stood and crossed to Uriel. The big angel looked up at him, suspiciously. Mephistopheles sat in a chair next to him and touched his shoulder.

"I know I joke too much," he said. "Maybe I do hurt people, but I'm not malicious—at least, I don't think I am. I'd forgotten about—things—or I wouldn't have brought up what I did. I hope you can believe that."

Uriel's eyes softened, but he still said nothing.

"Perhaps," Mephistopheles continued, dropping his voice still further, "I'm a bit jealous of you. I try not to be, but here you are, always next to Yaweh, seeing Michael and Raphael every day, getting in on their plans, speaking to them all, while I always seem to be on the outside and—never mind. I guess I'll be leaving now."

He stood up, but Uriel held out a hand to stop him. "Please," said Uriel. "I overreacted."

Mephistopheles paused, half-turned toward the door. Uriel touched his arm, and Mephistopheles nodded and sat.

"You have little cause to be jealous, believe me," Uriel continued. "Yes, I live here, but Yaweh spends his time with Asmodai of late, and Lucifer and Abdiel, as well as those others you mentioned."

Mephistopheles studied him. "Do you feel left out, Uriel? I doubt that you should. I'm sure it's just that his plans require—"

"Oh, I know that. No, I'm not hurt. And yes, there are good reasons for it. Lucifer understands more about cacoastrum than anyone else; Asmodai will be planning the construction of the globe itself. And Abdiel is helping to organize it."

Mephistopheles appeared uninterested in these details. "You have your role, though, do you not?"

"Oh, yes. I am content. I'll be working with Satan."

"Ah! That will be good. I'm told that he's pleasant to work with."

"I expect it will be well. Although, to be honest, Satan has been worrying of late. His task, and mine, is to make sure that everyone involved in the work does his job, and Satan worries that we may have to coerce some of the younger angels."

"Oh, but that's foolishness, isn't it?"

"I think so," said Uriel. "Who could fail to want this? A safe, *permanent* haven from the flux? A place large enough for, literally, hundreds of *billions* of angels? But come, this isn't what you came for, Mephistopheles. What can I do for you?"

Mephistopheles shook his head. "I really only came to see how you were. I had no particular errand."

"Are you sure there isn't anything I can do for you?"

"Yes. But thank you, Uriel."

Uriel stood. "Certainly. And, about our problems before—"

"I'm sorry. It was my fault. Don't think on it."

"Thank you. I'll walk you out."

"That won't be necessary. I'll see you soon."

"And I, you."

"Fare well."

"Fare well."

Mephistopheles strode evenly out of Yaweh's palace. As he left to report to his friend, Leviathan, a small, cynical smile came over his lips; a dry chuckle escaped his throat.

"Ah! Kyriel! What is this I hear of you and Bath Kol?"

"I don't know, Sith. What is it?"

"Be that way, then. Where are you going?"

"I'm helping out the Lord Michael, around his home. You know, keeping the fires going, and all."

"He's away, then?"

"Not gone on a trip, if that's what you mean, but he's spending most of his time at the Lord Yaweh's palace. I hear there's something big going on."

"I have heard that somebody is planning something. I haven't heard what, though."

"Neither have I. How are things with Raphael?"

"Slow. Just as well, though. I'm glad to see the illiaster wear down—not so many getting hurt."

"I suppose. Well, Sith, duty calls."

"A pleasant day to you, Kyriel."

"And to you. And if you hear any more about the big doings, let me know, will you?"

"Sure."

"Fare you well, then."

"Fare well."

Satan and Beelzebub met Lucifer and Lilith in a small, wooded area amid the grasslands near the southern border of Lucifer's dominion. For a while they walked in silence along a shallow stream, or through thick woods. Satan strode next to Lucifer, the former's long easy gait matching the athletic stride of the latter. Lilith held Lucifer's arm as Beelzebub trotted along beside her.

Lucifer was tall and strong and bronzed, and most of the mysterics of Heaven and creation that were known, were known because of his work.

He had explained how the angelic bodies had formed in response to the conditions of their creation, how illiaster had a tendency to become stagnant and thus rob them of their powers, and why it required two eyes in a single direction to see properly. It was through the arts of Lucifer and the devices of Asmodai that light had been brought to Heaven.

Lilith was small and dark—lithe, yet full-bodied. Her eyes, as black as Mephistopheles's, shone with energy and enthusiasm. Where Lucifer was indrawn and contemplative, she was outgoing and exuberant. Lilith it was who had invented differentiation of genders, and then taught the angels why. It was because she was female that most of them chose to be male.

After some little while of walking, Satan seated himself on a rock in the middle of a stream. He found a small stick and began tapping it on the stone.

Beelzebub looked up at Lilith and whispered, "Certes, he'll be at it, anon." She nodded agreement.

For a moment, the only sounds were the tapping of the stick, and the soft burbling of the stream. Then Satan gave a sigh.

"I'm not sure how to begin this, friend Lucifer."

"Is it about the Plan?"

"Yes."

Satan continued tapping the stick. Lucifer sat facing him in the middle of the stream, the clear water running over his crossed legs. Lilith sat behind Lucifer and rubbed her palm over his back. Beelzebub sat next to her, and occasionally leaned down to lap up water.

Satan began again. "Actually, it's about my own role in it."

Lucifer nodded. "Go on."

"I've been given the task—"

"I know. It suits you."

"Eh? Explain that."

Lucifer shrugged. "You may not know it, but you're the most respected of the Firstborn, excepting Yaweh himself. To have you leading them—"

"Leading them? I'm not leading them. I'm—"

"It amounts to the same thing. As I was told, you're to keep account of the work and make sure each angel does his job. That means that they'll be looking to you for guidance and inspiration—"

"And a good kick, when needed."

"Yes, that too."

Satan was silent for a moment, tapping the stick against the rock. "I admit, you make it sound better than Yaweh did."

"That's natural," said Lucifer, somewhat amused.

"To hear him describe it, I'm supposed to sniff around finding angels who aren't doing their job, and do whatever I have to do to make sure they perform."

"I'm sure there's truth in that, also."

"But—I guess it bothers me that he, and you too, think we might need it. It never used to be like that. We fought when we had to, to survive. No one had to force us to do anything. You remember how it was."

"I remember," said Lucifer softly.

Once again, for a while, the only sound was the stick, tapping rhythmically against a rock.

• • •

Twenty of the archangels fall in the Third Wave. Many others nearly do, as the Seven guide and rally the hosts. Yaweh is nearly overcome again, but is saved by Cherubiel, who is lost in the flux. Harut is pulled from the fray by Leviathan, but when he recovers, he finds that he cannot see or hear. Later, with great effort, Raphael restores his hearing.

Far to the North, Belial and four archangels are overcome. He survives by forming mountains above him and taking a new shape. The four archangels perish. Enraged, Belial lashes out. In his hate, he preserves his Regency, but such is the power of his fires that those who are newly created near him are destroyed immediately. Later, alone, Belial will curl himself up under the mountain and remember Seraphiel, an archangel who fell by his side, who was one of few Belial had considered a friend.

Ariel is fighting near Raphael when he is suddenly taken by the flux. Raphael sees this and grasps at his life thread. By main will, she holds him together. Only a small part of Ariel is left by the time he is safe, so he takes the form of a creature of the air and flies from the battle to the protection of Michael.

Michael walks slowly forward, his great arms swinging, and each time his sword cuts through cacoastrum, his companions pull in the new ones thus created and nurture them to life.

Abdiel is isolated in a small area of the Eastern Regency. All alone, he cries in terror, but somehow the flux doesn't find him.

Satan is everywhere, laughing in the face of the flux throughout the vast Southern Regency. His emerald flashes upon his breast, and cacoastrum burns, turns upon itself, and is gone. He comes to the aid of his friend, Beelzebub, almost too late. Beelzebub holds himself together, taking a new, smaller form, but he survives. Everywhere that spirits are flagging and angels are near to giving in to the flux, Satan is there, and the fight is renewed.

Yaweh is near the center, and from this distance, sees and directs all—for with the full power of illiaster present, his reach is all but endless. When, in the heat of battle, a structure is erected that ought to stand, he raises his sceptre and at that moment it becomes fixed.

Lucifer holds a single position, near the wall of his Regency.

His eyes are closed and his brow is furrowed. Around him trees are springing up. He occasionally makes remarks to Junier, who stands placidly at his side, oblivious to the chaos around them, calmly noting discoveries that Lucifer makes, to think upon later.

Like the universe, the Third Wave seems to go on forever. But, like the universe, it doesn't.

"Tell me this," said Lucifer. "How would you feel—are you listening?"

"Eh? Oh. Sorry."

"How would you feel," Lucifer continued, "if the Fourth Wave *did* come, and half of our new brethren—or more— were destroyed, and you knew you could have prevented it? By my figuring, that is just what will happen if we don't accept the Plan. How would you feel then?"

Satan studied the rushing waters at his feet. "I don't know."

"It's worth thinking about."

"You don't have any doubts at all, do you?"

"Not of that kind. I have knowledge; that implies a duty to use it. But let me ask you—have you spoken to Yaweh about this? It seems to be the next step, if you're still unconvinced."

"I suppose it is. But it was Yaweh who first had these doubts, and I tried to reassure him. If I'm wrong, Yaweh is the last one I should talk to; I'll just shake his confidence in the Plan, without getting any closer to having my questions answered."

"I see the problem," Lucifer admitted. "But what else can you do?"

Satan shook his head without answering. After a few minutes, he stood up and began walking back upstream, his eyes on the waters, his feet kicking small waves up onto the banks.

Beelzebub watched him, then nodded to Lilith and Lucifer.

"Dost thou know—"

"I understand," said Lilith. "It's all right."

Beelzebub ran to catch up. Satan continued walking, occasionally shaking his head. At length, he cursed softly and tossed the stick ahead of him. Beelzebub wondered at his sudden desire to chase it.

Two

I, who am called of men, The Beast, or The Master, or, The Supreme and Holy King, or The High Priest, and again the Black Maker of Magick, or The Betrayer of Oaths ... am in Thy sight none of these.

> —Aleister Crowley,
> *The Magical Record of the Beast*

The sneer, walking up the steps to Yaweh's palace, met the smirk coming down. Icy blue eyes locked with frigid black ones. The sneer noticed the crooked grin noticing the sneer noticing the amused contempt noticing the haughty disgust noticing the—

"Mephistopheles," said the sneer.

"Abdiel," said the smirk.

"I hope all goes well."

"All goes, Abdiel."

"What is this fascination of yours with black?"

"What is this fascination of yours with rude questions?"

31

"I don't think it was rude. I was just curious."

Shrug.

"Are you traveling again, Mephistopheles?"

"Perhaps. Are you out saving Heaven, as usual?"

"What?"

"Never mind."

Mephistopheles brushed past the sneer, not quite knocking into him. Abdiel, not deigning to look around, proceeded up into the palace.

"Page!" he called.

"Yes, lord?"

"Where is the Lord Yaweh?"

"In the throne room, lord."

"Alone?"

"Yes, lord."

"Well, announce me, then, or do you need it written out?"

The page opened his mouth once or twice, then quickly ran off. The sneer followed him into Yaweh's throne room on the heels of the announcement, vanished, and was replaced by a warm, pleasant smile.

"My Lord Yaweh."

"Welcome, Abdiel. Be seated. What are those papers?"

"The organizational plans, Lord. Completed."

"Well done! Let me see them."

Abdiel complacently handed over the parchment. He was a bit small, with fair hair and a full but neatly trimmed beard. Like Asmodai, he was compact, athletic in his movements.

Yaweh eagerly studied the papers, his eyes bright.

"So, two-thirds of our forces will be protecting the remaining third?"

"Yes, Lord."

"Need it be that many?"

"I think so, Lord. With this plan, it can all be completed in just over two days, and our losses will be less than a thousand."

"A thousand!"

"Yes, Lord. It's all down there."

"And everything else is worse, you say?"

"Yes, Lord."

"I see."

Abdiel studied him closely. What was the matter? Hadn't

he known there would be a cost? "If there is anyone you'd especially like not to be in the actual fray, I'm sure we can arrange—"

Yaweh motioned him to silence. He studied the papers.

"Lord?"

Yaweh looked up. "Yes?"

"I don't think we should mention these figures to anyone, just yet."

Again, an interlude of silence. Then: "I see what you mean. Leave me now. I have to think about this."

"Yes, Lord."

Abdiel took his leave. He nearly ran into the page, who was just entering. Abdiel scowled at him. The page muttered apologies and continued into the room.

"Raphael wishes to see you, Lord," he announced.

Yaweh looked up, blankly, then he nodded. "Good. Send her in, please."

The page stepped aside.

"Greetings, Yaweh."

"Good day, Raphael. I've been meaning to ask you a few questions about your beliefs."

She frowned. "I guess I believe in searching for truth in any direction it occurs to me to look for it," she said. "And then writing it down so people don't forget."

"Isn't that a little vague, Raphael?"

"Maybe." She smiled a bit and sat down. "I got the line from Lucifer; what would you expect?"

"He's never seemed vague to me."

"Have you ever spoken to him about anything as abstract as what one believes in?"

"Hmmmm. I suppose not." He chuckled. "You certainly have been feeling philosophical, lately."

Raphael studied the marble floor. She was a tall angel, yet full and sturdily built. Her hair curled a bit down her shoulders—blonde, with a touch of red. Her eyes were bright blue, and matched her gown. She wore nothing on her feet, and a silver chain around her waist held a six-pointed star fashioned of mother-of-pearl and set with rubies at each point. On her shoulders was the gold cloak of the Firstborn.

"Maybe," she said, "I'm just trying to justify myself. I'm not sure."

Yaweh shook his head. "You empathize too much, Raphael. I've been told that I have this fault, and I don't know if it's true, but it certainly seems true of you."

"I don't know if it is or isn't, but I don't think it is a fault in any case."

"Up to a point, it isn't. But what you call 'searching for truth' looks like refusing to hold to a position. When you're with me, and I speak of my doubts, you echo them. When you're with Satan, and he reassures you, you accept that, too. When you're with Lucifer, you catch his excitement. I don't mean to hurt you, Raphael, or make you angry, but this bothers me."

"Whatever the source of these doubts, Yaweh, I have them. And you're wrong about Satan, incidentally. The last time we spoke, he seemed to agree with every one of the doubts you have been expressing."

"What? But when he spoke to me—"

"Maybe you convinced him."

"I hope not. But it doesn't matter. Rather than figure out what to do if the hosts resist the Plan, I'd like to decide how we are going to make sure they don't. I gave the task to Satan because I don't feel that I can do it; I told him so."

Raphael started to argue, then thought about it. "Yes, it would be better if you didn't have to coerce them. Have you a way?"

Yaweh shook his head. "Not yet. But I think that is what we ought to be worried about. And," he added in a worried tone, "if Satan's feelings have been going the other way, I wish he would speak to me about them."

Raphael fingered the star at her side. "I think he hesitates to do so because of your doubts. He thinks the Plan is right, and doesn't want to make things worse for you. I think he'll speak to you when he has something definite to say."

Yaweh nodded. "That would be like him. But there is such a thing as being *too* kind."

"One returns from irksome task, sent by you in days gone by. He doubtless has a tale to tell. Come forth now; he draweth nigh."

Leviathan's head broke the water. "That was better, Ariel, but you're starting to sound like Beelzebub."

The owl fluffed his feathers and settled on a rock near the water's edge. "You mock my form, and rhymes, and tone, but this much I beseech: Leave my choice of words alone, and my style of speech."

Leviathan chuckled as Mephistopheles walked up. "Greetings, lady," he said. He nodded to Ariel. "And how is our flying iambic tetrameter?"

"I see and hear and speak the truth, not thinking loss or gain. The answer to your question is: You are a raging pain."

Mephistopheles was silent for a moment, then he said, "Go back to rhyming couplets."

Before Ariel had a chance to rebut, Leviathan broke in. "What did you learn?"

"There is, indeed, a plan afoot. It's pretty much a secret, but it involves Yaweh, Satan, Michael, Abdiel, Lucifer, Asmodai, and a few others. I don't know why they haven't discussed it with you, but I think they simply don't want anyone knowing about it who doesn't have to."

"I see," she said, her voice flat.

"It involves the creation of some kind of massive structure, to exist outside of Heaven, where, I guess, we'd all move. The idea is to make it a permanent thing, so we wouldn't have to be watching it all the time. The form of the thing, as far as I can tell, is to be a globe."

"But why such need for secrecy?"

"Well, there's danger in the construction. It means setting off a Wave ourselves, in effect, and there's some doubt that the new angels will cooperate willingly."

"Willingly? Do you think they'd *force* them to?"

"There's talk of it. Satan is responsible for that, and I hear that he isn't happy about it."

"No, I suppose he wouldn't be."

Ariel said, "It must be a worthy plan indeed, full of weighty gains, before I'll needless let them risk, what little of me remains."

"You see," said Mephistopheles. "And he isn't even one of the younger ones."

Abdiel walked alone through the streets near Yaweh's palace. Small dwelling places surrounded him. The streets were wide, winding affairs, large enough for two or three hand-carts to pass. Abdiel had spent a great deal of time walking and thinking in the last ten days, since delivering his plans to Yaweh and staying to eavesdrop on Yaweh's conversation with Raphael.

After this time, he was near to a conclusion.

"There is nothing wrong," he told himself, "with not wanting to be there when the Plan goes into operation. No one, in all the hosts, would actually *want* to be holding off the flux. I'm no different."

"True enough," he answered himself. "But can you do anything about it?"

"I'm not sure," he admitted. "Yaweh's talk with Raphael does bring up some interesting ideas."

"Eh? What?"

"The talk about Satan. Yaweh sounded almost irritated, if that were possible."

"I see what you mean," he admitted to himself. "If there is a falling out between Yaweh and Satan, it is certainly possible that I'll be able to replace Satan. And, if I can replace him, it'll be an easy matter to arrange to be somewhere safe while the battle is being fought. And certainly no one could fault me for that."

"No one except Mephistopheles, who can fault anyone."

"Ah! Mephistopheles! Yes, if I had Satan's position, I could manage to put *him* where I wanted to."

"And Lucifer, too, eh? And make sure Lilith stays safe?"

"Not likely, I'm afraid. The Firstborn will all do whatever they do, and I'm not going to be able to influence that."

"But it's still worthwhile."

"Oh, yes. But, would I do a good job of it?"

"Piffle! What's to do? All it takes is the willingness to see that the job gets done, no matter what. And that seems to be the thing that Satan doesn't have, for all his accomplishments."

"Why, you're right! The one angel who shouldn't have doubts is the one who does! If Yaweh does open his eyes, and tells Satan to step aside, it would be best for the Plan, too."

"Ah, but what if Yaweh doesn't open his eyes? He and Satan are the oldest friends in Heaven! Yaweh will probably just keep on, and let the whole Plan suffer for it."

"Well, is there anything that can be done about that?"

"I don't see what. Except stay alert, and see what opportunities present themselves."

"Couldn't I create an opportunity?"

"Maybe. I'll have to see what happens."

"Then why am I walking about here? I think it's time to look around a bit, and see what's going on. Maybe there's a way to push Lord Satan a bit in the right direction. Maybe there is, indeed."

"Sith! Hold a moment."

"Hello, Kyriel. Goes all well with you?"

"I'm not sure. Have you heard?"

"Since that question implies that I ought to know what it is about, and since I don't, I guess I haven't."

"I know what the big plan is."

"Really? What is it, then?"

"Well, I don't know exactly, but as I hear it, they want to do something to the walls so that nothing can get in anymore, and we don't have to worry about more Waves."

"Is that possible?"

"It's what I've heard."

"Where did you get this?"

"Rachsiel told me. She heard it from Cuniali, who heard it from Tetra, who heard it from Sagsagel, who heard it from Loquel, who lives right in Yaweh's palace, you know."

"Yeah, that makes it pretty definite."

"It sure does."

"Well, it's wonderful, if it's true."

"Wonderful? You think so? Well, then, listen to this: to do it, they're going to have to have *us* do the work, and some of us might be destroyed doing it."

"You can't be serious!"

"As serious as the flux."

"Where will they find angels willing to destroy themselves?"

"Where does the 'willing' come from?"

"Well, Lord Lucifer? Can you help me?"

Lucifer shrugged. "I don't see why not, Abdiel. It will be rather lengthy, but—"

"Excuse me," came a voice from behind Abdiel.

He turned around and said, "Greetings, my Lady Lilith."

She ignored him and spoke directly to Lucifer. "I happened to overhear."

Abdiel cursed under his breath. Lucifer looked an inquiry at Lilith. She addressed herself to Abdiel directly, then. "Why ask these questions? You've never been the curious type before."

Abdiel smiled, leaned back against a tree, stretched his legs, and pretended he was comfortable.

"Nor am I now," he said.

"Well then?"

Abdiel shrugged, but Lilith still looked at him closely, as if expecting an answer, and Lucifer was becoming curious as well.

"It's . . . an idea I had."

"What kind of idea?" asked Lucifer.

"For the Plan, Lord Lucifer."

"Then why haven't I heard about it?"

"It's my own idea, and, well, it isn't complete yet."

"I see. Well, tell me what you have."

"I'd rather not, until it's finished. I just want to find out if there is any chance of it working before I present it to Lord Yaweh. And you, of course."

"Of course," echoed Lilith.

Lucifer said, "Can you give me some idea, though? If I answer your questions, it'll take a lot of time. I'd rather not—"

"Of course, Lord Lucifer." Abdiel swallowed, his mind racing furiously. "It involves . . . drawing on the illiaster of a large group of angels at once and uniting it in a particular way."

"I see. *What* particular way?"

"To . . . ah . . . create something."

"To create *what*, Abdiel?"

"Well, I want to see if tools, like Asmodai makes, can be made between waves. I have a few specific ideas, but I'd really rather not speak of them until I've done some experimenting."

"I see."

"Well, Lord Lucifer? Will you answer my questions?"

Lucifer cocked his head and studied Abdiel for a moment, then shrugged. "I suppose. All right. Yes, it is possible to reach one's illiaster, even this far between Waves. It is difficult, especially for someone who is not of the Firstborn. For anyone of the Third Wave, it is very difficult, but not impossible. It is also, as we know, dangerous.

"The very least you can expect is some amount of fatigue, until the natural level of illiaster rebuilds itself. This takes from minutes to days, depending on what you have done. Those angels damaged by the Waves have had their natural level damaged, which is why their forms are either physically smaller, as Beelzebub or Ariel, or have some normal ability missing, such as Leviathan or Belial.

"Not only does this level differ depending on the Wave one is from, but it varies a great deal from angel to angel. Michael and Belial, for instance, have the highest levels of the Firstborn. Yaweh and I, while we have lower native levels, have more skill in using it.

"Also, many angels have particular, natural talents. Yaweh, for instance, is able to conjure images of what is taking place throughout Heaven. Raphael is able to repair damaged angels, and so on.

"As to how one uses it, go about it this way: Close your eyes. Now, try to imagine, in the middle of your belly, your free illiaster. Think of it as a ball of white fire. Get as clear an image of it as you can. . . ."

"Lucifer?"

"Yes, my love?"

"Did you get the feeling that Abdiel was making up that plan as he went along?"

"Huh. I'll say. That's why I kept asking him about it."

"Well then, why did you answer his questions?"

"I couldn't think of a good reason not to."

"Why do you think he wanted to know all that?"

"I imagine that he wants to use his illiaster, for reasons of his own."

"Aren't you worried about that?"

"Not especially. What harm can he do? He's a mischief-maker, but he would never do anything hurtful."

"No, I suppose he wouldn't."

"And if we see signs of someone running around creating snowstorms, or giving us bad dreams, we'll know where to look. He isn't ever going to be able to stand up to one of the Firstborn."

"That's a relief, anyway."

•   •   •

"Milord, word hath come to mine ears that doth cause me some measure of unease."

"What have you heard, Beelzebub?"

"Rumors do fly about the land, milord. These have little truth in them. Whoso they light on taketh the worst o' the lie and sends that forth; whoso that lights on them doth likewise. 'Tis a most potent distillation of falsehood; milord, it will fall like the dew and make every angel drunk unawares. Many hard words are spoken by those who fear to be sacrificed."

"Sacrificed?"

"Verily, milord. And yet we dare not enlighten these ill-sayers, for our lips are sealed by Yaweh's desires."

"True. Hmmm. This is serious."

"Aye, milord."

"All right. We have to make sure Yaweh hears about this."

"Aye, milord."

Michael was not the most brilliant angel in Heaven. He was one of the biggest, one of the strongest, one of the most constant and dependable, but he was not one of the brightest.

He had thick, curly brown hair to his shoulders and a broad, clean-shaven face with a well-formed nose. His eyes were brown and widely spaced. His shoulders were broad. He dressed in light grey, with brown boots, and on his shoulders was the gold cloak of the Firstborn.

The lights from the fires cast strange reflections on his face as he turned toward the doorway. Next to him, standing over the long, low table, Asmodai also looked up at the door.

"Enter," he called.

The door opened outward, and two figures were silhouetted against the night. They squinted down as Michael and Asmodai squinted up.

A voice called out, "Asmodai?"

"Lucifer! Come on down!"

The two figures walked down to the room where the lights were from fires from the forge, and the heat was unpleasant to everyone except Asmodai, who had gotten used to it.

"Good evening, Lucifer," said Michael as they approached.

"Michael! This is a surprise." They embraced each other, Michael being careful not to hurt the other.

"Yes, it is," he said, as they broke off, held each other at arms' length and smiled. "A pleasant one."

"Yes. You know Lilith, do you not?"

"Of course," said Michael, and smiled broadly at her. "Good evening, Lilith."

"Good evening, Lord Michael."

Asmodai coughed. "Let's go to the other room," he suggested, "where you'll be more comfortable."

"Yes, let's."

Asmodai lived a little to the north of the center, in the foothills of the mountains where Belial made his home. He had only two rooms. One was his workshop, with five forges scattered throughout, and the other held a bed, a small kitchen, and a few chairs around a fireplace. It was lit with naked torches and colored dark brown.

The three visitors followed Asmodai into this second room and found seats.

"What bring you here this evening, Michael?" began Lucifer, before anyone else could ask questions.

Michael grunted. "Asmodai was showing me where the work would begin on the globe, and how it would expand, so I can arrange the defenses."

"I see."

"And you, Lucifer?"

The Regent of the East bit his lip. Apparently liking the flavor, he chewed it for a while.

"I spoke with Satan several days ago," he said at last. "His talk disturbed me. I wanted your opinion of it."

"What did he say?"

"He was worried about our need for the cooperation of the hosts, and if we had the 'right' to force them to help us."

Asmodai shrugged. "Do we need to force them? And can we if we do? If we have the need, and the ability, then it seems that we have the right. I don't see the question."

"Odd," said Michael.

"What?" asked Lucifer.

"I've been wondering the same thing."

Lucifer and Lilith exchanged glances that Asmodai found unreadable. He looked from one to the other.

"Yes?"

Lucifer was silent. "We thought as you do," said Lilith. "But speaking with Satan—well—we aren't as sure now."

"I see. Well, maybe we'd better all hie off to see Lord Satan right now and find out about this."

"Now?" asked Lilith.

"An excellent idea," boomed Michael.

"And say what to him?" asked Lucifer. "The last time we spoke—"

"I wasn't there," said Asmodai.

"True."

"Well?"

"Let us wait a few days, anyway," said Michael. "Now that I think of it, I must turn these plans over to Yaweh."

"Very well," said Asmodai. "Four days from now? In the evening? Meet here?"

"Agreed."

"Agreed."

"Agreed."

Yaweh studied Michael for a moment before saying anything. Michael broke the silence himself: "Is something wrong, Yaweh? You look—I don't know—unhappy. We did the best we could."

"No, it isn't that. Your plans are fine, Michael. It's—this." He drew from his robe a scrap of parchment and held it up. "This is a message from Satan. In it, he says that he's noticed a growing worry among the hosts, and the spreading of rumors about the Plan—false rumors, he says. He recommends that we announce our whole Plan to the hosts at once. What do you think?"

Michael furrowed his brow. "I'm not sure," he said at last. "Are the hosts unhappy because the rumors are false? I mean, would the truth make them happier, or less happy?"

"Who can say? I certainly can't. What does Satan think, do you suppose?"

"Well, he must think that it would be best—"

"There is more."

"Yes?"

Yaweh relayed Raphael's mention of Satan's attitude. Michael nodded. "This echoes my own thoughts," he said.

"I know," said Yaweh. "But I happened to overhear something as I was entering here. It was Abdiel's voice, but I'm not sure to whom he was speaking. I heard him say, 'Nonsense.

These are mere rumors, and not fit to disturb Lord Yaweh. If the Lord Satan *were* to oppose the Plan, as you say, he would certainly speak of them to the Lord Yaweh directly.' There, Michael—now do you see why this bothers me?"

Michael thought for another while. "No," he said at last.

Yaweh looked hard at him. "But then, you agree with him, don't you?"

"I'm not yet sure. We'll be speaking to him soon, to try to find for good and all what his—"

"We, Michael? Who is this 'we?'"

"Why, me, and Lucifer, and Lilith, and Asmodai—"

"What? You're all going to speak to Satan about our Plan? Why is this the first I've heard of this?"

Michael furrowed his brow. "I don't know, Yaweh. I guess it never occurred to anyone to mention it."

"It never occurred. . . ."

"Would you want to be there? I'm certain you are welcome."

Grief and anger seemed to compete in Yaweh's voice, as he said, "I think that if the Lord Satan wanted me there, he would certainly have informed me of it."

"Oh, but he doesn't—"

"That will do, Michael. I don't wish to hear more. Leave me, please, I have to think about this."

"Of course, Yaweh. Excuse me."

"The Lord Abdiel!"

"Very well. Send him in."

Abdiel entered, looking full of doubt and worry. "I'm sorry to disturb you, Lord Yaweh, but—"

"What is it, Abdiel?"

"I have just spoken with Michael, and he related something of what had passed between you." (This wasn't far from the truth. Actually, Abdiel had hidden himself in a cloakroom, from where he had heard the conversation.)

"What of it, Abdiel?"

"I think you are being too harsh on the Lord Satan, Lord."

"I appreciate your thoughts, Abdiel, but I don't feel that I'm being harsh. It's just that I'm worried."

"I think Lord Satan is just as firmly committed to the Plan as you or I, but he has some doubts on exactly how we ought to do it. I think you ought to speak to him directly, Lord, so all of these questions can be answered. Forgive me for being so presumptuous—"

"No, that's all right. I feel that it is he who ought to come to me; that's all it is."

"But—as you wish."

"How go things otherwise, Abdiel?"

"Well, Lord Yaweh. I'm working on an idea to solve the problem that the Lord Satan is concerned with, but I'd rather not tell you about it until it's complete."

"Excellent. But don't take too long. I'm becoming impatient to begin. It won't do to have another Wave begin just as we're about to start."

"I understand, Lord."

"Page!"

"Yes, Lord Yaweh?"

"I need a message delivered to the Southern Hold. Prepare yourself for a long journey."

"Yes, Lord."

"Tell the Lord Satan that I am anxious to speak with him as soon as possible. Present my respects, and say that I would be grateful if he would journey to the center and speak with me. I think it very important, and urgent."

"I will set out this evening, Lord Yaweh."

"It isn't that urgent. Make it the morning. Get a good rest first."

"Yes, Lord. Thank you."

"Don't mention it, Gabriel."

He waved the page away and returned to his reflections.

"Welcome back, Beelzebub."

"Thanks, milord."

"Did Yaweh say anything about the rumors?"

"My message seem'd to displease him, yet he had naught to say to't."

"I hadn't thought he'd be pleased. But he didn't give an answer?"

"I was to say he'd think on't. And yet, milord, there was somewhat in his tone that did make me to feel unease."

"Hmmm."

"There is more, milord."

"Yes?"

"I spake to Michael, and he did say that he and others would come to speak unto us."

"Who? About what?"

"I know not, milord."

"Hmmmm. Guesses? Speculation?"

"Perchance some have heard of thy questions on the Plan and wish to question thee on them, or to convince thee that thou art wrong."

"Interesting."

"Verily."

"Well . . . suggestions?"

"Be sure of the wine stocks, milord."

Four archangels walked along the Southern Road, which dwindled to a path, and then a trail, and finally disappeared altogether. As one got closer to the Hold, a trail or two emerged as if from nowhere and came together to form another path, and this became a full road again, several leagues from the Hold.

But these archangels were still near the center, walking steadily southward. Two of them wore gold cloaks. Such a sight was enough to excite great interest in those who saw them go by. None spoke to them, but many spoke of them.

They walked all four abreast, for this part of the Southern Road, passing through flat and rolling farmland, was wide. Michael walked to the right, Asmodai next to him, then Lucifer and Lilith. These latter touched hands from time to time. The braver among those they passed would step out for a better view of her walking away.

"It has been awhile since I've traveled," said Michael.

"And I," said Asmodai.

"What will we say to him?" asked Lucifer.

Michael shrugged and said, "We'll tell him—whatever we tell him."

"I'm sure of that," said Lilith.

"Wait till we get there," suggested Asmodai.

"Do we know why we're going?" asked Lucifer.

Michael opened his mouth and closed it again. Asmodai said slowly, "Because he has to be confronted with what he's doing—creating doubt and dissension. If he's right, he should bring his arguments to us. If not, he should remain silent. This state is intolerable."

There was silence for several paces. Then, "Quite a speech," said Lucifer.

"Thank you," said Asmodai.

Mephistopheles sat with his back against a stone, his feet stretched out in front of him, and his head resting on his hands, which were locked behind his neck. If Mephistopheles looked relaxed, he was. He could easily have waited there half a day. This was good, because it was nearly half the day before Leviathan happened to look over at that rocky opening in the cliff and saw a figure seated there.

"I thought you'd left already," she said, swimming up.

"I came back."

"Where is Ariel?"

"I expect he's around, looking for a four-footed tercet or something."

"Or something. Did you want something?"

"Not especially. Did you want me for something?"

"Why, yes. How did you know?"

"A little bird told me."

"Ariel? How did he know?"

"I couldn't say."

"He's sensitive, that one."

"Yes. The soul of a poet." He smirked. "So, what can I do for you?"

"How long since you've been to the Southern Hold?"

Abdiel wondered why he was walking. His feet took him further and further away from the center, as if they knew they had a mission. He was fully a day ahead of the page, whom he had overheard Yaweh send this way, and that was certainly interesting, but how could he use it?

Perhaps, he decided, the best thing would be to wait until the message had been delivered, then find out what the answer was.

But he knew what the answer would be. Satan would certainly go along, and he and Yaweh would talk, and either settle their differences or not. Was there a way to make sure it was not?

No, he decided, there wasn't. As soon as the two of them got together, it was out of his hands.

He stopped in the middle of the road.

As soon as the two of them got together. . . .

Slowly, a smile spread across his face. He closed his eyes and stood while he worked out the details.

After several long moments, he started up again, briskly. He had a long way to travel. It wouldn't do for the page's trip to be too short.

Three

For neither man nor angel can discern
Hypocrisy—the only evil that walks
Invisible. . . .

—Milton, *Paradise Lost*, iii:682-684

Thrumb thrumb thrumb.
"Do you hear it, Asmodai?"
"Hear what, Lucif—oh, yes."
Thrumb thrumb thrumb.
"Where is it coming from?" asked Asmodai.
"Around the corner, I think," said Michael.
"Do you know what it is?"
"No."

Lucifer and Lilith smiled as the sounds got louder, but didn't enlighten the other two. Presently they turned a corner and saw the small, dark-skinned angel seated by the road, his back against a tree. They stopped and listened for a while. Soon the music stopped. The angel continued to look straight ahead, but said, "Who is it?" in a low, raspy voice.

49

"It's Lucifer and Lilith, with two friends," said Lucifer.

"Why, hello!" Harut said, breaking into a bright smile.

"You're blind!" said Michael.

"You're right," said the other, his expression not changing.

"This," said Lilith, "is our friend, Harut. Harut, the one who spoke is the Lord Michael, the Firstborn. The other is the archangel Asmodai."

"Good day, Harut. Your music is pleasing."

"Hello, Asmodai. I've heard of your work. And Michael, I've heard of you, too, of course."

"Thank you," said Asmodai. "May I see your lyre?"

"Sure! Only it's a cithara." He grinned even more and handed it up. Asmodai gave it close inspection, whistling appreciation from time to time. He tapped the wooden base, studied the strings and where they joined to the heads, and handed it back.

"Lovely job," he said. "Yours?"

"Yeah. Lucifer gave me the wood."

"Excellent workmanship."

"May we join you for a while, Harut?" asked Lilith.

"Why, sure."

Lilith seated herself next to him in a graceful sweep. Lucifer dropped next to her, sitting cross-legged. Asmodai stiffly lowered himself to a stoop, then rocked into a sitting position. Michael moved next to Asmodai, grunted, started to lower himself a couple of times, then creakingly bent over, supported himself with both arms, and maneuvered himself to the ground.

"Quite a company you have here," said Harut.

"We're going to visit the Lord Satan," said Asmodai.

Harut nodded.

"How did it happen?" asked Michael.

"Third Wave done me in," said Harut. "Raphael pulled me out 'fore it did a full job, though. She done that for a lot of us."

"I know," said Michael. "But couldn't she heal you?"

"She did, some. It was worse. I was lookin' away when I got hit. I knew what was happening, and I thought I was going to *change*, you know? Isn't that funny? I wasn't afraid to die, but I didn't want to lose my shape, like Beelzebub or Ariel. All I could think of was holding myself together. I guess Raphael pulled me out then. There were a lot who needed her, though.

By the time she got back to me, it was all she could do to make me hear again. But that's a lot. I'm thankful."

There was silence for a time.

"I'm thankful," he repeated.

Asmodai cleared his throat. "You did change, you know," he said. "I didn't recognize you at first."

"I know. I lost a bit off the top, and I don't weigh so much now. But that don't matter. That much I could fix myself, if I wanted to."

Michael said, "Some of the injured ones from the Second Wave were actually healed in the Third. Do you think...." His voice trailed off.

"The Fourth Wave? Maybe. I'm not expecting anything. I'm not anxious for it."

"None of us are," said Lilith. "As you know."

"Yeah, I know. I've heard some folks aren't happy about the big plan."

Asmodai stared. "How did you hear of that?"

Harut shrugged. "I guess it isn't as big a secret as some would like. For me, I'll just wait. When it happens, I'll live, or I won't."

"I wish I had your attitude, Harut," said Lilith.

He shook his head.

"What have you heard about it?" asked Asmodai.

"Lots of stuff. I don't listen a whole lot, since I don't think much of that kind of talk. But I know that *somethin'* is up, and it has to do with starting the Fourth Wave. And I know that some don't like it much."

"I see," said Asmodai. He looked around at the others. None of them said anything. Michael seemed lost in thought, Lucifer met Asmodai's look, but his face was blank. Lilith seemed amused.

After the silence had stretched across the road and back a few times, Harut said, "You don't have to tell me nothin' if you don't want."

"No," said Asmodai, "it isn't that. It's just that I had thought it a better-kept secret than it is."

"I'm not uncomfortable with you knowing," said Lilith.

"Nor am I," said Lucifer. "In fact, I'll tell you that the Lord Satan has doubts, and we're going to see him now to try to resolve them."

Harut nodded, but didn't say anything.

"Are you curious, Harut?" asked Lilith.

"Some," he said.

"Lord Satan isn't sure it's right to coerce the hosts into helping, if they don't want to."

"Why wouldn't they want to?" asked Harut.

"I expect," said Asmodai, "that they will. We want to build a place that will be safe from the flux—forever. Where we won't have to worry about Waves—ever. Why wouldn't everyone be in favor of that?"

"I don't know," said Harut. "How many will die doing it?"

Lucifer licked his lips, but didn't answer.

"Abdiel was studying that," said Asmodai. "I never heard his results."

"That may be an answer," said Harut.

"Certainly, it could be a lot," said Asmodai. "And it might be any of us—we're not asking anyone to do something we aren't doing ourselves. We take risks every Wave. But this time, it would be the last."

"Is Satan the only one who thinks this way? How did he think of it?"

"His task," said Lucifer, "is to make sure everyone does what he must. So he had to think about it."

"Why?"

"Because," Asmodai explained, "they *might* object, and we have to be ready."

Harut nodded. "Maybe, if the only way to handle those who don't like it is to force them, something's wrong from the beginning."

Asmodai looked at him and started to say something, then stopped. He remained silent until the four rose to continue their journey. Then he said a brief farewell to Harut and resumed his silence.

"You've got something on your tail."

"Thou mayst bite it off, Lord Mephistopheles."

"I may, at that."

"And kiss what doth lie beneath."

Mephistopheles chuckled. "It's nice to find you in a good mood, Beelzebub."

"'Tis thy pleasure, Mephistopheles."

"So, how are the plans?"

"Perchance thou should'st ask nearer the center, where such are made."

"No, no, not those plans. I mean the ones for the rebellion."

"What?"

"It's all over Heaven, Beelzebub. How you and Satan—"

"Lord Satan!"

"Lord Satan, then. How you and Lord Satan are planning to raise the entire region in rebellion and—"

"Hold, thou!"

"Eh?"

"Art thou quicker than I, Mephistopheles?"

"I'm not sure, Beelzebub."

"Canst thou move faster than these teeth can find thy throat?"

"Well, that would be hard to say."

"Then know this: the Lord Satan and I have certain doubts and fears. We know not if 'tis right to force upon the hosts risks that they choose not. An these doubts thwart our obedience, we shall go unto the Lord Yaweh and speak them. Naught else shall be done by the Lord Satan or me. He that saith else, shall discover whether he be quicker than these teeth. Grasp thou that?"

"Quite."

"Then, if thou hast business here, thou mayst enter. Else, get thee gone ere my patience wanes."

"Perhaps it would be best if I just left."

"Perchance 'twould."

"Farewell, then, Beelzebub."

"Fare quickly, Mephistopheles."

Mephistopheles turned from the doorway of the Southern Hold, holding his smile with some difficulty.

"Where can he be going, or coming from?" asked Abdiel. Since he was alone, no one answered. He hunched behind the rocks as Mephistopheles passed within fifty feet of him.

"And smiling, too. What has he been up to?" Abdiel watched the retreating figure with some apprehension. He was in the secluded area, and well-hidden, but he was close to the Southern Hold. It wouldn't do to be seen at all, and it would be disastrous to be seen while he was about this business.

How long? He had nearly a day's head start, but Gabriel moved quickly.

He bit his thumb and continued walking.

• • •

"Well, well, Gabriel! Good day to you."

"Good day, Lord Mephistopheles."

"You don't need the 'Lord,' Gabriel; my name is too long as it is."

"Thank you, Mephistopheles."

"What brings you out here, Gabriel?"

"An errand, Lo—Mephistopheles."

"An errand? Out here? Nonsense! Admit it, Gabriel, you're taking a vacation, aren't you?"

"No, I'm not. Really!"

"It's all right. I won't tell anyone."

"Really, I'm on an errand."

"Who is there to deliver a message to, out here?"

"Lord Satan. I've—oops."

"What, you weren't supposed to tell me that? Well, don't worry. And I suppose you can't tell what the message is, can you?"

"No, I can't."

"Well, that's all right. I can guess it pretty well. All of this fuss about the Big Plan. But I suppose, even being right there, you aren't told a lot about it."

"Well, I'm not exactly *told*...."

"It must be frustrating, after a while."

"Frustrating?"

"Well, being that close to all of the planning and agitation, and not knowing what is really going on. For instance, I understand that the Lord Satan is angry with Yaweh over some little matter, but I imagine you'd know even less about that than I would."

"I don't think that is quite the case, actually."

"Well, you probably haven't heard of it."

"Oh, no. You have it just backwards. I—uh, I shouldn't say any more."

"Of course. Well, will it be a while before I see you back at the palace?"

"Oh, no. We should be returning right away."

"We? The Lord Satan will accompany you?"

"Yes, he—uh, I must go now, Mephistopheles. My errand is urgent."

"Certainly, Gabriel. A pleasant day to you."

"And to you, Mephistopheles."

• • •

Beelzebub padded into the large chamber. Wine and glasses were placed throughout. As he entered, he announced solemnly, "My Lord Lucifer of the Firstborn, Regent of the East. The Lady Lilith. The Lord Asmodai. The Lord Michael of the Firstborn."

He stepped out of the way as they entered. Satan rose and greeted them, then motioned to the chairs.

This room was done in dark blues, but well lit, so it seemed bright. A painting of Lilith was against one wall. She smiled as she saw it, and exchanged glances with Satan that implied memories.

The other walls were bare, except for a cupboard against one. The total effect was spaciousness, but not enough to make one uncomfortable, and the chairs (soft and white) were close enough together to make conversation easy.

Beelzebub nudged the door closed with his nose, then leapt onto the couch next to Satan.

Satan poured wine and gestured to the others to do the same. Lilith and Asmodai did.

Lucifer said; "This is a continuation of our last discussion."

"I see."

Asmodai cleared his throat. "I wasn't there. Could you fill me in?"

"We didn't resolve anything," said Satan. "My feeling was—is—that I'm not sure it's right to force the hosts to risk themselves in this if they don't want to."

"You seem," said Lilith, "more certain than you were."

"Hmmmm. I don't *feel* any more certain."

"Why not?" shot Asmodai.

"Eh?"

"You have questions. Why, after all this time, haven't you resolved them? What makes you—if I may—doubt your doubts?"

Satan nodded. "Good question. Why is it," he asked suddenly, "that I feel as if I'm being judged?"

The others looked at each other. "I don't know," said Lilith at last. "*I'm* not judging you."

Satan shrugged. "It doesn't matter. To answer your question, Asmodai, it's just what Lucifer told me before: How can we sit here, knowing that we can save thousands or millions of lives, and not do anything about it?"

Michael stirred, then spoke for the first time. "I remember hearing about you during the Third Wave, friend Satan. You were holding things along your eastern border when there was a breakthrough far to the west."

"I remember."

"As the story goes, you decided, no matter how hard pressed you were, that the western area was in more peril because there were few defenders."

"I remember."

"It turned out you were right. Those you abandoned, survived. And you arrived at the western area in time to—"

"What is your point, Michael?"

"That there are times when you have to decide. You've shown that you can do so in battle, but—" He fanned the air, as if he could churn the right words from it.

"He is saying," said Lucifer slowly, "that you must be able to make hard decisions even if there doesn't seem to be any urgency. Sometimes there is an urgency that you can't see."

Satan looked away. "Acting on impulse is fine for some things," he said. "But there are times. . . ."

Lilith bit her lip.

"Word of your doubt has spread," said Asmodai. "There is growing unease, Lord Satan. Yaweh is worried. The rest of us are worried. I—"

He stopped. Satan looked at him. "Yes?"

Asmodai sighed. "I've been wondering about these things myself."

Satan chuckled wryly.

"It isn't funny," said Lucifer.

"No, it's sad. So sad I have to laugh at it. Well, what do you want from me?"

"A decision," said Lucifer.

Asmodai nodded. "Either put aside your doubts and do your task, or declare yourself opposed."

Satan chewed his lower lip for a while. "It sounds so easy. But it isn't that easy, it's—" He stopped. The others remained silent. At last, Satan said, "I realize what you mean, Asmodai. Yesterday, Mephistopheles came by to worm some information from us, and in doing so he spoke of talk that we were plotting rebellion."

Next to him, Beelzebub growled softly.

"There is no truth in it, but it is interesting that he chose that approach. Now, I've known him since long before the Third Wave—I know him as well as I know any angel in Heaven. I'm not worried about Mephistopheles, but I recognize that, though he made up that story, there are seeds there that I can't ignore."

Asmodai nodded. "That's what I meant."

"I know. But what you four are doing to me is what I'm afraid of doing to the hosts. Now that I see it, I like it even less than I did when I was just imagining it."

Asmodai shrugged. "Is that your decision, then?"

"I'm not sure."

Asmodai slammed his palm against the arm of the chair. Then he poured himself a glass full of wine and tossed it down.

"Lord Satan?" said Lilith.

"Yes."

"It isn't by our desires that we are doing this—forcing you to decide."

"I know."

"We are being forced as much as we are forcing you. By the Plan, yes—but more: by the flux itself."

Satan turned to Beelzebub. "Sound familiar?" he asked wryly.

Beelzebub nodded without speaking.

"All of this is beside the point," said Asmodai, his lips tight with anger. "You must decide *now*. You must—"

"Why all the heat, Asmodai?"

"Because—" he stopped, looked away, and shrugged.

"Methinks," said Beelzebub, "that Asmodai doth fear his own doubts, and would have thee as target that he need not have himself."

"I see," said Satan.

"Whatever Asmodai's reason," said Michael, "he is right."

Satan shrugged. "Telling me 'decide' doesn't help me do it. Which way? Why? What are the effects? Can you answer these questions? Can you answer them for yourselves, if not for me?"

No one spoke.

"I thought not. Then here is my decision: I will leave tomorrow, and travel to the center, and speak with Yaweh. If he can't give me the answers I want I'll . . . do whatever I do. Does that satisfy you?"

Michael nodded thoughtfully. Lilith said, "Yes." Lucifer nodded once, abruptly. Asmodai remained silent and unmoving.

"Perhaps," Lucifer told Asmodai, "you should go along and get your answers at the same time."

"No," he said. "I'll get my own answers, in my own way, or live without them."

"An thou canst live without them, thou art better than I."

"Good day to you, Kyriel."

"And to you, Sith."

"I've been hearing things."

"It's as I told you, isn't it?"

"Worse, if anything. They don't care about us, it seems. They need angels to work on the walls, and whatever happens to them doesn't matter."

"It isn't the walls."

"It isn't?"

"What I've heard is that. . . ."

"Why did you shudder, Kyriel?"

"I've heard that . . . that we're to go out there and—build something. I don't know what."

"Go out there?"

"You know, *outside.*"

"Oh."

"Now *you're* shuddering, Kyriel."

"I know. It's hard to believe. I've heard the stories."

"Yes."

"Do you remember your creation, Kyriel?"

"Somewhat."

"I also, somewhat. Would you go back to that?"

"Not if I didn't have to!"

"Is there nothing we can do, Kyriel?"

"Well, I suppose we could do nothing."

"What do you mean?"

"Well . . . look, Sith: We're going to hear about this before it happens, aren't we?"

"Well, yes. I suppose."

"They have to gather us together, somehow or other, to go marching out into it."

"Yes."

"Well . . . what if we're not there?"

"Huh? Where would we be?"

"Somewhere else."

"I don't understand."

"Hide! We go off somewhere—to the north maybe—"

"Where Belial is?"

"Not that far north. Just somewhere that we can hide."

"Then what?"

"We wait until it's over, then come back. They'll never miss us, two out of the thousands."

"Three."

"Three?"

"Bath Kol."

"Oh! So it's true about—"

"Shut up, Kyriel."

"Right. Three."

Yaweh walked alone in the throne room. He walked around the perimeter, or back and forth across the middle. Sometimes he walked slowly, lost in reflection; other times he moved quickly, as if he actually had somewhere to go. He wondered whether Satan would return with the page. He thought so, but then he thought not.

Yaweh remembered the beginning—how the two of them had perceived each other, almost before each had perceived himself. During the first battle, they fought on and on, side by side, striving for their lives without understanding that that was what they were doing. Then suddenly discovering by accident that perhaps there could be more to existence than this struggle. He remembered how they had shared the joy when he who would later be called Michael was born of their battles with the flux, and then others.

He remembered the time, brief as it seemed now, after the First Wave, when they knew peace. He shook his head. Satan remembered these things too, didn't he?

Yaweh walked about the large room. He wondered whether Satan would return with the page. He thought so, but then he thought not.

"'Twas painful, was it not, milord?"

"It was painful, Beelzebub. But they're only doing what they think is right."

"As art thou, milord."

"I suppose. What about you?"

"Milord?"

"Do you think I'm doing the right thing?"

They stood at the door of the Southern Hold, watching the vanishing figures of their friends. Beelzebub was silent.

"Well?" inquired Satan after a suitable time had elapsed.

"Methinks to speak to Yaweh is good, milord. Yet methinks 'twill not solve what thou hopeth to solve. 'Tis thyself thou must answer to, and none can do it for thee."

"I'm afraid you may be right."

The four figures before them dwindled into nothingness.

It was just a few minutes after Michael, Lucifer, Lilith and Asmodai had passed by where Abdiel hid that he saw a lone figure walking toward him. About the right size, from the right direction—yes.

He concentrated on feeling a ball of white fire in his stomach.

"Gabriel!"

"What—? Lord Abdiel!"

"Ah! You recognize me."

"Of course, Lord Abdiel."

"I am pleased, Gabriel. What brings you here?"

"An errand, lord."

"Yes, of course. To the Southern Hold, no doubt. But I meant, what errand?"

"I'm afraid I can't speak of it, lord."

"I see."

"I'm sorry, lord."

"That's quite all right, Gabriel. I understand."

"Thank you, lord."

"And please call me Abdiel."

"Why, thank you—Abdiel."

"And, as to your message, you don't have to tell me. I can guess it."

"You can?"

"Certainly. You are going to summon the Lord Satan."

"How did you know?"

"I guessed. But I can save you the rest of the trip."

"Lo—Abdiel? You can?"

"Yes. By giving you the answer. The Lord Satan will not return with you."

"How—?"

"He feels he cannot be bothered just now. Lord Yaweh will have to wait. Perhaps in twenty or thirty days something could be arranged."

"I don't understand."

"What is there to understand, Gabriel? You spoke to the Lord Satan, and that was the answer he gave you. Should I repeat it?"

"No, but—"

"Then where's the problem?"

"But I haven't spoken to him, so how—"

"Gabriel."

"Yes, Abdiel?"

"I notice a certain tension in your shoulders and neck. Try to relax—you won't tire so quickly."

"And yet, Abdiel, it seems—"

"You're still tense, Gabriel."

"I don't understand how—"

"Wait. Do as I say, now. Relax your shoulders. Breathe evenly and deeply. There, that's better. Do you feel better?"

"Yes, but—yes, I do, Abdiel. But still—"

"Look at me, Gabriel. You have known me for a long time, haven't you? Would I give you false guidance? Of course not! You are about to waste your time and energy, and I wish to save you from that. Also, the Lord Yaweh will want to learn this news as soon as possible. Don't you trust me, Gabriel? Come, remember now, you came to the Southern Hold, and spoke with the Lord Satan in his great hallway, with his friend, Beelzebub, standing there. And the Lord Satan explained that he had nothing to say to the Lord Yaweh and directed you to inform him of it. You pleaded, remember? But he wouldn't listen. Is it coming back? Think . . . do you see it? Think of his voice. Can you hear it? Now you are going to return to Yaweh, and report to him. You met no one on the journey, except for those four archangels. You will report to me, later, what Yaweh says. You will do this secretly. Until it is time to do so, you will not know that you are going to. You will remember no part of this conversation. Now go."

Gabriel turned without a word and began the long journey back to Yaweh's Palace. Abdiel tiredly watched his departing back.

Four

Some think they see their own hope to
    advance
tied to their neighbor's fall, and thus they
    long
to see him cast down from his eminence;

Some fear their power, preferment, honor,
    fame
will suffer by another's rise, and thus,
irked by his good, desire his ruin and
    shame.

—Dante, *Purgatorio,* Canto xvii:115-120

Abdiel got as close to the Southern Hold as he could.

"This is probably stupid," he told himself. "There isn't anything I can learn here, and eventually someone will see me." He shook his head. "What did I come here for, anyway? I should be on my way home by now."

Some feeling, after he'd finished with the page, had told

him that he should see the Southern Hold. He could think of
no reason for it, but his instincts had been good in the past.

He had gone slowly, recovering from the exhaustion that
he'd felt after his efforts with Gabriel. His strength had returned
now. He made note of how long it took, munching blueberries
picked from bushes near the side of the road, occasionally
wiping purple juice from his lips and beard with a white linen
handkerchief.

He wondered what he was waiting for, and whether he would
recognize it if it came, and how long he would wait before
giving up and heading back.

Periodically, there would be travelers to or from the Hold,
and he would strain to make out what they said. It was never
anything important, though.

He sighed, continued his vigil, and ate blueberries.

"I'm not used to not being tired when I head back this way,"
remarked a traveler to his companion.

"I know what you mean," said the other. "It's going to be
nice to get home with some energy left."

The corners of his mouth rose a bit as he said this. The first
noticed and grinned.

"I see. What's her name?"

"What's the difference?"

He shook his head. "Sometimes I wonder about you."

The other shrugged.

"When will he be back?" asked the first.

"I don't know. Beelzebub said we shalleth be informedeth.
But look: we have enough oil done for fifty days, right? It's
twenty days each way to the center, if you're not hurrying, so
I'd guess he's visiting Lord Yaweh, and it'll be at least forty
days."

"Again? He was there a hundred days ago. . . ."

Abdiel cursed under his breath. Satan, going to the Palace!
All that work, wasted. He bit his lips with rage, and mangled
a handful of blueberries in his fist without noticing. Was there
any way to stop him?

Abdiel ran through his resources, and decided that there was
no way to prevent him from setting off. How about preventing
him from arriving? Maybe. But how?

By getting him to go somewhere else? Where? And again, how?

He concentrated. Maybe he could do *that* . . . which would mean . . . hmmm. He wondered how fast a dog could run. On the path, or off? Yes. . . .

He turned and began running toward the palace. He was going to need at least a day or two. Probably two.

The thought of what he was planning made him a bit uncomfortable. But it would be stupid to pull back now, and he wasn't really going to hurt anyone. Not exactly.

He pushed himself over the road that would become a path, and then a trail. . . .

Gabriel entered the palace and went to see the Lord Yaweh before he had so much as dusted himself off from the trip. Yaweh being alone, Gabriel coughed. Yaweh looked up.

"You're back."

"Yes, Lord."

"Alone?"

"Y-yes."

"I see."

"He—he said he was busy, Lord. That perhaps in a few days he'd have time—twenty or thirty days, he said."

"Twenty or thirty days."

"Yes, Lord."

"Did you speak to him personally?"

"Yes, Lord."

"How did he seem?"

"Haughty, Lord. He said that he had nothing to say to you. I tried to convince him, but—"

"Very well."

"I'm sorry I failed, Lord."

Yaweh shook his head. "No, Gabriel, you didn't fail. The Lord Satan made his choice." Tears began at the corners of Yaweh's eyes. Gabriel started to take a step forward, then caught himself.

"You may leave now," said Yaweh, thickly.

"Thank you, Lord."

Gabriel bowed and left, sick at heart. Behind him, Yaweh buried his face in his hands.

• • •

Under the open sky in daylight, in a place of long, thick grasses with oak and cedars commingling around and above them, they lay. They held hands without speaking, then she put her head on his shoulder, then he put his head on her shoulder.

They turned and held each other close. Above them the sky slowly darkened, and the winds around them grew still. They held each other through Heaven's long, slow night, without speaking.

Sometime toward morning, they kissed, and it was an exchange of vows—promises and hopes. They looked at each other, and knew that before many days had passed they would be seeing something new. It was too soon to know what.

Their robes fell away, and they touched each other as they had taught each other, and there was movement beneath the trees.

"Comfort me," they said without speaking.

"I will," they said in the silence.

Beneath the trees, upon the grass, upon each other, they did.

It was a statue in the water, a statue of a great, monstrous head supported by a massive neck that was long and sinewy and scaled, and disappeared into the waves. The eyes of the statue, no doubt by some trick of jewel-craft, seemed to glow. The statue had appeared three days ago, emerging from the sea, staring at the cleft at the edge of the small cliff.

Mephistopheles walked into the cleft from the path on the other side and saw the statue at the same time the statue saw him. The statue spoke first.

"I've been waiting for you for three days," she said.

"Sorry. It's been a long trip."

"Any luck?"

"Depends on what you mean by luck. I had a talk with Beelzebub. I don't think he likes me," he added thoughtfully.

Leviathan chuckled. "What did you do to the poor fellow?"

"I think I struck a nerve."

"Oh?"

"I accused him and Satan of fomenting rebellion, and it seemed like a sore spot."

"Why did you do that?"

"So that in denying it, he'd let slip their objections to the Plan."

"Clever," she said.

He shrugged.

"Well," asked Leviathan, "did you find out?"

Mephistopheles summarized his discussion with Beelzebub. Then he said. "I met Yaweh's page on the way back."

"And?"

"He had a message for Satan."

"Did you find out what the message was?"

"It was a summons. I got the impression that Yaweh wants to see Satan right away. I think Yaweh is angry about something."

"I could take a guess about what, Mephistopheles."

"Exactly."

"So, what does this mean?"

"It means that something is going to happen."

"Yes. I think I'd like to see Satan myself."

"Before or after he speaks to Yaweh?"

"Either will do."

"Good. My feet need rest. And, anyway, I doubt that I could catch up to him before he gets to the palace."

"I hadn't asked you to."

"Oh?"

"Could you find Ariel for me?"

Mephistopheles sighed. "My poor feet. Sure, I'll find him."

"Good."

"I'm on my way."

"Mephistopheles. . . ."

"Yes?"

"Thank you."

He bowed his head. Then he turned and went looking for Ariel, because he was uncomfortable showing strong emotions.

"Ho there, Sith."

"Hello, Kyriel."

"There's more news, from Chesetial out by the Southern Hold."

"Oh?"

"She says the Lord Satan is on our side."

"What do you mean?"

"He's going to see Yaweh, to tell him off."

"When?"

"He left from the South a bit ago. He could be here any day."

"Do you think they'll call it off?"

"They might."

"Well, it's nice to have one of them on our side, anyway."

"Yeah. Maybe we won't have to hide."

"Maybe."

It was early evening. Michael was sitting in an easy chair before the hearth, his feet bare, and resting from the journey. He heard shuffling noises outside, groaned to himself, then decided not to get up.

"Lord Michael?" came the voice, weak but recognizable.

"Come in, Abdiel," he said without turning his head.

"Thank you." Abdiel stepped inside and collapsed on the floor.

Then Michael was up, kneeling by his side. "Abdiel? What is it? Are you—"

"I'm . . . fine, Michael. Just let me . . . catch my breath."

Michael nodded, got up, and brought wine. Abdiel, meanwhile, had heavened himself up to a sitting position and was breathing in gasps. He accepted the wine and drank thirstily, nodding his thanks to Michael between gulps.

"What happened?" Michael asked when Abdiel's breathing was about back to normal.

"Nothing happened—but something nearly did."

"Tell me."

Abdiel nodded and got to his feet, supported by Michael. He made it to a chair and collapsed. He closed his eyes, as if gathering strength, then said, "I was near the Southern Hold, just twelve days ago."

"Twelve days!"

Abdiel nodded. "Something happened, and I didn't know what to do, so I came here."

"Well, what was it?"

"Satan," said Abdiel, "is after me."

"After you? What do you mean?"

"I'm afraid he may be chasing me. I'm not sure. He started to, but I escaped from the Southern Hold and ran. I looked back once and he had set out after me. I didn't look back again."

"I'm surprised Beelzebub didn't catch you."

"So am I! Happy, also. But I had a good start, and I guess Beelzebub can't run as long as I can."

"But, Abdiel, why was he chasing you?"

"Because I wouldn't go along with his plan."

"What plan?"

"He told me that he intends to overthrow Lord Yaweh and set himself up as ruler of Heaven. He explained that the Plan was folly, would never work, and that he wanted to end it once and for all."

"I don't believe it! He said—"

"I know. He told me that you had spoken to him, with Lucifer and Lilith and Asmodai. He said he'd managed to take you in, to convince you that he had nothing planned. But he wanted my help. He said that I had 'Yaweh's ear,' was how he put it."

"By the flux!" cried Michael. "Can this be true?"

"He tried to persuade me, but my ears were roaring and I couldn't hear his arguments. I just stood before him and shook my head."

"And then?" asked Michael.

"He tried to make me promise that I wouldn't tell anyone what he'd spoken of."

"Did you?"

"No."

Michael nodded. "Go on," he said. "What did he do then?"

"He . . . grew angry," said Abdiel. "He began walking toward me. I backed up, but he kept coming. Finally I turned and ran. I got out of the place, and when I looked back, he was running after me, yelling and shaking his fist."

"Did you hear what he was yelling?"

Abdiel shook his head. "Not clearly. I think it was something about finding me, but I'm not sure."

"He said he'd find you?"

"I think so. That's why I came to you. I didn't know what else to do."

"I think, Abdiel, that you ought to go to the Lord Yaweh and tell him what you've told me."

"Do you . . . do you think so, Lord Michael?"

"Why not? Shouldn't he know?"

"I'm afraid Lord Yaweh will take it hard."

"That may be true, Abdiel, but he should hear of it."

Abdiel sighed. "All right. I'll go to him now."

"The morning will do. You should rest first."

"No," said Abdiel, shaking his head. "By morning I'll have lost my courage."

"Lilith, my love?"

"Mmmmm."

"What did you think of the trip?"

She pulled her head up from the crook of his arm, turned over, and pulled his cloak up around them.

"What do you mean?"

"Well . . . I don't know. Never mind."

"If you want me to say that Satan has me half convinced, I won't."

"No, I—"

"Not until you do."

Lucifer lifted his head up to look at her. Then he smiled and dropped it again.

"All right," he said to the sky above them, "he has me half convinced."

"Me, too."

He sighed. "So what do we do?"

"We go see Yaweh."

He raised his head again. "You sound pretty certain of that."

"I am."

"Why?"

"Because I heard you whispering to Asmodai to set up an appointment with him."

He dropped his head back and laughed quietly. Then there was stillness in the glade.

They covered the leagues without effort. They didn't stay quite on the path, but always varied their journey just a bit, to admire a meadow they hadn't noticed before, or a brook that had carved a new trail.

The path had long ago petered out, and, after several days, they had found the one going toward the center. They stayed close to it as it grew into a stronger path that would soon become a trail.

"It's been a while since we've been here, Beelzebub."

"Verily. 'Tis much changed."

"I wonder if Yaweh will have changed."

"Milord? In a hundred days?"

"Well, I've changed, haven't I?"

"Thy meaning escapeth me, milord."

"I was thinking of what Michael said, about the Third Wave. It seems as if I can't make that kind of quick decision any more. Everything seems—I don't know—more important, or something. It's as if I have to watch every step, or I'll hurt someone. Haven't you noticed?"

"I . . . perchance 'tis true, milord. This conversation likes me not."

"Never mind, then."

They walked another league or three. Beelzebub said, "An the Lord Yaweh be changed, what then?"

"Then, maybe, I won't be able to convince him, or he won't be able to convince me."

The path did, indeed, turn into a trail. They found themselves on it again and continued, looking for a place to spend the night.

"Tomorrow, methinks, or the next day should see us to the Palace."

"The next day, more likely."

"Thou wilt speak unto Yaweh, then wilt thy questions have answers."

"In other words, I worry too much, right?"

Beelzebub chuckled. "'Twas not my meaning, milord, but 'tis true nevertheless."

Satan shrugged. "I hope you're right. About my questions being answered, I mean. You know, don't you, that at first it was only the two of us?"

"Milord?"

"Yaweh and I, I mean. At the beginning."

"Aye, milord."

"It was our battle that created the other Firstborn, or so Lucifer tells me."

"Aye."

"And the rest of the Firstborn, in the Second Wave, created you and the other archangels."

"Aye, milord."

"And so on in the Third Wave. So, one could say, all of

Heaven is the product of Yaweh and me."

"By the selfsame logic, milord, art thou the product of Yaweh."

Satan stopped in the middle of the trail and looked down at his friend. "You know, I never thought of that."

"Methinks, milord, that yon clearing will do well for us this night."

"I never thought of it that way at all."

"Shall we stop, then, and rest?"

"It never crossed—what? Oh, this'll do fine, I think."

"Then let us rest, milord, an it please thee."

"All right."

They moved off to the side. "Will he listen to me, do you think?"

"Aye, milord. Yaweh hath no small measure of love for thee."

"I hope so. Rest well."

"And thou, milord."

Abdiel found a door at the rear of Yaweh's palace and made his way inside as quietly as he could. He removed his sandals and crept down the narrow hall.

He came at last to an arched doorway with a plain brown curtain across it. He moved the curtain and slipped inside.

The only sound was even breathing from the bed as he set his sandals down. He moved to the head of the bed and tapped the form sharply on the shoulder.

"Who's th—"

"Shhhh!"

"Who's there?"

"Abdiel."

"What is it, lord? Why are we whispering?"

"It's the right time and place, Gabriel."

"For what . . . oh. . . ."

"Report."

In a steady, whispering voice, Gabriel told how Yaweh had taken his news.

"What will happen tomorrow? Limit your speech to things concerning the Plan."

Abdiel endured a seemingly endless stream of small doings, until—

"Wait! Repeat that last!"

"The Lord Lucifer has asked for an audience with the Lord Yaweh, to be held early in the morning."

"I see. Bide a moment."

Abdiel made a quick decision.

"Gabriel."

"Yes, Abdiel."

"The meeting is canceled."

"Yes."

"The Lord Yaweh will notify him when he has time to speak to him."

"Yes."

"The Lord Yaweh understands how urgent it is, but has no time just now."

"Yes."

"When the Lord Lucifer leaves, you will tell the Lord Yaweh that the Lord Lucifer has changed his mind, and no longer has any need to see him. The Lord Lucifer was no more specific than that."

"Yes."

"Continue your report."

Gabriel did so for another few minutes, but Abdiel found nothing else of interest. When the page finished at last, Abdiel said: "I wasn't here tonight. You didn't see or speak with me."

"Yes."

"Go to sleep."

Abdiel took his sandals, slipped out of Gabriel's room, and made his way out of the palace. He went to the top of the hill and into a small wooded area. There he put his sandals on and headed back toward the palace, this time circling around to come in the front way.

Satan stretched hello to the morning, relieved himself off from the clearing a ways, and nudged Beelzebub.

"Time to set off," he said.

Beelzebub rose. "Ready, milord."

As they walked, Satan remarked, "Another day until we get there, I think."

"Aye."

"Not more. We'll be on the road in another hour."

"Aye, milord."

"I'm beginning to despise traveling."

"Aye."

"And there's still the trip back."

"'Twill seem shorter, milord."

"I suppose."

"Art thou better . . . content today, milord?"

Satan chuckled. "Yes and no. I'm still worried about how Yaweh will react to me. We only spoke about the Plan once, you know, and before that I hadn't seen him for a long time."

"All will be well, milord."

"I hope so. By the flux! Sleeping on the ground makes one stiff!"

"Forsooth? To me, it seemeth not so."

"Thou dog, Beelzebub."

"Aye, milord."

Yaweh came down the wide sweeping stairs at almost the same moment that Gabriel appeared from the back of the hall, having emerged from the small doorway that connected to his chamber.

They saw Abdiel at the same instant. Abdiel ignored Yaweh and spoke to Gabriel. "Please tell the Lord Yaweh that I wish to speak with him, if it is convenient."

Yaweh smiled, nodded at Gabriel, and entered his throne room. Gabriel motioned Abdiel in, then returned to his post outside the door.

Presently, Lucifer arrived, and Gabriel was forced to turn him away, regretfully. It was then that Yaweh's voice came from the other side of the door.

Gabriel rushed to open it, and Yaweh said, "Ask Michael to come and see me at once. And send in Lucifer as soon as he gets here."

"Lord Yaweh, the Lord Lucifer has been here."

"What? Why didn't you tell me?"

"Lord, he said that he changed his mind, and no longer needed to speak with you."

"I see," said Yaweh. "Well, bring Michael. Hurry."

"Yes, Lord," said Gabriel, and he rushed off to do so.

"What is it, Yaweh? Is it about Abdiel's story?"

Yaweh nodded. "He said you sent him to me, is that right?"

Michael nodded.

"I'm glad you did. He waited all night in my hall, rather than waking me up with bad news." Yaweh smiled at Abdiel as he said this. Abdiel blushed and lowered his eyes.

"But it *is* bad news, Michael," Yaweh continued.

"I know, Yaweh. I don't know what to think."

"It's worse than you suppose," said Yaweh. "I have some indications that Lucifer has turned against me as well."

"Lucifer?"

"It seems that way. I'm not certain yet."

"It's hard to believe."

"I know," said Yaweh. "What should we do?"

Yaweh, who had been standing next to the throne, sat down on one of the chairs before it. Michael took another one and, after some urging, so did Abdiel.

Michael shook his head. "I don't know *what* to do, Yaweh."

"Have you turned against me also?"

Michael's nostrils flared, then his brows furrowed and he seemed more doubtful than angry.

"I—don't think so," he said.

"Good. I'm running out of angels I can trust."

"I understand," said Michael. "When Satan gets here, if you'll speak to him—"

"Gets here!" cried Yaweh. "Where?"

"Here. To the Palace. To see you. If you speak to him about—"

"What makes you think he's coming here? He told me he wasn't."

"He told you? But he told us—"

"When?"

"When we saw him, twenty-some days ago."

"My page was there, to ask him to see me."

"Gabriel?"

"That's right."

"We saw him on the way back, just after we left. But why would Satan have lied to us when he knows we'd find out in just a few days, when he failed to arrive?"

"To gain time, perhaps," suggested Abdiel.

Michael nodded. "Then he did fool us."

"It seems he did," said Yaweh.

"What can we do?"

"I don't know. Leave me for a while. I want to think about this. But please, stay around the palace—both of you."

"Yes, Lord."

"All right."

"That's the story, Raphael."

"It's hard to believe."

"So everyone has told me."

Yaweh was still in the small chair next to the throne. Raphael was seated beside him, her arms folded. She was frowning.

"I'd like to speak with Satan myself," she said.

"So would I. So would Michael."

"But perhaps he'll listen to me. We always got along well."

"So did we." Yaweh sighed and shook his head.

"Yes," she said softly, looking at him sympathetically, "you did."

Yaweh shook the mood off, forcing himself to think clearly. "But you think it will do some good for you to speak with him?"

"It might."

"Lucifer went with the same idea, and now it seems that he's been 'converted' also. And without the decency to let me know about it. That's what hurts, Raphael. None of them seems willing to tell me what he doesn't like."

"I know."

"Well?"

She shook her head. "I heal during the Waves. I see those who can only barely be saved, like Ariel, and those who can't be saved, like Seraphiel. Whenever an angel dies, part of me dies with him. This is our chance to stop that."

Yaweh nodded and placed his hand on her shoulder. She leaned a cheek against it.

Then, abruptly, he sat back, shaking his head. "But is there a plan left?" he asked. "Without Satan, without Lucifer—"

"So what? Lucifer has done his part, has he not?"

"Well, yes. . . ."

"And, as for Satan, it would be good to have him, but he can be replaced. Abdiel could do his job, could he not?"

"Yes, I suppose he could."

She was quiet for a moment, then she spoke softly, almost in a monotone. "Yaweh, do you remember the day you gathered us together, Satan, Abdiel, Michael, and me, and told us of this?"

"I remember."

"Do you know what I did after I left?"

"What did you do, Raphael?"

"I returned to my home, Yaweh, and I cried." As she said it, tears began to form in the corners of her eyes, as if the memory were the event. "I remembered how grateful poor Harut—do you remember Harut?"

"The musician? Somewhat."

"I remembered his face when we restored his hearing. And Leviathan. I'm told that she's as happy as she can be, under the circumstances, but do you remember how beautiful she was, before we even knew what beauty was?"

"Of course."

"I remembered that night, and I cried, because I thought that maybe we had the chance to end that. If you take that hope away from me now, Yaweh, now when we're almost ready to do it, well—who will heal *me?*"

Yaweh bowed his head.

Michael walked up to Raphael. She stood, and they held each other for a moment. Then he turned to Yaweh. "You wanted to see me?"

"Yes. Thank you for coming."

"You're welcome, Yaweh."

"I'd like you to do something for me, if you would."

Michael nodded, waiting for him to continue.

"Find our friend, Satan. Bring him here if you can; speak to him for me, if you can't."

"Happily!" said Michael. "I'll find him!"

"Thank you. If he won't return with you, tell him—tell him I love him."

Michael bowed his head.

"Raphael, accompany him, if you would. You speak to him, too. Tell him what you told me."

"All right."

Michael cleared his throat. "There is one thing," he said.

"Yes?"

"Abdiel. He fears Satan."

"I know."

"May he stay here? I'd feel better."

"Of course."

"Then I'm ready to leave at once," said Michael.

"And I," said Raphael.

"Good luck to you both."

When they left, Yaweh sent the page to bring Abdiel.

He came and bowed low. "You wished to see me, Lord Yaweh?"

"Yes, Abdiel. You fear Satan, don't you?"

Abdiel suddenly turned pale and could only manage a nod.

"Well, you may stay here until this matter is settled."

Abdiel swallowed. "Th-thank you, Lord. But—forgive me, it isn't safe here."

Yaweh furrowed his brow.

"What?"

"I fear for you, Lord, as well as myself. There are none to protect you here, and Satan—he will try to harm you."

"What, Abdiel? Harm? Me? Nonsense!"

Abdiel shook his head, but speech seemed beyond him.

"Why do you say that?" Yaweh asked.

"I feel it, Lord. And from the way he spoke. He hates you, Lord."

Yaweh bowed his head. He had never understood hate, or even dislike. The idea of it was unthinkable, so having it directed at him from one he loved as much as he loved Satan was no more unthinkable.

A deep anguish filled his heart, and he suddenly wished there were someone who could tell him what to do. He looked up after a moment, and Abdiel was still there, on his knees now, his eyes pleading.

Yaweh spoke in a whisper. "What do you wish me to do?"

"Bring in angels, Lord, and have someone make weapons for them, weapons that will make Satan fear them. Station them around you, and in the halls, and outside your palace, so none may get past who you do not know you can trust. Then I'll be free of fear for you, Lord."

Yaweh buried his face in his hands. "Has it come to that?" he asked.

Abdiel didn't answer.

"I'll think about it," said Yaweh at last.

Abdiel nodded, bowed low, and left the room. When he was out, he left the Palace, running as fast he could toward the south.

So far, everything was working as planned.

Five

Then Satan first knew pain,
And writhed him to and fro convolved.

—Milton, *Paradise Lost,* vi:327-328

The owl circled the clearing a few times, looking down. It made wider and wider sweeps and angled out over the sea. Soon a monstrous head broke the water. Spotting it, and seeing himself spotted, the owl returned to the cleft and landed there.

Leviathan swam as close as she could and stretched her neck out so she was nearly face to face with the owl. "Welcome, Ariel," she said. "I see Mephistopheles finally found you."

"He found me in forest in light of the day, and asked if by chance I would still know the way, to where you await me near rocks by the sea."

"'Near rocks by the say?' Oh. Never mind. Not bad, Ariel. Well, what did you learn?"

Ariel cleared his throat and began: "I found out that Yaweh has grow-en full sore, at Satan who turns down invites to his door, and Lucifer, Lilith, and p'raps many more. I saw then that Michael does hunt for this one, to ask him for reasons for what he has done, with Raphael, he's going forth at a run."

"I can see," said Leviathan, "that it's going to to take a while to get the whole story. I may as well relax."

Abdiel was well ahead of Raphael and Michael, but he hadn't yet found Satan and Beelzebub. With the added strain of having to find Satan before either of the others saw him or each other, he could barely keep going.

"This is stupid," he told himself. "But unavoidable," he added.

He moved along the road as quickly as he could, without the risk of being spotted too soon. It was still fully day, so both parties would be moving. One way or another, he decided, something would happen before nightfall.

Yaweh paced back and forth within the chamber, feeling more alone than he had ever felt since he had discovered, back at the beginning, that there was such a thing as un-alone.

Deciding that he needed company, he called his page.

"Yes, Lord?"

"Bring Abdiel. I want to speak with him."

"Abdiel is gone, Lord."

"Gone? Don't be ridiculous. Where would he go?"

"I don't know, Lord. But he left soon after Michael and Raphael."

"But—are you sure?"

"Yes, Lord."

Yaweh stood silent, then noticed the page. "You may go."

"Yes, Lord," said the page, who bowed and left.

Yaweh remained, feeling very much alone indeed.

"This doesn't make sense, Ariel. No, don't answer. But it doesn't. Mephistopheles tells me that Gabriel has summoned Satan for Yaweh. Now I learn that Satan refused the summons. But I also hear that he's left the Southern Hold and is going toward the center. Why?"

Ariel started to speak, stopped at a look from Leviathan. Her tail swirled the water behind her as she said, "Let me think for a minute."

She did so, with Ariel looking around him absently.

"No," she said, "I was right in the first place. There is something wrong, and I'll never find out what without speaking to Satan." She sighed. "Sometimes, Ariel, I hate being stuck like this."

"I grieve for you, lady, with all of my heart, I do what I can to aid for my part; so tell me my mission—anon will I start."

"Thank you, Ariel. Your help means a great deal to me. As to your 'mission,' if you wi!l, I want to speak to Satan as soon as possible. Tell him so. Say please. I think he'll come."

"I go to find Satan and bring him to you; I fear I'll be gone for an evening or two, but I promise to do all the best I can do."

As he finished, he bobbed his head, spread his wings, and launched himself into the air. He circled once over her head and was gone.

"Fare thee well, Ariel," she said softly. She sighed. "It's good to have friends."

"Yes, it is, honey."

"Harut! How long have you been there?"

"Just got here. Thought I heard Ariel's voice, but I guess I missed him."

"Yes. Harut, are you sure you saw Satan and Beelzebub leaving the Southern Hold? I don't mean to offend you, but—"

"I know. It's all right. Well, they weren't saying anything, and they didn't seem to notice me, but one was an angel, and I'd say he was an archangel at least by the way he walked, and—"

"The way he walked?"

"Yeah. You know, some people kind of step lightly, as if they aren't sure what they're about. An' some kinda march, like they aren't carin' who's in the way. Well, this guy knew where he was going, and he was sure of himself. And he was the right size for Satan, too—I could hear how far apart his feet planted themselves."

"I see."

"And whoever was next to him had four legs and wasn't very big."

"Yes, I guess that does sound like Satan and Beelzebub."

"That's what I thought."

"But it's strange."

"What's strange, honey?"

"There's a lot going on, Harut. I wish I understood it. But I don't think anyone does, two legs, four legs, or no legs. Eyes or no eyes."

"There somethin' I can do?"

"No . . . yes. Follow Ariel. See if you can find Satan and learn whatever you can. Ariel doesn't always see everything he might."

"Sure."

"But play me a song first."

Harut smiled. Leviathan wished for a moment that he could see his own smile. It would brighten his day, too.

Abdiel heard them before he saw them, which was lucky for him.

"This road is in good shape, isn't it?"

"Aye, milord. 'Tis said there are those who work at keeping it."

"Really?"

"So 'tis said. And that they extend it, so that someday it may link the Palace and the Southern Hold."

"That would be good, I think."

"And I, milord."

"But if we're going to be leaving Heaven, I guess we'll never see it."

"Think'st thou that we shall leave, milord? What of thy doubts?"

"Hmmm. Beelzebub, are you under the illusion that anything we're going to do or not do will stop the Plan?"

"Well, milord, my thought hath been—"

"Well, it shouldn't have. I'm not interested in stopping the Plan, nor am I capable of it. The only question is whether or not I'm going to participate. Do you think I'm irreplaceable? I'm not."

"As thou sayest, milord."

By this time Abdiel was well up the path. He found a spot amid the trees to one side where he could see the road, but was still partially sheltered.

He sat down to rest and wait, and think about a ball of white fire, burning in his middle.

• • •

"He wouldn't see me, Asmodai."

"Oh, hello, Lucifer. Who wouldn't? Yaweh?"

"That's right. I went to see him as I said I would, and he wouldn't talk to me."

"Why?"

"He said he was busy."

"That's absurd."

"Yes."

"How did he seem?"

"I don't know. I didn't actually see him. His page relayed the message. He seemed very apologetic."

"The page? Gabriel?"

"That's right."

"Hmmmm."

"What are you thinking?"

"I'm thinking that it was this same page who was to bring the Lord Satan. And he's the one who relayed the Lord Satan's answer, which wasn't anything like the answer we, who'd just spoken to him, would have expected."

"I think I see what you mean."

"Yes. I'd like to speak to Yaweh."

"You're right. I don't think he can keep us out no matter what he does, if we really want to get in. Are you with me?"

"Yes! When?"

"Now."

"Let's go."

Alone in the dark, Yaweh nursed his sorrow and his doubts.

If he could have solved the problem by abandoning the Plan, he would have done so, but it was beyond that now—Raphael had made that clear to him.

If he could have convinced himself that Abdiel was wrong, he would have done that, but he couldn't—it fit the pattern too well. First Satan, then maybe Michael, perhaps Lucifer—no, this was organized, not random. He could feel it. And that meant that Abdiel was right.

If he could have been sure the Plan could go on without him, he would let them destroy him when they wanted to, because he could see no more pleasure in life, with his friends deserting and hating him. But he couldn't. Of them all, he was the only one who could see the Plan through.

The conclusion was inescapable—he would have to do what Abdiel suggested.

Since Yaweh had no understanding of hate, he couldn't know that, as he summoned his page to bring Uriel, he hated himself.

Uriel bowed very low. "How may I serve you, Lord?"

"Uriel," said Yaweh, "you know much of the Plan, do you not?"

"I know somewhat of it, Lord."

"And do you like it?"

"Like it, Lord? It hadn't occurred to me to wonder. Yes, I like it. I think it would be a wondrous thing."

"Good. Do you know that there are those who would stop it?"

"I've heard it rumored, Lord, but I don't know if it's true or not."

"It's true."

"This grieves me, Lord."

"And me also."

"Is there something I can do, Lord?"

"Yes, Uriel, there is."

"I am ready, as always, Lord."

"Good. Find two hundred angels and bring them here."

"Two hundred?"

"Yes."

"Very well, Lord."

"But before bringing them, have each of them find a sapling—a straight sapling of good wood about his own height, and sharpen one end of it."

"Sharpen it, Lord?"

"That's right."

"Very well, Lord."

"Have them back with the prepared saplings in one hour."

"As you say, Lord."

"Then find the archangel Albrot, who worked with Asmodai. Have him fashion swords, to look like Michael's, only smaller. I want them soon. When they're ready, replace the saplings with the swords."

"Yes, Lord."

"Go, then."

Uriel bowed and left. Yaweh leaned back and closed his eyes, trying not to think of what he had just done.

"One thing about these sticks."

"What's that, Sith?"

"Well, if we poked someone with them, it would hurt, wouldn't it?"

"Huh? It sure would! So what?"

"Well, I wonder if that's what they're for?"

"To poke someone with?"

"Well, what else?"

"I don't know. What makes you think of that?"

"The Plan."

"You mean we might have to poke angels who don't go along with the Plan?"

"It could be."

"You don't really think so, do you?"

"I don't know. How's this?"

"Uh . . . that's good. Check mine?"

"Ow!"

"I guess it's good enough, huh?"

"Oh, shut up."

Yaweh stood before his throne. To his left were twenty angels; to his right were eighty angels; in front of him were another hundred. Also before were Uriel, Gabriel, and an archangel named Raziel.

Yaweh cleared his throat and began. "Greetings to you, my loyal and true angels."

The angels before him looked at each other.

"I have called you here because I need you," he continued. "Some of you may have heard of a great Plan being formed. It is true that there is such a Plan. We are trying to make a safe place for us all to live. That is the Plan. You are to be its guardians.

"Why does it need guardians? Because some of your brethren wish to stop it. I will not say who, because I'm not sure of them. I cannot say why, because I don't know. None of them has spoken to me.

"But I know this is the case. I am deeply saddened—" He stopped for a moment and looked away. When he looked back, his face was normal. "I am deeply saddened, but it cannot be helped. The Plan is for all of us equally. I cannot let them stop it by destroying me, as they may wish to do.

"I might be wrong. I hope I'm wrong, but, for the sake of the Plan, I cannot risk myself now."

He looked at the hundred angels directly in front of him. "You," he said, "will guard the outside of the palace, so that none may come near in force. There must be some of you there at all times. You may let groups of four pass; you must stop any group larger than that. You will be called Thrones, for you will extend my throne outside of the palace, and any gathering that wishes to appear before the throne shall appear before you, instead." He pointed with his right hand. "You will guard the inside of this palace. You will stand together, taking turns while your comrades sleep, so that none may enter without my leave. You shall be named Cherubim, after Cherubiel who fell in the Third Wave." He pointed with his left hand. "You," he said, "will stay near me, around my throne, so that any who get past the Cherubim will be stopped. You will be called Seraphim, after Seraphiel, who also fell in the Third Wave.

"Raziel shall be chief of the Thrones, Gabriel shall lead the Cherubim, and Uriel shall lead the Seraphim.

"And know this, also: No one, be he angel, archangel, or Firstborn, shall give orders to you, save only myself, and your chiefs."

He looked around at them.

He saw Raziel, Gabriel and Uriel as their faces swelled with pride. Throughout the room, this same reaction was occurring. To be on the same level as a Firstborn? Even above a Firstborn in some ways? Yaweh frowned. There was something wrong about this reaction, but yet . . . he sighed inwardly.

"Go now to your appointed places. The future of all the hosts of Heaven rests with you."

With some disorder, as Gabriel and Uriel got used to telling others what to do instead of being told themselves, they made their way to their positions.

Once more, he sighed too himself. He had done what he had to do. Now he had only to learn to live with it.

Abdiel relaxed and controlled his breathing. Soon, he knew, they would be before him, and he would have to act quickly.

And carefully. He wanted to hurt the one, but not too badly. He had only a vague idea of how strong he was going to have to be, because, so far as he knew, nothing like this had ever been done. He knew that a blast of illiaster that would only annoy a Firstborn could destroy a mere angel, and that one that would injure a healthy angel could destroy one who was wounded. He knew all of this, but he didn't know precisely how much to use in this situation, so he was going to have to be careful.

He concentrated on his illiaster, because that way he wasn't so nervous.

Lucifer and Asmodai wondered at the angels outside of the palace carrying sticks, and resolved to ask Yaweh about this, too. Inside they found Gabriel. On either side of him was an angel holding a stick, and there were several more around the main hallway. Lucifer and Asmodai ignored them.

"We're here to see Yaweh," said Lucifer.

Gabriel bowed. "He doesn't wish to see you, lord, as I explained earlier."

Neither noticed how perfunctory the "lord" was.

"That won't do," said Asmodai. "We're here to see him. If he doesn't want to speak with us, he can tell us so."

"I'm afraid that isn't possible."

"Indeed?" said Lucifer.

They began to brush past him—and stopped. In front of them stood six angels, each holding a stick sharpened to a point, and the point was aimed at them.

"What is this?"

"You cannot go inside," said Gabriel.

They looked around and saw twelve more angels looking determined and excited.

Asmodai turned to Lucifer. "Do you know, I think they're going to poke us with those things."

Lucifer nodded. "I think you're right."

"Well, have we found out what we came to find out?"

"I guess we have. We were wrong after all."

"Yes. Unless—"

"Yes?"

"How do we know this is by Yaweh's will?"

"I see what you mean."

They looked around themselves and saw the same determined faces, still pointing the sharpened sticks at them.

"I'm going to try something."

"Okay."

"Be ready!" called Gabriel. "At the first sign—"

His voice caught. There was the sound of clattering as sticks fell from hands which dropped to sides. The angels around them were staring forward, dumbly.

"Go!" hissed Lucifer between his teeth. "I can't hold them like this for long. Speak to Yaweh and find out!"

Asmodai ran forward and flung open the door to the throne room. Ten angels with sticks surrounded the throne, Uriel at their head.

The angels spun and stared. "An attack!" cried Uriel. "Stop him!"

"It's true, then," said Yaweh.

"That answers my question," said Asmodai, and bolted.

When he returned, he found a dozen more angels with sticks running toward Lucifer, who was beginning to look worried.

"I've found out!" he called. "Let's go."

Lucifer and Asmodai, as one, raced for the door. The Cherubim, released, growled and reached for their spears.

"After them," called Gabriel.

"I hope we're faster than they are," said Asmodai.

Lucifer saved his breath for running.

Ariel spotted them from above, despite his poor eyesight. He was pleased with how short a time it had taken. He began circling down to hailing distance, and composing the proper introduction.

As he dropped, something caught his eye. Where was it? There! In the trees off to the side.

He went closer. Abdiel! What was he doing here? He seemed to be watching the road. For what? Was he waiting for Satan and Beelzebub? If so, why not wait where they could see him?

Ariel wondered whether he should stop and ask him. He came a little closer, landing in a tree between Abdiel and the road.

There was a funny feeling in the air, he decided. He tried to think of what it was. It was certainly familiar. Where had he run into it before?

He suddenly remembered and was even more puzzled than before. It was the feeling of illiaster, controlled and ready for use.

In his shrunken, damaged form, Ariel was particularly sensitive to illiaster. He sensed for it and immediately found himself led to Abdiel.

Abdiel? Controlling illiaster? Why? He shook his head and tried to work out the puzzle.

"Methinks all is not well, milord."

"Eh? What do you mean?"

"There is that in the air which likes me not."

"I don't understand, Beelzebub."

"Nor I, milord. Yet—" He shook his head. "All is not well," he repeated.

Michael and Raphael walked on in silence. There was nothing to say. If Satan were, indeed, on the way to the center, they would meet him on this road. If not, they would ask after him until they found him, however long it took.

Raphael was sad that it had come to this, but she hoped to reason with him. She felt strongly for the Plan. If she couldn't convince him to join, at least he would agree not to hinder it. Wouldn't he? They had been so close, once.

Michael was angry. He knew that there were others in Heaven who were, well, quicker than he. He didn't resent it. But to be made a fool of! That was uncalled for.

But he wouldn't be hasty. He would give Satan every chance to explain. Better yet, let Raphael do the talking. Maybe she could make him see that what he was doing was wrong, was something that was hurting everyone. No, I have a right to be angry, he decided, but I don't have a right to act on my anger. Not yet, anyway.

They wandered down the road, following its twists and turns, oblivious to the beauty around them.

Soon, thought Michael, soon there would be a reckoning.

Gabriel returned, tired and worn. He entered the Throne room.

"I'm sorry, Lord. We have failed."

"Failed?"

"We didn't catch them."

"I didn't expect you to. You are of the Third Wave. They are of the First and Second."

"As you say, Lord. Then you know who they are?"

"Certainly. I recognized them."

"So did I, Lord. We can continue to hunt for them."

"If you do, there will be fewer to guard the palace."

"As you wish, Lord."

"You've done well, Gabriel."

"Lord? They got past us."

"Yes, and they were stopped inside. You slowed them down; Uriel and his folk stopped them. Neither of you could have done it alone."

"But they shouldn't have gotten this far!"

"Gabriel, there is no greater master of illiaster than Lucifer. I am not surprised that he was able to confound you. But it took all he had—he had nothing left to help his friend."

"Yes, Lord."

"And, further, I hadn't known until now that Asmodai was with them. I suppose I should have suspected it, because he was one of those who went to see—that one—in the South. But I hadn't known it. Now I do. You have done well this day, Gabriel. I am proud of you, and of Uriel, and of the Cherubim and the Seraphim. You have all proven your worth."

"Thank you, Lord."

"Thank you, Lord."

"You may tell your people so."

"Yes, Lord."

"Yes, Lord."

"Now, back to your posts."

"Yes, Lord."

"Yes, Lord."

It was good to know, Yaweh decided, that he could appear strong when it was needed. Had he told them how he felt— but there was no point in that.

It occurred to him then to wonder if something wasn't wrong when he had to lie to those who should be helping him. Yes, something was wrong. So many things were wrong that it was pointless to count them. What caused this? Who could say? Had he more energy, he would have tried to think it through, but not now, he decided. Not now.

• • •

From the top of the tree, Ariel saw Satan and Beelzebub approach. A little later, Ariel saw Abdiel lean forward and extend his hands toward the road.

Stranger and stranger, he thought. The feeling of controlled illiaster grew stronger, and Ariel realized that Abdiel was about to release something.

Toward the road.

Where Satan and Beelzebub were walking.

From a concealed position.

Everything he had heard about Satan and Gabriel and Yaweh suddenly flashed through his mind. In that instant, he understood.

"It groweth stronger, milord."

"What?"

"'Tis only a feeling, milord, but much is amiss."

"Should we stop?"

"Perchance 'twould be best, milord."

"For how long, Beelzebub?"

"I know not, milord, but soon! I feel—"

He was interrupted by a cry from above. They looked up.

"Ariel! What—"

Ariel swooped down, his wings wide apart as if shielding Beelzebub.

Then Satan felt it. Illiaster, controlled, funneled and focused. To him, it would have been an annoyance. To Beelzebub, it may have caused some pain. But it hit Ariel directly.

He screamed, a long wail of agony to come from so small a form. Then his body seemed to collapse upon itself, as paper burning without a flame. It turned to a sheet of black ash, then the ash collapsed upon itself and even that was gone.

Satan looked to where Ariel had been a moment before and felt a great emptiness sweep over him.

He fell to his knees and bowed his head.

Six

Behold, he put no trust
in his servants, and his
angels he charged with folly.

—Job, 14:8

For the space of four breaths nothing moved. It was Beelzebub who spoke first. "'Twas from off the road, milord," he said softly. "That way," he added, looking directly toward Abdiel without seeing him. Satan looked at him, his eyes vacant.

Then there was a crashing sound before them, and Beelzebub saw the figure moving through the trees. He growled and sprang into the brush. After a moment, the figure emerged onto the road, sprinting away from them. Beelzebub appeared after it.

"Abdiel!" called Beelzebub.

"Abdiel," said Satan, standing. He reached for the emerald at his breast, but when he looked up again Abdiel had vanished around a turn in the road.

Without another word, they set off in pursuit.

• • •

"They are gone," said Lucifer, leaning against a small building near the edge of the center of Heaven.

"At least they aren't fast runners," remarked Asmodai.

"I don't understand this," said Lucifer. "It doesn't make sense."

Asmodai shrugged. "Let's figure it out later. What should we do?"

"I don't know. I'm going to find Lilith."

"Good idea. Then meet me at my home."

"Why there? That's where they'll look for us."

"Let them. I have—things there."

"I see."

"And with your help, I'll build more."

"Hmmm. And do what?"

"I'm not sure. But I'll not be humiliated like that again, Lucifer. I will not tolerate it."

"I see your point."

"Good. Then will you meet me?"

"All right."

"You may have to fight your way through."

"I know. I still have the last gift you gave me—somewhere."

"Oh, yes. That. Good. Until later, then."

"Until later."

They weren't of the quality that Asmodai could have produced, even between Waves. They were not especially strong, nor especially sharp. Nor did they hold what edge they had very well.

But the Cherubim put down their sharpened sticks and took up spears with metal tips. The Seraphim and the Thrones took up swords.

Some time was consumed by all of this, as they had to compare their weapons and engage in swaps. But at last Yaweh looked over those who guarded his palace.

"Now," he told himself, "I am defended. I hope I don't find a need to attack as well."

Michael and Raphael felt something happen. They stopped where they were and considered.

"You felt it?" asked Michael.

"Yes," said Raphael. "What was it?"

"I'm not sure. It reminded me of a Wave, somehow."

"Do you think it's starting?"

"No, I don't think so. It was different, but—what's that?"

"Abdiel!"

He came running up to them and collapsed at their feet.

"He . . . help me."

"What are you doing here, Abdiel?" asked Michael, kneeling at his side.

He gasped, "I . . . felt . . . something was . . . wrong. I wanted . . . to warn you. . . ."

"What happened?" asked Raphael.

"He's . . . after me!"

"What?" cried Michael, standing and looking up the empty road.

"Who?" asked Raphael.

"Satan," said Abdiel, and began trying to stand.

As if by cue, Beelzebub came into sight, his teeth bared.

"Help me!" cried Abdiel, springing forward and covering his head.

Raphael moved to stand over him, her hand going to the star at her side. Michael advanced to meet Beelzebub, not without some fear.

Satan appeared then, running, his eyes flashing as only the eyes of the Firstborn can.

Beelzebub stopped. "Thou shalt let me pass," he told Michael flatly.

"No," said Michael.

"That one hath—"

Abdiel gave a great cry. Michael looked up as Satan leaped over him and was upon Abdiel before anyone could move.

Abdiel screamed again as Satan's hand found his throat. There was a flash of movement from Raphael's arm, and Satan dropped without a sound. Raphael stood breathless, tears at the corners of her eyes, holding the chain which held the star.

"I had to," she said. "He would have—"

"It's all right," announced Michael. "Help Abdiel return to the Palace. I'll take this one with me." He indicated Satan on the ground before him.

In an instant, Beelzebub was past him, standing over Satan's body.

"Thou shalt not," he said.

Michael flung his cloak back. "Can you stop a Firstborn, small one?"

"Art thou faster than my teeth, Firstborn?"

They considered each other for a moment.

"I guess we'll find out," said Michael softly.

Harut, from leagues away, felt it.

He stopped and wondered at the sudden tears that came to his eyes. He concentrated for a moment and felt where it had come from. He changed direction accordingly and started walking again. The stick he used to guide himself made little sound against the soft dirt. His feet made less.

He wondered why he suddenly felt that some of the freshness had gone out of the air.

He made himself walk a little faster.

"Hold, Michael!"

Without taking his eyes from Beelzebub, he said, "What is it, Raphael?"

"Can he best you?"

Michael chewed on his lower lip for a moment. "It's possible," he said.

"Then what? What about Abdiel?"

"Then it's up to you."

"And if I fail? We must protect him, Michael."

"What about you? Help me now with this one."

"I . . . can't, Michael. I can't hurt someone like that."

"Hmmph. You did well enough with Satan."

"That just happened. It was different."

"You mean we should leave these two here?"

"We must."

"Our task was to bring them back."

"Maybe. But in a sense, we have accomplished our task, have we not? We have found out what we wished to, at least in part."

Michael thought this over, then nodded. "If we leave, what will you do, four-legged one?"

"Why dost thou defend—"

Abdiel whimpered, and clutched at Michael. "He's going to spring! Help me!"

"Answer my question," said Michael.

Beelzebub nodded. "Thou hast answered mine full well."

"I'll ask once more, small one. What will you do if we leave with our friend?"

"I will wait until the Lord Satan awakes."

Michael nodded. "All right then, we'll leave. When he awakes," Michael gestured at Satan, "tell him there will be another time."

"An he were awake," said Beelzebub, "like words would he give unto thee, Lord Michael."

"I'm sure of it."

Michael turned his back on Beelzebub. "Let's go, then."

Abdiel stood. He looked fearfully back at Beelzebub. Michael and Raphael each took one of his arms and assisted him back down the road.

Michael looked back once and saw the eyes of Beelzebub fixed on him like the coals of the furnace of Asmodai.

"Well, now, isn't this a fine-looking troop?"

"Get out of our way, Mephistopheles."

The one addressed opened his eyes wide and quickly stepped out of the way.

"My apologies, Lord Michael. May I be of assistance?"

The three of them walked past him, Michael and Raphael each holding an arm of a pale and shaking Abdiel.

"Yes," said Michael as they passed. "If you see Satan, hold him for me. If you can't hold him, tell him to keep looking over his shoulder. One day soon, I'll be there."

They continued down the road.

"Odd," thought Mephistopheles. "Why is Abdiel over-acting?" After some thought, he decided to continue traveling south.

"Beelzebub!"

"Who art thou? Ah! Harut. Thou mayest approach, an thy intentions toward the fallen be not evil."

"My intentions aren't evil. The fallen?"

"Ah! Thou canst not see. I had forgotten. My Lord Satan doth lie at my feet."

"Satan! He's hurt then!"

"Certes is he hurt. He lieth not on the road by my choice or his."

"What happened? Should I get Raphael?"

Beelzebub made a sound that could have been a laugh. "Methinks that Raphael needs us least of all."

"What happened, Beelzebub? Ah! His face is warm. What's this?"

"Where he was struck, Harut."

"Struck? I don't get this. Struck by who?"

"Raphael."

"Raphael! You sure?"

"Harut, it doth hurt me to tell thee, for he was thy friend more than mine, but—"

"Who?"

"Ariel."

"Ariel? What does he have to do with this?"

"Harut, Ariel is no more."

"What?"

"He hath been struck down, e'en to save me. A traitorous blow from a hidden spot did fell him but hours ago."

Harut tried to speak, but found he couldn't. Tears welled in his eyes and a lump in his throat.

"'Twas Abdiel who struck the blow, but Michael and Raphael aided him, for they protected him when the Lord Satan and I would have torn him asunder for his deed. 'Tis an evil day, Harut."

As Satan had done before, Harut, on his knees, covered his face with his hands and sobbed.

When Mephistopheles found them, something told him to be careful—that this wasn't a time to be snide or sardonic. Maybe it was the way they stood, huddled over Satan who lay stretched on the ground. Maybe it was Harut, who knelt with his face in his hands. Maybe it was Beelzebub, who glared and said, "Come no closer, or thou shalt feel my teeth, black one."

Mephistopheles came closer, steadily, and said, "I mean you no harm, Beelzebub. Nor do I mean to harm the Lord Satan. Tell me what has happened."

"Wherefore?" shot Beelzebub.

"He should know," said Harut in a whisper. "He was a friend of . . . of. . . ." His voice trailed off and he covered his face again.

"I was a friend of whom?"

"Ariel," said Beelzebub.

"What do you mean, was?"

"Ariel hath fallen."

"What do you mean, fallen?"

"He will not rise again. Abdiel hath destroyed him by a blow of the flux, which he did aim at me."

Mephistopheles stood, staring. His mouth formed the word, "No," but no sound came forth.

Beelzebub looked down then and said, "He stirreth!"

"What is this?" demanded Michael.

"My Lord, these are the Thrones of the Lord Yaweh, Lord King of all Heaven."

Michael studied the small, thin archangel before him. "Your name is Raziel, isn't it?"

"Yes, Lord."

"Where did you get all that about Lord King of Heaven?"

Raziel cocked his head, as if this weren't a fit question to come from the lips of a Firstborn.

"It's what we call him," he said.

"We? The Thrones?"

Raziel nodded.

Michael shook his head. "I don't understand this, but never mind. I'll find out."

Raziel stepped aside, and Michael, Raphael, and Abdiel took the steps up and into the palace. Inside, they found more angels standing in the hallway. These had spears and stood in front of the door to the throne room.

Michael located Gabriel among them and said, "Who are these angels, and what are they doing here?"

"My Lord, these are the Cherubim," said Gabriel.

"That doesn't answer my question. Why are they here, blocking my way?"

"None may pass, Lord Michael, save at the Lord Yaweh's request."

"This is outrageous!" he roared, and was reaching for Gabriel's throat when Raphael said, "Peace, Michael. This is Yaweh's Palace, and he may do as he will, here."

She turned to Gabriel. "Please tell the Lord Yaweh that Michael, Abdiel, and I have arrived with news."

Gabriel turned to an angel at his side and nodded to him.

The other bowed and departed.

"I don't think I like this," said Michael.

Raphael only shook her head.

"What happened, Beelzebub?"

"Thou hast taken a blow to thy head, milord."

"Well, that explains why it hurts so much. From whom? Or what?"

"The star of Raphael, milord."

"Oh. Yes, she was sort of on top of me, wasn't she? Did I do anything to Abdiel?"

"Naught more than affrighting him, milord."

"That's a shame."

"Verily, milord."

"How did you make out?"

"I spake with the Lord Michael, milord. We did argue upon thy body, and where it should be."

"I see."

"We did compromise our differences, at the end."

"Compromise?"

"He left, thou didst remain, and Abdiel didst escape with an whole throat."

"I think you did well, Beelzebub."

"As best I could, milord."

He looked around, and nodded at Harut and Mephistopheles. "What are these two doing here?"

"Mourning, milord."

Lucifer found a stone beside a fast-flowing stream. He lifted it up, and, from a pocket in the sand beneath, he picked up a rod of scarlet light by its handle of gold. He looked at it, nodded his approval, and attached it to his belt.

Lilith studied it for a moment. "What is happening, Lucifer?"

"I don't know, Lilith. But I was threatened in Yaweh's Palace. Asmodai was also threatened. I'll not allow myself, or you, to be threatened and harassed."

"What are you going to do?"

"Now? As I told you, we're going to visit Asmodai. Beyond that I don't know. Whatever we're forced to, I guess."

"This is worse than a Wave."

"I know."

"Will it end?"

"It'll have to end."

"I wish it were over, then."

He shrugged, looking through the forest that separated him from Asmodai's home.

"Welcome, Michael, Raphael. And you as well, Abdiel, though I wonder about your behavior."

"Yaweh, what does this mean?"

"What, Michael?"

"This!" He gestured around him at the impassive angels who surrounded the throne, each holding a long, heavy, double-bladed sword.

"It means, Michael, that I no longer feel safe. I need to have angels near me to protect me from those who would destroy the Plan. I don't think I need to name names."

"Do you really think they would harm you?" asked Raphael.

"I know they would. Two of them, Asmodai and Lucifer, tried to force their way in."

Michael and Raphael looked at each other. "Are you sure they would have harmed you?" asked Michael.

"If they'd wanted to talk, they had the opportunity to do so when I requested to see Lucifer. And if you'd seen them, you would have known that they had no intention of talking. For a moment, Asmodai was in here. I won't try to describe the look he gave me."

"I see," said Raphael.

Michael's lips tightened. He turned away from the throne and covered the distance to a glass case in three long strides. With a sweep of his fist, the glass shattered. Heedless of the damage he did to his hands, he swept away the remaining pieces, reached in and took the sword. Still without a word, he strode out of the throne room.

Yaweh, Abdiel, and Raphael watched him leave.

"I suppose," said Raphael, "I'd better tell you what happened."

Mephistopheles left without committing himself to anything or giving a definite answer as to where he was going. His last words were to warn the others away from the road itself, thus leaving them with the impression that he was with them.

Mephistopheles couldn't commit himself yet. Not only did he not know which side was right, he wasn't sure what the sides were.

That, he decided, was the first thing to find out. He felt free to leave because Harut had promised to tell Leviathan about Ariel. For that he was grateful. That was a task he didn't care for.

On reflection, he realized he might have many tasks ahead of him that he wouldn't enjoy, no matter which side he ended up on.

He set himself one task, however, that he would relish, and all it would take to perform would be a minute, alone, with Abdiel.

"I understand most of what you have told me," said Yaweh at last. "But, Abdiel, how did you come to leave here, where you were safe?"

"I don't know, Lord. I just had the feeling that I should be with Michael and Raphael—that they were going into danger without knowing it." He shrugged. "Unfortunately, I found Satan first. Fortunately, he hadn't found them."

"Raphael," Yaweh said, "is there anything to add?"

"No, Yaweh. That's everything."

"All right. Raphael, you can go if you like. Abdiel, please stay for a while."

"Of course, Lord."

Raphael bowed her head a bit, then left.

"How may I serve, Lord?" asked Abdiel.

"First, know that from now on, you will be taking over the task of the Lord Satan, who has refused it."

"Then the Plan goes on?"

"Yes!"

"I am glad, Lord. And I'll do my best to live up to the trust you have shown in me."

"Good. And I have another mission for you."

"I am ready, Lord."

"Gather together the two hundred angels that I call Thrones, whose chief is Raziel. Tell Raziel to come and see me, for I have something special for him to do. You will be the new chief of the Order of Thrones."

"Yes, Lord."

"The first thing I want you to do is to find Satan."

Abdiel swallowed. "Find Satan?"

"Yes. And bring him to me, whether he wishes to be brought or not. Find a way to secure him, if necessary."

"Very well, Lord."

"Good."

"May I make a request, Lord?"

"Of course, Abdiel."

"I'd like to rest, first. The events of the day. . . ."

"Of course. Tomorrow will be soon enough, Abdiel."

"Till tomorrow, then, Lord."

"Till tomorrow, Abdiel."

He made a deep bow and left. He had gotten what he wanted—and, unfortunately, more than he wanted. But, at least for the moment, he had survived.

"Well, not bad, eh, Sith?"

"What do you mean?"

"From the bottom to the top in one day?"

"Oh. Yeah."

"Seraphim. I like it. It has a nice sound to it."

"Did you see the look on Asmodai's face, Kyriel?"

"How could I miss it?"

"Well, I don't know about you, but I wasn't sure about the whole thing."

"Why not? There were ten of us, plus Uriel. Why worry?"

"I don't know, but I was worried."

"There's strength in numbers, Sith. Remember that."

"I suppose. What do you think about the Thrones setting out after Satan?"

"Well, I wouldn't like to be there, I'll admit."

"Oh? What about strength in numbers?"

"It isn't that. It's—well, I still think of him as on *our* side, if you know what I mean."

"Hmmmm. Kyriel?"

"Yes?"

"You're right."

"Yeah."

"But you know what it means, don't you? *We* aren't on our side anymore."

• • •

Lucifer and Lilith met Mephistopheles outside of Asmodai's door. They looked at each other for a long moment. Finally, Lilith said. "Good day, Mephistopheles. What brings you here?"

He shrugged, never taking his eyes off Lucifer. "Oh, the usual. War, rebellion, strife, death. That sort of thing. And you?"

"Answer her question, dark one," said Lucifer.

"Answer mine, light-bringer."

"I'll answer it this way: if you intend to harm Asmodai, you will have to deal with me first—or afterwards. Is that clear to you?"

"Clear enough. If *you* intend to harm Asmodai, I'll look the other way. But if you don't, I have news for him that may concern you, too. Okay?"

Lucifer spat. He took a step toward the door and yelled down, "Asmodai!"

They waited for a moment, then the small, strong archangel appeared from below.

"Hello, Asmodai," said Lucifer. "This one," he gestured toward Mephistopheles, "says he has news for us. Do you want to let him in?"

Asmodai shrugged. "Sure. All of you can come in. Find chairs. Get as comfortable as you can, considering."

They did this. Lucifer turned to Mephistopheles. "All right, speak."

Mephistopheles studied his thumbnail. Then he said, "Do any of you know Ariel?"

There were nods from all around.

"Then you should know this: Abdiel destroyed him today."

"What?" cried Lucifer, standing.

Lilith and Asmodai registered shock.

"As near as we can tell, Abdiel was trying to get Beelzebub, and Ariel interposed himself. He used his own illiaster to send out a blast of some kind. I wouldn't know much about that. It destroyed Ariel instantly.

"If it matters to any of you," he added bitterly, "it was over quickly."

There was silence. Then Lucifer said, "What happened to Abdiel?"

"Nothing," spat Mephistopheles. "Michael and Raphael

helped him get away from Satan and Beelzebub. Raphael struck Satan as he was attacking Abdiel."

"What I'd like to know," said Asmodai slowly, "is how Abdiel learned to control his illiaster that way. There aren't many other than Firstborn who can do that."

Lilith looked at Lucifer, her face without expression. Lucifer hung his head and was silent.

Yaweh studied Raziel. Raziel met his gaze honestly and frankly. Yaweh nodded after a while and spoke: "I am told that I am now called King of Heaven."

Raziel nodded. "Yes, Lord. You are."

"Whose idea was that?"

Raziel blinked a couple of times and brushed a blond forelock out of his eyes. "It just seemed to happen," he said.

Yaweh nodded. "I do not wish to be King of Heaven, Raziel."

"Lord?"

"I do not wish there to be a King in Heaven, Raziel. We've never needed one."

"Excuse me, Lord, but—may I speak?"

"Of course."

"If there are those who oppose you—"

"Exactly! If there are those who oppose me, and who oppose the Plan, then we need a king. *If* there are those who oppose me."

"I don't understand, Lord."

Yaweh leaned forward. "I feel that I can trust you, Raziel. That is why I made you Chief of the Thrones, and that is why I now want you to do something else for me."

Raziel studied him. "Anything I can do, Lord," he said.

"Then go out, using whatever wits and skills you have, and find the truth for me. Is there opposition to the Plan? From how many? Is it organized? How does Satan really feel about all of this? What about Lucifer and Asmodai? Are they really trying to kill me?

"I need to know, Raziel. I *must* know. I want you to find out for me—whichever way it is."

Raziel nodded. "I'll do it, Lord."

"Thank you, Raziel," he said, feeling a semblance of peace for the first time in days.

• • •

The seas raged. Waves the size of the Southern Hold built themselves up and crashed into nothingness. Valleys of the same size opened up, almost showing the bottom. All along the shores, great waves swept up and drew trees, rocks, and flowers into the deep.

Sometimes, far out in the middle, a great head would appear and then plunge beneath again, with a flickering as the tail showed above the waves for a moment. After a time, the sound would drift back—a long, mournful wail.

Harut, high upon a rock wall above the worst of the waves, heard these sounds. Someday they would become part of a song called "The Grief of Leviathan," and it would evoke pain and beauty at once, as if they could be a single thing.

In this way, songs can lie. There was nothing of beauty in the grief of Leviathan as she sundered the ocean wishing she could have her small friend back, if only for a moment, and understanding death as only one can who has lived from the beginning and seen it from every side.

Silently, Harut mourned with her. Perhaps she knew this, and perhaps it comforted her somewhat.

Seven

I'm only a dream but I've come from on
  high,
To free you from the chains that bind you
  tight.
To give you the freedom of the clouds in the
  sky;
It is simpler to run than to fight.

—Nate Bucklin, "The Road"

Satan and Beelzebub wandered away from the road, not going in any particular direction but heading more or less westerly. For long, slow hours they walked without speaking, each lost in his own thoughts.

They rested at times by unspoken mutual consent, and they both seemed to know when it was time to get up again and continue.

At last Beelzebub spoke: "Milord," he said, "perchance 'twere best to consider where we walk."

"All right, Beelzebub. Consider. Where should we walk?"

"Harut hath said that Leviathan wisheth to speak with thee."

"Yes. But I'm not sure she wants to speak to anyone just now."

"Mayhap thou'rt right, milord. And yet will come a time when she shall desire conversation, e'en more than she did ere this."

He shrugged. "Maybe. Well, if you think so, we can go that way."

"We do so walk, milord."

"Eh? Oh. All right, then. Do you know where to find her?"

"I think so, milord."

"All right, then."

"Milord, I. . . ."

"Yes?"

"'Tis nothing, milord."

"I guess I'll be going, then."

"Where to, Mephistopheles?"

"I don't know, Lilith," he lied, "wherever I end up. I'm going to think all of this over."

"Where do you stand?" asked Lucifer suddenly.

"I'm sitting, now."

"I meant—"

"I know what you mean, Firstborn. You'll know sooner or later, but not until I do. If that isn't good enough," he shrugged, "here I am."

Lucifer's eyes narrowed. Lilith set a hand on his arm. Asmodai stood up smoothly and opened the door. He stepped to the side and waited.

Mephistopheles rose, inclined his head to Lilith and Lucifer, turned his back and went out the door, nodding to Asmodai on the way out.

After shutting the door, Asmodai returned to his chair.

"I don't trust him," said Lucifer.

"It doesn't matter," said Asmodai.

"No, I suppose it doesn't. And, in any case, he did give us news, as he promised."

"Yes."

"Although, in fact, I think he got more from us than we got from him."

"He's like that," said Lilith.

"That's why I don't trust him."

"In any case," said Asmodai, "what should we do?"

"About what?" said Lucifer. "About Yaweh? About Satan? About Ariel? Which one?"

"I think it's all one problem," said Lilith.

"In some ways, yes," said Lucifer. "But—never mind. All right, then; what should we do?"

"I think," said Asmodai, "that we have to find Satan."

"Find Satan! Find Satan! My whole life seems to be one long day of finding Satan! I think all of Heaven is spending its time finding Satan!" Lucifer shook his head.

"Whether he meant to or not, he started it all. We can't do anything without at least speaking to him—it would be wrong."

"I suppose. But whatever we do—"

"My Lord."

They turned to her. "Yes, Lilith?" said Asmodai.

"You both continue to avoid the subject. You keep saying, 'whatever we do,' or 'we can't do anything,' without saying what it is you're talking about."

Asmodai shrugged. "We can't —"

"Put it this way. I'm Satan. You've tracked me through all the trails and paths of Heaven. Finally you've found me. I say," she lowered her voice into a fair imitation of Satan's low, melodious tones, "greetings, my lords, may I do something for you?

"Now," she continued, "what do you answer?"

Asmodai opened and shut his mouth, then did it again. Lucifer smiled. "I think she has you," he said.

"Well, what's your point?"

"That what we have to decide is this: What are we proposing here? You were right when you said that all of these things were tied together, but tied together how? What do they have in common?"

"The Plan, of course," said Lucifer.

Lilith nodded. "The Plan; yes. Then what? I'll put it another way: what is Satan threatening that Yaweh is trying to protect, which led to Ariel's death?"

"Power!" cried Asmodai.

"Yes," said Lilith.

"Power?" said Lucifer. "I don't understand."

"Take the long view. The First Wave—all it was, was the seven of you against the flux, right? There was no confusion, no time for thinking about it, or for conversation, or art, or anything else we prize. But then there was a pause, and things started to develop. After the Second Wave there were only a few hundred of us—that much I remember. We all knew each other; we got along pretty well. But now, after the Third Wave, there are too many for that.

"Before, we were living from Wave to Wave. You know how many of us are destroyed each time—that's a big price to pay for living peacefully in between. But now, with all of the angels created during the Third Wave, we have the potential to end that—as Yaweh knows. But at the same time, that brings up the question of who tells whom what to do when. Yaweh simply did it—he was the obvious one. But now, Satan has called all of that into question. Now, the angels aren't sure just who is telling whom to do what, or who has the right to. So the *real* issue, when you strip away everything that's just a facade or a side point, is—"

"Rebellion," said Asmodai softly.

"Exactly."

She looked around the room. "And the Lord Satan is aware of that, whether he's admitted it even to himself or not. That's what's scaring him."

"Then why," said Lucifer, "doesn't he just come out and do it?"

"I can tell you that," said Asmodai. "The reason that he objected in the first place was because he felt uncomfortable with the idea of coercing the angels into helping with the Plan."

"So?"

"So he knows that the Plan is necessary. If he leads a rebellion, he'll only have to do the same thing Yaweh is doing. So, for him, where's the gain?"

"I see," said Lucifer. "I think I see. So where does that leave us?" He chuckled. "If we're going to revolt," he said, "it would be nice to know what we're revolting about."

"I don't think there is any, 'if we revolt,'" said Lilith. "It's too late for that. Mephistopheles knew it; I could tell as soon as I saw him. The factor that Satan never thought of was the angels themselves—those of the Third Wave. They see this as Yaweh telling them to sacrifice themselves—you've heard the rumors as well as I. No, there's a rebellion already. If we try to do nothing until it's so obvious that everyone can see, it'll be too late to direct it. We can get out of it—maybe—but we can't stop it.

"So, as I said earlier, my lords, what are we going to do?"

Alone, with a chance to rest for the first time in days, Abdiel found himself thinking. This wasn't something he wanted to do, but he couldn't stop it.

Everything had been working well until that owl—he squeezed his eyes tightly shut and shook his head. He covered his face with his pillow, as if he could block out the memory of Ariel being hit, screaming the horrible, horrible scream, and then, nothing.

It was an accident, he told himself. The illiaster would hardly have hurt Beelzebub. How could he have known the owl would be there and misunderstand?

He couldn't, he finally decided. There was no way. His motives were certainly reasonable, and, with Satan feeling as he did, there was nothing wrong with his methods, either. Certainly, it would have caused Satan some trouble, and there might have been a small falling out between Satan and Michael, but that was natural—they were on opposite sides. Abdiel hadn't put them there.

He took a deep breath. No, he couldn't go on beating himself over an unfortunate event that had been beyond his control. He had to go on, and do what he had to do.

But now there was another problem—Raziel! Naturally, he had listened in on the conversation between Raziel and Yaweh. He was a little surprised that Yaweh hadn't accepted all of the evidence that Abdiel had manufactured for him, but it was too late now. Raziel was going to have to be made harmless.

Ha! All very well to say, but how to do it? Abdiel knew Raziel somewhat, and he would do what he set out to do, if he wasn't stopped. How could he be stopped?

A thought came to Abdiel quite suddenly. But he rejected it as he remembered, once more, Ariel screaming and vanishing. No, that would be wrong, he decided. And he'd certainly never do anything wrong.

Certainly not that. • • •

Mephistopheles, for one, knew where Satan was going. Whatever Ariel had done after he had found Satan, he hadn't been near him by accident. And the presence of Harut confirmed it, if any confirmation was necessary.

Mephistopheles set off at once for the Western Regency. He wasn't sure where he stood on the larger issues, and preferred not to decide until and unless he had to, but there were loyalties and friendships he respected.

Satan would be going to see Leviathan. Mephistopheles might be needed there.

"Not that it solves anything," said Asmodai, "but I'm curious: Why hasn't Yaweh come after us?"

Lilith cocked her head. "He may be so interested in Satan right now that everything else comes second to him. Do we know where Satan is going?"

"I have a guess," said Asmodai. "Mephistopheles mentioned that Harut and Ariel were there. Does that suggest something to you?"

The others spoke with one voice: "Leviathan!"

"That's what I thought."

"So should we go meet them?" asked Lucifer.

"If we're right about Yaweh," said Lilith, "he'll have sent either Michael or Raphael after him."

"No," said Asmodai. "You forget the—what were they?"

"Seraphim, Cherubim, and Thrones," said Lucifer.

"Right. He'll send them."

"Or more like them," said Lucifer. "He won't want to leave himself undefended. After all, one of us could break in and kick him in the knee."

"Speaking of defending," said Asmodai, "we're going to have to protect Satan from whoever went after him. Will the three of us be enough?"

"I don't know. What do you suggest? Trying to raise our own host?"

"It's a thought," put in Lilith.

"I don't like it," said Asmodai. "It may come to that, but I don't want to push things to it any sooner than we have to."

"Do you have another idea?" asked Lucifer.

"Yes. If you and Lilith can stand to be parted for a while."

"Why?"

"Lilith is the fatest runner I know, and what I have in mind is going to take speed."

"Tell us about it," said Lilith.

Raziel didn't attempt to understand what he had overheard. That would come later.

He had never actually done this sort of thing before, but he felt it was best to learn all he could before trying to understand any of it. Had he thought about it carefully, he would have realized that the stories he had gotten from Michael, Raphael, and Asmodai didn't quite add up. But he wasn't ready to think about that yet. No doubt, when all was said and done, the conversation between Lucifer, Lilith, and Asmodai would be important. But not now.

Now, the only important thing about it was that it told him to head west, toward Leviathan, because that was where things were going to happen.

There were no roads, trails, or paths heading from the center to the Western Regency. This mattered little to Satan or Beelzebub, who enjoyed tromping through woods or over bare rocky ground.

They took their time, and spoke little. Leagues fell slowly before them. From time to time, they tested the air for a trace of the sea, but even Beelzebub couldn't catch the scent.

That was all right. They knew the way, and were in no hurry.

The forces of chaos gathered around them.

Lilith ran north. Her footfalls were a blur, yet her breathing was light and easy.

In a few more hours she would slow to a walk, and after an hour of walking she would stop and rest. Then she would run more.

Time, to her, was everything.

Her friends would be going more slowly, and her enemies as well, but none had so long a distance to travel. She couldn't run in a straight line; this part of Heaven grew gradually more and more hilly, until at last mountains appeared.

To her, these mountains appeared as far lumps, ahead, when her path took her to the top of hills. This happened less often as time went on, for she began to pick her way between the hills to save energy.

Lilith knew the forces of chaos were gathering around her, and responded to them. Fleetest of all the angels of Heaven, she ran on through the day, through the night, through the mountains of Heaven.

Michael took his time, but not because he wanted to. Had he been Beelzebub, he could have followed Satan's scent. Had he been Mephistopheles, he would have immediately noticed the signs of where they turned off the road. Had he been Yaweh, an effort would have brought forth a vision of them, fleeting and imperfect though it was between Waves.

But he was Michael. His eyes weren't the keenest, his feet not the swiftest. But he was determined, which counts for much.

Painfully, he read the signs. After some hours, he became certain of where they had left the road. After a few more hours, he was sure that they were heading west, although not in a straight path. He guessed that they were heading toward Leviathan, but since he wasn't yet sure, he took his time.

He wasn't aware of the gathering of the forces of chaos; he was one.

Abdiel marched at the head of two hundred angels.

Well, perhaps "marched" is too strong a word. He walked, and they walked behind him. Before leaving, Yaweh had told him, "West," so he went west.

He didn't know if he would find Satan, and more than half hoped he wouldn't, but he had his assigned task, and the risks of ignoring it were even greater than the risks of carrying it out.

Behind him, two hundred kept pace, through brush and over rocks, each with a tall sword in his hand. Some looked grim, others looked worried, others excited. They were setting out to capture a legend—a Firstborn. As they walked, the chain and the manacles made clanging sounds, so they couldn't forget why they were there.

It occurred to Abdiel that if Satan (those hands!) or Beelzebub (those teeth!) were waiting for them, he, Abdiel, would be the one in front. And yet, he could hardly lead them from behind. Quite a dilemma.

After some thought, he signaled an angel to come forward. He directed the angel, whose name was Zaphkiel, to walk ahead and keep his eyes open for any traces of Satan. Zaphkiel obeyed without a word.

That much safer for his efforts, Abdiel continued westward.

Mephistopheles negotiated the boulders with lithe efficiency and found level ground again. He surveyed it, pleased with his progress. From here, the way was mostly flat, with occasional rocky areas and scattered small woods until he reached the sea. There were no obstructions in his view of— There was an obstruction. Wasn't there? Way off, a little to the left? Was it moving? Well, well! Who could this be?

He hurried to catch up, noticing for the first time that there was a faint sea-tang in the air.

"We're getting close, I think."

"Aye, milord."

"Another day?"

"Less, methinks. By dusk, perchance."

"Good. It's been a long time since I've seen her. I hear she's pretty much adjusted, though."

"Aye."

"It was horrible at first. Yaweh, Raphael, Michael and I were with her nearly every minute after the Second Wave. She tried to destroy herself once. Lucifer stopped her."

"So I've heard spoken, milord."

They walked a little further.

"Milord?"

"Yes, Beelzebub?"

"It hath been said that thou and she were . . . close, on a time."

Satan smiled. "That was long ago, Beelzebub. Before the Second Wave. We didn't know what we were doing, then, if you know what I mean."

"Aye, milord."

Nearly exhausted, glistening with sweat, thinner, flushed and drawn, Lilith collapsed inside the cavern. Sounds filled the chamber, as of thousands of angels breathing in perfect unison. It was at the end of a tunnel, massive, yet twisted and convoluted, which burrowed down into the mountain.

There was not the least trace of light.

She lay on her back and tried not to close her eyes. She had come so far, so fast. It would be horrible to fall asleep here and be just that much too late. On the other hand, she thought, her face twisting into a mockery of a smile, it would almost be worse if none of this turned out to be necessary.

Lilith had paced herself during the run, so she was not completely exhausted—quite. She rolled over on her stomach, then fought her way to her hands and knees.

She held herself there until her breathing settled, then grasped a ledge in front of her that she'd felt before falling. She hauled herself painfully to her feet.

From inside her shirt, she removed a small stone that Asmodai had given her. As she brought it forth, a faint glow began within it. Faint as it was, it allowed her to see her surroundings.

The chamber was even larger than she had imagined it. The ceiling was far beyond the range of her small light, but extended at least to many times her height. The walls appeared dark grey and rocky and uneven. Yet the floor of the cavern was strangely smooth.

Her eyes were drawn toward the source of the sounds of breathing. She couldn't quite make out anything, so she haltingly stumbled forward.

After ten paces, she saw the massive object before her—twice her own height in length, half of that in breadth. After another five, she realized that this was only his head.

Her hand began to shake harder, from reasons having nothing to do with exhaustion.

She whispered, almost soundlessly, "Belial."

"Good day, Michael."

"Wha—?"

Michael spun and saw Mephistopheles, hands on his hips and smiling, about four paces away.

"How long have you been behind me?"

"Most of the day. I would have spoken sooner, but you kept moving faster. I'd have thought you were trying to get away from me if you'd ever looked back."

"I see," said Michael. He'd been marching with his great sword resting on his shoulder. Now he gripped it with both hands and swung it as he advanced, stopping with the blade a hair's breadth from the other's chest. Someone with keener eyesight than Michael's might have noticed Mephistopheles's face going the least bit pale.

"Does this gesture mean something, Lord Michael?"

"Why have you been following me, dark one?"

"To catch you. It *is* necessary, you know."

"You could have hailed me."

"I did."

"From farther back!"

"I dislike shouting."

Michael bit his lips. "What are you doing here?"

"Well, we seem to be going in the same direction, and I prefer to walk with company. If you're of like mind, we can solve this problem for each other without discommoding ourselves."

"My business is my own."

"Of course. I assure you, I have not the least interest in why you pursue the Lord Satan."

"How did you know?"

"Why, Lord Michael, you just told me yourself. But it doesn't concern me. I'm here to visit Leviathan. We're friends."

"You have friends?"

"Tsk, Michael. Don't be nasty. Would you mind pointing that somewhere else, by the way?"

"Yes."

"Suit yourself. Shall we be going?"

"Why do you think I'll go anywhere with you, dark one?"

"Because if you don't, you'll have to destroy me, which you can't justify to yourself, or allow me to follow you, which you wouldn't like at all."

"I could have you walk in front of me."

"That will be fine. Although, to think of it, Leviathan might be vexed with you."

Michael spat and lowered his blade. "Walk to my left, and stay at least two paces off."

"Certainly." Mephistopheles began whistling tunelessly between his teeth.

"And don't do that," added Michael.

"Who's there?"

"Hello, Harut. It's me."

"Well, Lord Satan. Glad you came. The lady, she's been asking about you."

"Where is she?"

"Swimming," said Harut dryly.

Satan and Beelzebub approached the water's edge. They stood there for several moments before, far out to sea, they saw a long, thin neck with a powerful head break the surface. It scanned the shoreline, and her eyes came to rest upon them. They felt her gaze almost as a physical blow.

The head dived and, almost at once it seemed, reappeared directly in front of them.

"Satan," she said, affection coming through her rich, thick voice.

He bowed deeply. "Greetings, lady. I'm told you wanted to see me; I'm here."

Her great head nodded. "Who is this, though? This must be Beelzebub, whom Harut and . . . and others have spoken of."

Beelzebub inclined his head until his nose touched the ground. "I do greet thee, lady," he said. "In all I have heard of thee there is no ill."

A sound that was probably chuckling came from her as she nodded slightly in acknowledgement.

"Well, what can I do for you, Leviathan?"

She closed her eyes, then opened them and spoke: "I want to know everything that led up to the loss of my friend, Ariel. Everything you know or guess. From the beginning. I ask this as a favor, relying on old friendships which, I know, are falling apart all around. But, please, tell me."

"And tell me, too, if you would."

They spun. Asmodai had spoken, and Lucifer was standing next to him.

Leviathan stared at the newcomers, and took in Beelzebub and Satan, who faced them in an attitude of alert anticipation, as if they were expecting an attack.

"Lucifer," she said, "I withhold my greeting until I know why you are here. You are in my Regency now, and the Lord Satan is my guest. If you mean any ill toward him, you should leave."

Lucifer bowed. "I mean no ill toward my friend Satan, and I hope I may continue to call him that. I understand why he may think otherwise, but I pledge that this is not the case. I, too, have a story to tell that may have some bearing. I ask only that you listen."

"And I," said Asmodai, "ask that you don't."

"What?" said the others as one voice.

He turned toward Lucifer. "You aren't thinking. We don't have time for this; they'll be here soon."

"Who will?" said Leviathan, raising her head higher and looking past them.

"I don't know exactly, but—well, I think I'd better tell you this much of the story. If we have time."

Asmodai began speaking, closing his eyes often to remember details. For as much as he was going to tell now, it was important that the got it right.

She screamed it, finally. For ten minutes that had felt like an eternity, she had been saying it in gradually louder tones. Finally, she threw her head back and screamed at the top of her lungs.

"BELIAL! AWAKE!"

By some ancient property of the chamber, no doubt left from the Third Wave, her voice seemed to come back to her from the walls. She thought that nothing would happen, but then the great beast stirred. A tremor seemed to move down the length of its body—or as much of its body as she could see.

After a moment, one great eye opened. She had the sudden feeling that she could walk into the pupil and be lost.

He saw her, suddenly. His voice came as a low, rumbling sound, as if from out of the ground: "Who?"

Lilith felt ridiculous. "I'm Lilith," she said.

"Who?" he repeated.

"I'm a friend of the Lord Satan, who needs your help, and the Lord Lucifer, who sent me.

His eye closed again, then opened.

"What?" came the great voice.

"They need your help. Please."

"Where?"

"The Western Regency," she said. "And hurry, please! They are in danger."

She would never, in all of her existence, have believed that he could move so quickly. Suddenly he was up, two massive legs supporting him. He looked down at her for a moment, then his great head lowered. At first she thought that he was going to destroy her. Then she thought he was bowing.

But his head came down next to her until it touched the ground.

"Get on," he said.

Trembling, she did.

Zaphkiel reported, "I saw five angels by the water, lord. I don't think they saw me."

"Describe the terrain."

"There is a path," said Zaphkiel, "that begins about two leagues from here. It is narrow at first; then, after half a league, it expands to a width such that ten may walk abreast. Then, after another league it opens up into a cleft that is perhaps three leagues deep and two wide. There, all is flat, and there I saw Leviathan, Beelzebub, and three others, all speaking together. If we emerge there, they will see us at once."

"Are there any other features to the cleft?"

"There is a narrow path on the other side, wide enough for three, that goes for two leagues and opens out onto a large plain. This plain is hidden from the cleft itself."

Abdiel contemplated. "Not wide enough," he said.

Abdiel motioned Zaphkiel back, then turned to the angels behind him and motioned them to gather round. As they did so, he desperately tried to figure out what to do.

"All right," he said at last, "you ten in front. If you see the Lord Satan, point him out to," he motioned again, "you ten. You'll have the chain." There were clinking sounds as the chain was passed. "Get him manacled. The rest of you, ah, make sure no one interferes. If the Lord Satan isn't there," he added, "don't do anything. I'll explain."

Without giving them time to think about his plan, he held his sword up, and brought it sweeping down. Somewhat to his surprise, the two hundred Thrones ran past him, yelling at the top of their lungs.

"Odd," he told himself. "I wouldn't do that."

As the last of them passed, he fell in and brought up the rear.

"Kyriel?"

"Hummm?"

"Does the Lord Yaweh seem—different?"

"Different how?"

"I'm not sure. But he seems to have changed, somehow."

"I'm not sure what you mean."

"He seems to be more, well, active. I'm not sure that's the right word."

"Nervous?"

"Maybe that's it."

"The way he keeps pacing back and forth?"

"Yeah."

"Or grabbing those papers and looking through them?"

"Yeah."

"Or demanding to see Raphael, and talking to her for two minutes, then forgetting about her and starting something else?"

"That's right."

"I hadn't noticed."

"Huh."

Then, "You know, Kyriel?"

"Vaguely."

"Shut up. You know, I'm getting worried."

"Me too."

"I'm starting to think about what you said, way back, about running off somewhere."

"What about it?"

"Well, if someone showed up, like Lord Asmodai, well, I wouldn't let him attack Lord Yaweh, but I wouldn't feel good about attacking him, either."

"Well . . neither would I."

"So what do we do about it?"

"Things can't last like this."

"I guess not. But what if they do?"

"Hmmmm. Ask me again in a few days."

"I will."

Too many sensations. Her eyes flickered from the mountains, rivers, and plains below her—those tiny figures were angels?—to Belial's mighty wings at her sides. The motions, like walking into a heavy wind, but more, and the feeling of Belial churning beneath her, almost like a lover. His hard, cool scales against her hands; biting wind against her cheeks.

The sound of the air in her ears; Belial's musky odor. Fear and exhilaration. Joy, and—

Below her, a new sight. She wondered if she had come too late.

"What's that?"

Asmodai, interrupted by Lucifer's exclamation, stopped and looked. He didn't see anything, but he began to hear something like shouts in the distance.

Leviathan raised her head. "Angels," she said. "More than a hundred. They're heading this way and waving sticks. Metal sticks, I think. Odd."

Satan turned, his hand going to the emerald at his breast. Beelzebub rose and stood next to him. Asmodai stood with his hands behind his back, inside his cloak, fumbling at something. Lucifer drew the wand from his side.

The Thrones came into view around a rocky structure several hundred paces away. They kept appearing for quite a while, yelling and waving their swords over their heads.

"More like two hundred," observed Lucifer.

"Two hundred angels," said Asmodai. "Against two archangels and three Firstborn. This could be interesting." From behind his back he brought a short rope, which he began whirling over his head. After a couple of turns it began to emit a soft red glow. As he spun it faster, the red became brighter. Then Asmodai moved his arm and wrist until the rope was spinning in front of him.

"Something new," commented Lucifer.

The distance between them closed. Leviathan reared up and opened her mouth. Her teeth were very white.

But even as the distance closed to nothing, there was a sound which made everyone look up. A great bellow, louder than anyone had heard between Waves, came from the sky.

Those in the front ranks of the charging angels faltered, and those behind them ran into them. And so on.

From above, a great dark shape was descending, gouts of flame appearing from its mouth.

"Belial!" cried Leviathan.

"Belial!" cried Satan.

"Lilith!" cried Lucifer, seeing the small form perched atop Belial's neck.

Down and down he came, and the two hundred Thrones turned and scattered, leaving their swords here and there about the field. As they scattered, a long figure was revealed standing near where the rear of the troop had been. Satan would not have noticed him, except that Beelzebub suddenly stiffened at his side and growled.

Separated by three hundred paces, Satan saw him, and, from that distance, their eyes locked. Satan and Beelzebub began walking forward, slowly and evenly. Abdiel turned and broke into a run.

Satan and Beelzebub began jogging, letting Abdiel get ahead for now, content to allow him to exhaust himself. They were willing to follow him forever.

For a few minutes they lost sight of him, as he passed through the pathway. But then they found him again, still running, only now he seemed exhausted.

He looked over his shoulder, apparently saw that they were gaining on him, stopped, and waited. As they got close, they could see he was trembling, his eyes wide and vacant.

Zaphkiel suddenly appeared beside him, leaping down from the rocks above, still holding a sword.

Without a word being spoken, Beelzebub stepped up ahead of Satan and crossed in front of him, so he was opposite Zaphkiel.

It was the same thing, in miniature, that had happened before. Each side waited for the gap to close. On the other side of the path, Belial was spouting flame and holes appeared in the rock walls and the ground. Behind them, Lucifer and Asmodai had finally seen what was going on and were moving forward.

Then, as if by prearranged signal, Beelzebub and Satan sprang. Zaphkiel held his blade before him, but Beelzebub leapt under it and was upon him.

Satan dived for Abdiel's throat and would have had it except that Abdiel, screaming, fell over backward, leaving Satan above him.

Satan reached for his throat and—

"Look out!" called Lucifer behind him.

Satan ducked and twisted. Michael stood beside him, his great sword swinging. Them Mephistopheles caught Michael squarely in the back with both hands. Michael stumbled forward, and his sword, with all of his strength behind it, struck the ground.

There was a sound like a thunderclap. All of Heaven seemed to shake, and there was a flash of light, blinding and white, from where the sword had struck. Satan had a confused glimpse of Michael flying through the air over his head and Belial tumbling toward the ground out of control, then all was darkness.

Eight

But certainly, if I am not mistaken,
it was just before the coming of Him who
    took
the souls from Limbo that all Hell was
    shaken

so that I thought the universe felt love
and all its elements moved toward harmony
whereby the world of matter, as some
    believe,
has often plunged to chaos....

           —Dante, *Inferno,* Canto xii:37-43

Michael never lost consciousness. As the ground split before him, he was in midair, hurled by the force of the explosion.

"I don't know my own strength," he muttered, which was the first time that line was used.

He landed hard, and was recovering his breath when a sud-

den flood picked him up and carried him inland. He was able
to control himself well enough to avoid the occasional obstacle
that appeared in his way.

After a few leagues, he found that his feet were beginning
to touch the ground. After another couple, he stood up, waist-
deep in water.

It was, he decided, going to be a long walk in water. He
shrugged. Satan had either survived—or not. For now, Michael
must return to the Palace, defeated again.

He looked at his sword for the first time since the explosion
and saw that it had taken no damage. He rested it on his shoulder
and began slogging his way toward the center of Heaven.

Belial was thrown out of control by the explosion. He had
nearly hit the ground when he recovered, his great wings straining to cup the air.

He managed to halt himself before hitting and began to work
his wings to climb when he heard a cry from the small angel
on his neck. Abruptly, he felt lighter, and he saw her dive into
the waters below him.

He wondered at this, but had no time to do anything about
it.

He was curious, however, about the sound of Lilith's scream.
He wondered what "Harut" meant.

Satan woke to the sound of rushing water, the taste of salt,
and the feel of a sharp pain in his right calf. He realized that
he was moving quickly, and along with this awareness came
a mouth full of sea water.

He forced himself up, choking and spitting, and looked at
his leg, which had miraculously stayed above the surface.

The reason for the pain and buoyancy was obvious at once:
Beelzebub had fastened himself to Satan's leg with his teeth.

Beelzebub looked at him apologetically, but couldn't speak.
Satan gave him a brief smile and looked around.

He noticed, with more than passing interest, that they would
soon collide with a large boulder, directly in the path of the
waters.

He gave this his full attention.

Lucifer saw the explosion and was knocked to his knees.

He heard the sounds from behind him, turned, and saw the waves rushing in. He grabbed Asmodai with his left hand and pointed as he stood up.

Asmodai's eyes widened as he saw the wave towering over them; then he began twirling his rope again. Lucifer raised his wand over his head, and a scarlet glow issued forth that formed a shield above them.

The wave front crashed over and around them, and they soon found themselves in a small pocket of dry land beneath the sea.

It was, decided Lucifer, an interesting view.

Soon the water began to recede, and Asmodai faced the other direction until it had passed. Belial landed beside them.

Asmodai bowed low. Lucifer began to bow, then stopped and looked sharply at Belial.

"Where is Lilith?" he asked, his voice utterly flat.

Leviathan had felt it all.

She had been sitting in the water, watching as Belial scattered the attacking angels, when she felt the sea itself shake, as if a Wave were coming out from the land.

Then it had come back, seemingly magnified, and Leviathan was swept up and over the land on a mountain of water. It carried her far inland. She had fears of being left stranded and helpless, but she managed to stay in deep enough water to flow back out with it.

As she went, she saw angels, some conscious, some not, floating with her. She relized then that all of the angels would be sucked back into the sea when the waters receded. She laid her will upon the tide then, and the tide responded.

It receded slowly, settling angels gently onto the ground.

Leviathan also receded slowly, occasionally scraping the ground with her belly. She held her breath, to keep herself as buoyant as possible, and at last made it safely back to the sea.

She let the air out of her lungs with a great sense of relief and began the business of causing the silt in the water to fall to the bottom. She hated bathing in dirty water.

Harut had heard the sound of many feet running toward him, and then the shouts and cries. By the time he realized he was directly in the path of an oncoming mass of angels, it was too late. The Thrones knocked him down without seeing him, and he felt himself kicked and cursed and stumbled over. Then something, probably a foot, hit him in the head, and all was darkness.

He awoke, much as Satan did, spitting water and coughing. His head was being held up and there was the sound of gasping next to his ear.

He tried to relax in the grip and found that it was easier to stay up this way.

Neither of them spoke for what felt like hours, until they felt ground beneath their feet.

They waded forward, at last coming to dry land, and collapsed there, panting.

"Who is it?" he gasped.

"Lilith," she said, also gasping.

"Thank you," he said, and passed out again.

She nodded, then fell asleep also.

Belial had all but forgotten how to speak, but he managed to convey to Lucifer what had happened and where. This was more of an effort for him than the flight itself had been. When Lucifer understood, he and Asmodai immediately set off in the direction indicated, leaving Belial alone.

Belial reflected on what had happened as best he could, and decided that he didn't understand it. Cacoastrum he understood. That was the source of pain, and when he saw it, he either fled or destroyed it. Angels were friends, and Satan and Lucifer were old friends. They had been old friends even back before— before it had happened. That terrible, burning pain, the twisting inside and outside as the cacoastrum had torn into his body.

But this was confusing. It almost seemed as if angels had been fighting each other, which wasn't the way things worked as he understood them.

Mentally, he shrugged. He knew who his friends were. He still remembered the names of his six friends—Yaweh, Satan, Michael, Lucifer, Raphael, and Leviathan. These he'd help, and if that meant that he must harm others, well, so be it.

Lilith had known where to find him; therefore others would know where to find him.

He spread his wings and cupped the air. He skimmed along the ground until he found an updraft. He allowed it to carry him to a sufficient height, then he turned toward his home—to wait.

Abdiel allowed the waters to carry him wherever they would, and was finally deposited on a small hill. He looked around, but saw no one. Just as well, he decided.

He determined which way the center of Heaven lay, and began walking toward it.

He reflected on failure.

He could not have known that Satan would be in the company of two other Firstborn, and he certainly could not have known that Belial would show up. But none of that mattered; he had failed.

He had built himself up on successes, and a single failure would bring it all crashing down upon him. He was, he decided, going to have to find a way to repair the damage—and quickly. He looked back the way he had come. Find Satan? Then what? He shuddered at the thought. No, something else.

Well, what problems were there that he could solve? He continued toward the center, his brow furrowed. And, if furrowing the brows is actually useful, he got his reward.

Morale, he realized, was the problem. There were rumors, and words of ill tidings. This was the kind of problem he could address.

Well, then, how? His pace increased as he began to concentrate. Something would have to happen to unite Heaven. Or some new rumor would have to be spread. Or both.

Then he remembered something that he, himself, had said. Idle mouthings at the time, but—

"Ho, there, Abdiel. A word with you, if I may."

Abdiel turned and saw Raziel approaching him. He found that his pulse was racing. He had forgotten his most immediate problem, he realized. His mouth was suddenly dry.

"May I walk with you a ways, Abdiel?"

Abdiel swallowed. "Of course," he managed. "What—what brings you out here?"

"What? Oh, I was following you. You certainly are right about Satan having it in for you!"

"Yes. How did you follow me after the flood hit?"

"I didn't. That was merely good fortune. Excuse me, Abdiel, but I still don't understand something about the previous in-

cident with the Lord Satan. Why it was that you left the safety
of Yaweh's Palace and put yourself in such danger? Could you
tell me again?"

Raziel was looking at him with frank and open curiosity.
Abdiel felt a pounding in his head.

"As—as I said before: I had a feeling that there was danger
for Michael and Raphael, and that I should warn them."

"Hmmmm. Yes. But how did you miss them? They were
on the road, as you were and as Satan was. How was it that
you missed seeing Michael and Raphael, and yet Satan found
you?"

Abdiel swallowed hard. The pounding in his head got
stronger, and there was a roaring in his ears.

Then he realized that he was still carrying his sword.

After resting for a few hours, Satan stood up. Beelzebub
opened his eyes, saw him, and stood up also.

"How fares thy foot, milord?"

"Sore, but I don't think it's anything serious. It could have
been a lot worse."

"Aye, milord. Hadst thou not awoke ere we reached the
boulder, 'twould have been worse indeed."

Satan nodded. "Well, where to now?"

"I know not, milord. Back to Leviathan, perchance?"

"Hmmmm. Maybe. But that didn't work out too well, last
time."

"Verily, milord. But then?"

"I don't know."

"What would'st thou do, milord, an thou could'st do as thou
pleased?"

"If I could, I'd find Abdiel. But who knows where the waters
left him? I doubt we're so lucky that he didn't survive."

"Aye, milord."

"Maybe I should try to get in and see Yaweh, after all."

"An thou would, milord. The Palace doth lie in that direction, and the way is clear."

"I don't know. Would he see me? Do I want to see him?"

Beelzebub didn't answer.

Satan shrugged. "Let's rest here for another day or so. I'll
think it over."

"Aye, milord."

• • •

Looking for Lilith, they met an angel they didn't know. He'd been walking toward the center, a sword in his right hand. He was tall and thin, with short, light hair. He turned, saw them, and waited.

They strode up to him and stopped. The three of them stood for a moment, then the tall angel inclined his head.

Lucifer spoke: "You were one of those who dared to attack the Lord Satan."

"That is right," said the other, laconically.

"Well?"

"We failed."

"What is your name?" snapped Lucifer.

"Zaphkiel."

"Do you know who I am?"

"I see by your cloak that you are a Firstborn."

"I am Lucifer."

"A pleasure," said Zaphkiel.

"This is the archangel Asmodai."

"A pleasure," Zaphkiel repeated.

"We should destroy you for what you tried to do—you and all your companions."

Zaphkiel shrugged.

Asmodai and Lucifer looked at him in silence. Asmodai spoke at last. "Forgive him, Lucifer; he doesn't know what he's doing."

Lucifer nodded, still staring up at the other. "I suppose. You may go," he said. "Hope that you don't meet me again, Zaphkiel."

"Thank you," said Zaphkiel.

"Well? Why aren't you going?"

"Since you've given me my life, I'll give you something in return."

"Yes?"

He raised his arm, and stiffly pointed southwest. "She's that way," he said, "walking toward the center." Then he walked back toward the center, himself.

Lucifer and Asmodai stared, open mouthed, for a moment. Then they turned and began running in the direction that Zaphkiel had pointed.

• • •

Leviathan saw him standing by the shore, at the edge of the cleft, and swam over. He bowed his head to her.

"We never got to talk, Leviathan."

"I know."

"I'm very sorry about Ariel."

"I know that, too. Thank you."

"If there is anything I can do. . . ."

"There was a lot that I never heard, from Lucifer and Asmodai. How much do you know?"

"Not enough, I'm afraid. Still, here it is."

The dark angel sat down, closed his eyes, and began speaking.

Abdiel stared at the spot where Raziel had been. He continued looking at it for long moments. He squeezed his eyes shut and opened them again, as if willing the place to vanish, and take the act with it.

At length, he shook his head. "I didn't know what I was doing," he told himself. "I panicked. I couldn't help myself. I wouldn't have done it on purpose."

Still he stood there for long moments, wishing his mind were clear of the sight of Raziel's face as the sword had cut into his stomach. And then Raziel had dropped to his knees, still amazed. Abdiel had stood there trembling, but Raziel didn't seem ready to die. So Abdiel had struck him again. He had aimed for his neck, but the sword had struck Raziel's shoulder.

Then Raziel had pleaded—first with his eyes, then aloud. Abdiel had struck him again, jabbing him in the chest. Raziel fell back, yanking the sword from Abdiel's hands.

Abdiel, nearly blind, had pulled the blade free, had seen the sick, orange glow coming from Raziel's chest. Abdiel's next blow had cut his neck, and then, finally, Raziel had vanished.

Abdiel began walking again. Then running, hoping to drive the memory out of his mind.

He had been running for a long time when he saw two Thrones slowly heading back toward the center. Yes, he decided, they would be useful as a test.

He slowed to a walk, took a few deep breaths, and hailed them. They saw him and bowed. He nodded sharply and motioned them to fall in next to him.

"I'm pleased that you two are well."

"Thank you, Lord Abdiel."

"Have you seen any of the others?"

"No, lord."

"I see. Stop for a moment."

"Yes, Lord?"

"I'd like you to do something. Here, look at me. Watch my hands. Try to relax, now. Watch the way my hands are moving. Think of it as a path you walk along. From you to me, but only in your minds. No, you don't have to understand, just think of it that way, and try to relax. . . ."

He left them there, pale and shaking, telling them that they would recover soon, and to make it back to the center when they could.

He felt as he never had before—powerful, full of energy and life, as if he could run forever and not feel it.

May as well not waste time, he decided, chuckling, and broke into a run toward the center of Heaven.

"It's nice to know it'll work," he told himself.

Lucifer spotted them first and gave a shout. He and Asmodai started running as Lilith looked up.

Lucifer and Lilith met, and held each other without saying anything. Asmodai met Harut, and clasped his shoulder. "Are you all right?"

Harut nodded. "Banged up some. Okay, I guess."

"Good."

"Lilith told me what happened."

"And?"

"If I can do anything to help out, you let me know, right?"

"Good. We will. And if I can do anything for you, let me know about that."

Harut chuckled humorlessly. "You can do something for me, but I don't know when you'll have time."

"What is it?"

"My cithara. It got lost in the flood."

"I'll make you another."

"I'm obliged."

Asmodai looked at Lucifer and Lilith, who were still holding each other tightly without moving or speaking. He turned back to Harut.

"You can play me a love song on it."

• • •

Abdiel nodded haughtily at the Cherubim by the door and brushed past into Yaweh's presence. Raphael was there, going over the parchment on which the Plan was inscribed. He noted that the case that had held Michael's sword had been removed.

They looked up, and the Seraphim moved aside for Abdiel to pass.

"You're back quickly," said Yaweh. "What have you to report?"

"We failed," said Abdiel.

For the briefest moment, it almost seemed an expression of relief crossed Yaweh's face.

"We found him," Abdiel continued, "in company with Leviathan, Lucifer, and Asmodai. We approached him, but as we got close, Belial appeared from the north and scattered us. Satan attacked me, but I was rescued by the Lord Michael. In the process of rescuing me, his sword struck the ground, and there was an explosion that knocked us all down and seemed to make all of Heaven shake. Then—"

"So that's what it was!" said Raphael. "We felt it."

"It couldn't have been that," said Yaweh, looking closely at Abdiel. "That was only two days ago."

Abdiel shifted on his feet. "I'll explain that in a moment, Lord. After the explosion, there was a great flood, which completed the scattering of our forces. I don't know if the explosion caused it, or if Leviathan set it off. There may have been some lost in the flood; I don't know. I returned as soon as I could. The other Thrones should be returning in a few days."

Yaweh nodded. "All right, then. How is it you are so far ahead of them?"

"I moved very quickly to bring you the news. I have found a way to run for long periods of time without needing to rest."

"Indeed?"

"Yes, Lord. It's part of something else. Do you recall mention I made some time ago of a plan I was working on?"

"Yes, I believe so."

"It is now complete, Lord."

"It involves running without resting?"

"No. That was just a test of part of it. I still don't know if it will work, but I'd like to explain it to you, Lord."

"Very well."

"First, Lord, let me discuss the problem I am hoping to solve. . . ."

As he spoke, Raphael studied him through slitted eyes.

"This is quite some tale, Mephistopheles."

"I know. And that is only what I know—there is a great deal that I don't. Maybe enough to change the meaning of the whole of it; I'm not sure."

"Yes. It certainly is something to think about, though." She ducked her head under the water, and brought it up again, accidentally showering Mephistopheles.

"Sorry."

"It's all right. Is there more I can do for you?"

"Yes. I still wish to speak to the Lord Satan. Do you think you can find him?"

"I don't know. He could be anywhere. I'll try."

"I appreciate it."

"It may take a while."

"That's all right. And, Mephistopheles—"

"Hmmm?"

"Try to find Harut, too."

"Okay."

Lucifer, Lilith, and Asmodai made their way toward the center of Heaven. They took their time, and spoke often of their doubts. What should they do? Who was on which side? What of Mephistopheles?

They decided to return to Asmodai's home, there to build them weapons of war, which which to oppose Yaweh. None was happy with this decision, but none could escape its inevitability.

They knew, also, that Yaweh now considered them opposed to him without room for doubt, so they often looked around as if they expected to see a hundred angels with swords uplifted running toward them and screaming. They knew that Asmodai's home might not be safe. But they knew that to go to Leviathan, now, would be to draw danger to her. And there was no way to find Satan.

Harut had left to return to Leviathan to reassure her. He had made his choice of sides by his statement to Asmodai.

Occasionally Lucifer, Lilith, and Asmodai would pass by

Thrones, who had recovered from the flood and were returning to Yaweh's palace. None of the Thrones spoke, and the arch-angels ignored the Thrones.

They passed the night in silence, setting no guard, daring any of Yaweh's minions to attack them as they rested.

At last they reached the center, and Asmodai's home. The house was undisturbed, and empty.

Asmodai lit the fires, which needed a day to become hot enough to use. They shared wine, and companionship, and tried not to think about Ariel.

"You wished to see me, Lord?"

"Yes, Abdiel. Thank you for coming." He motioned the Seraphim out of earshot and indicated to Abdiel that he was to approach. Abdiel did so, bowing.

"I've considered your scheme. Indeed, I've done little else for the past several days."

"Yes, Lord?"

"Raphael and I have spoken of it at length. She agrees that what you brought up about morale, and the attitudes of the angels, is a problem. She agrees that this will solve the problem. But she doesn't like it.

"Nor do I, Abdiel. I don't like it at all."

"Lord, I—"

"Peace, Abdiel. I don't like it, but I think it's necessary. Raphael and I have been up nights trying to decide if there is any other way to solve the problem, or if we can get by without solving it. We finally admitted that we had no choice. We are going to do it."

"I feel gratified, Lord."

"There are things which make me very unhappy, Abdiel, but it is a chance to solve the problem with Satan once and for all—and we can't pass it up."

"That is, indeed, how I saw it, Lord."

"We will begin at once."

"At once, Lord?"

"Nearly. I've sent out messengers this morning. The entire host—all of Heaven—is being asked to gather on the hillside behind the palace. In fifteen days."

"Fifteen days, Lord? But, excuse me, Lord Yaweh, there are those who live more than seven days distant. They will not receive the message in time to come."

"My messengers are faster than you think, Abdiel. They're using your method. They'll arrive, at the latest, early tomorrow in the most distant areas of the Southern Regency. If those who live there hurry, they will be able to be here in fourteen days. And they were asked to hurry."

"I see, Lord. That leaves little time for preparations."

"I know. We must begin at once. What will we need?"

"Need? Nothing, actually, Lord. But we must be certain that we know how to do it, without fail."

"Then let us begin. I'll summon Raphael."

"All right, Lord. But . . . Lord, I still don't understand why we are rushing like this. Excuse me."

Yaweh shook his head. "It isn't necessary that you undersand, good Abdiel. It is necessary; that is enough."

"Yes, Lord."

Yaweh signaled to a Seraph, who received his orders, and went to find Raphael. Yaweh closed his eyes. He knew very well that they had to do this soon—because, if they delayed, he wouldn't have the courage or the will to do it at all.

"What do you suppose it is, Kyriel?"

"How should I know? Everyone sure is excited about it, though."

"Yeah. I've heard that everyone is going to be there."

"That's what I've heard, too. Is there going to be room on the hill for them?"

"I hope so. You know what I think, Kyriel?"

"Not often, Sith."

"Cut it out."

"Sorry. What?"

"I think this is *it*."

"You mean the Plan?"

"Yeah. I think he's going to start it, right then."

"Already? Don't be foolish."

"Well, then, what is it?"

"I don't know. It probably has to do with the Plan. Maybe he's going to answer the rumors, and the talk about Satan."

"I guess that's possible. It sure will be something to see, though. Twelve more days."

"Yeah. I'm getting anxious."

"Ha! Not half as anxious as Yaweh is, I'll bet."

"Watch your mouth, Sith."

"Sorry."

Harut and Mephistopheles met on the barren plains near the eastern border of Leviathan's realm.

"Are you heading back to see her?" asked Mephistopheles.

"Yup."

"Good. That saves me some trouble. She was asking about you."

"I'll be there in a day or so. I don't move too fast, you know."

Mephistopheles smiled a bit and clasped Harut's shoulder. "Say," he said suddenly, "have you seen Satan, by any chance?"

"No," said Harut. "I can guess where he is, though. There's talk all over about a big get-together in the center, in eleven days. If he's heard of it, he'll be there."

"What kind of get-together, Harut?"

"Dunno. But everybody is supposed to show up."

"Hmmmm. What about you?"

"I'll be with Leviathan."

"I see."

"Afternoon, Mephistopheles."

"So long, Harut."

Michael strode up to the Throne, and the Seraphim made way for him lest they be trampled.

"Welcome," said Yaweh.

Michael nodded.

Yaweh continued, "I've heard what happened."

"From Abdiel?"

"Yes."

"I'm glad he made it back safely. I'm sorry I failed again."

"In failing, you saved Abdiel's life—again. And Abdiel had an idea along the way. I'm going ahead with it. You won't like it, I think. I don't like it either. But we're going to do it."

Michael studied Yaweh for a moment, then he slapped himself on the chest. Dust sprang out. Michael brushed at his right arm and sides.

"I see," said Yaweh, "that you've had a long trip. Would you like me to wait before describing Abdiel's scheme?"

Michael shook his head. "No. Does it have to do with the gathering of angels I've been hearing about?"

Yaweh nodded.

"All right. You'd better tell me about it, then."

"All right. But first—did you see Raziel, by any chance?"

"I saw him near the battle, just before it began. He asked me a few questions about Satan's attack on Abdiel."

"Good," said Yaweh. "Now let me tell you what your task is to be—if you are willing."

Michael nodded sharply.

"You will be leading a new order of angels that I am creating. They are to number one thousand. I have, in the last few days, created an order of which the archangel Yahriel is chief. They number five hundred. They are called Dominions. They will be in amongst the angels we are gathering, to make sure there are none within who wish to disrupt the assembly. Your order is to be called Virtues. You will keep your forces at the edge of the gathering and watch for anyone trying to disrupt it."

Michael's brows came together. "Before I answer you," he said, "I want to hear what this is about."

"Of course. Sit down, and I'll explain."

Yaweh motioned to a Seraph, who brought a chair for Michael.

"Now, here's the idea. . . ."

Nine

So spake thc Omnipotent, and with his
    words
All seemed well pleased; all seemed, but
    were not all.

—Milton, *Paradise Lost,* v:616-617

"I'll speak for about half an hour," said Yaweh some days later. "Then you and Abdiel will begin."

"Begin what, exactly?" asked Raphael.

"The first step will be to unify them, to get the energy from all of them flowing to me, through you."

"I think I can do that."

"And what," said Michael, "will I be doing?"

"As I told you before, Michael, you and your Virtues—do you have them yet, by the way?"

"Yes. One thousand angels, with swords."

"Good. You will encircle the gathering and look for any danger from outside."

"You're worried about Satan, then?"

"Somewhat," admitted Yaweh, looking uncomfortable. "Also Lucifer and the rest."

"I see."

"Good. As to the details of the casting," he told Raphael, "you must speak to Abdiel. I will be holding in my mind the image of what I want to appear, and I will always have control of the energy. I can direct it, but Abdiel knows best how to gather it."

"All right. I'll go speak to him then."

"Good. And when you're done, tell him I'd like to see him."

"All right."

Raphael swept gracefully from the room.

"Yaweh?" said Michael.

"Yes?"

"Is this . . . necessary?"

"Yes, I think it is."

"All right."

Michael left. Yaweh stared straight ahead. Necessary? Yes, exactly as necessary as the Plan itself. Unless Raziel had found something. That one "unless." But where was he?

Yaweh was shaken out of his reverie some time later by Gabriel announcing Abdiel's arrival.

"Come in, Abdiel."

"Thank you, Lord. You wished to see me?"

Abdiel took a seat near the throne. Yaweh studied him as if looking for something in particular, then spoke.

"Yes. I take it all went well with Raphael."

"Yes, Lord," said Abdiel.

"Good," said Yaweh. He shifted his position, gripping the arms of the throne. "I've been thinking about the speech I'll be giving."

"Yes, Lord?"

"Your idea was for me to make these statements as if they had always been true."

"Yes, Lord. I think that is best."

Once more, Yaweh shifted. "But Abdiel—I am not at all sure that it is the case."

Abdiel's eyebrows came together. "But—" he stopped, and considered things for the space of a dozen heartbeats. "You aren't sure, you said. I don't understand—how could it not be the case?"

Yaweh shook his head. "It isn't exactly wrong, but—it's a new way of looking at things. I'm not used to it. I've always looked at it as something that just happened. I'm not saying that another interpretation is untrue, merely that I see it differently."

"But why do so, Lord? If you present it as I suggest, it will help our project. And, as you just said, it isn't *wrong* to look at it this way. At worst, you are being more positive about things than you normally would. But you are doing this in order to help. What is wrong with that?"

Yaweh chewed his lip for a while. "I'm not sure, Abdiel. I'll think it over."

"Thank you, Lord."

"Now here's another thing...."

"Good afternoon, Lord Satan."

Satan spun and dropped to one knee, his hand going to the emerald at his breast. Beelzebub whirled and bared his teeth. Satan stood then, and nodded. "Good afternoon, Mephistopheles. Have you been following me long?"

"This conversation suddenly sounds familiar."

Beelzebub growled.

Mephistopheles shrugged. "Not more than an hour or so."

"I see. Well, I'm glad you're here. I wanted to thank you."

"For what?"

"For what you did for me—back there. With Michael."

"I don't remember doing anything with Michael. You must have mistaken me for someone else."

"Have it that way then."

"Mind if I ask where you're going?"

"Not at all."

"Well?"

"Well what?"

"Where—oh. Very good." Mephistopheles chuckled. "Where are you going?"

Beelzebub began, "Milord, methinks—"

"I know, Beelzebub. I'm heading toward the center."

"Oh. Then you've heard about it. Well, what are you going to do? Do you think you can influence it in any way?"

Satan shrugged. "You know me. What do you suppose I'm going to do?"

"I'd say that you'll try to stop it, unless you know what it's really about."

"What makes you think I don't?"

"Do you?"

"Maybe."

"All right. But you have a few days to decide. Maybe you don't know."

Satan smiled but didn't answer.

"Or it could be," continued Mephistopheles, "that you hope for a chance at Abdiel. While everyone is standing there, listening to Yaweh talk about whatever it is he's talking about, maybe you think you can find Abdiel. After all, not everyone knows you. You could find him, do whatever you do, and be gone before anyone notices."

"I like the way your mind works, Mephistopheles. But I don't want to dominate the discussion. What brings you out here?"

"Much the same as what brings you. I want to get there a day early to see what's going on, and who's saying what. The same as you, I imagine."

"You have a good imagination."

"Thank you."

They looked at each other, Satan in his green and gold standing a bit taller than Mephistopheles in his black. Beelzebub looked back and forth between them, aware that they were communicating on some level that he couldn't reach.

"You know what my problem is?" said Satan at last.

"As a matter of fact, I don't, Lord Satan."

"I have trouble making up my mind."

"Hmmm."

"I do. After all this time, I still haven't decided whether to oppose Yaweh's Plan. I've been wrestling with it for hundreds of days, now. Isn't that something?"

"It's *something*, but—"

"You, on the other hand, are different."

"Yes?"

"You *won't* make up your mind. You spend your time tearing other people down, and exercising the power of your mind and intellect over them, more for the delight of doing so, it seems, than to accomplish anything. Because there just isn't anything you want to accomplish. You have friends, and you help them, and you think that that is enough. It isn't.

"There are lines being drawn, Mephistopheles. And the lines can cut across friendships as though they weren't there. If you try to balance in the middle, you make enemies on both sides.

"You're clever, all right. I'll give you that, and then some. But that isn't enough. I hope that I'm going to be allowed to make up my mind, in my own time, in my own way. But if I'm not, I'll commit myself. You won't, though. You'll wander along, taking potshots at everyone, and when the roll is called you'll be alone in the middle, with both sides looking at you. And the best you can hope for is that they'll only spit."

He looked down at Beelzebub. "Let's go."

They turned their backs on Mephistopheles and continued toward the center.

After a league or so, Beelzebub ventured, "Milord?"

"Yes, Beelzebub?"

"Thou spake on some event at the center of Heaven, of which I knew not."

"Ah, yes. That. There is to be a gathering of all the hosts near the Palace. Yaweh is going to speak to them, and there may be more to it."

"I knew not of this, milord. How didst thou learn of it?"

"Why, Beelzebub, Mephistopheles just told us. Weren't you listening?"

They continued walking in silence.

"Well, my friends, that's all that I know. What do you think, Lilith?"

"I don't know, Asmodai. It is certainly important, and it must be connected to the Plan in some way, but I don't know how. Lucifer, have you any guesses?"

"I don't know what it means, but I think we ought to be there, whatever it is."

"I agree."

"And I also, but—what do we do there? Just watch?"

"Why not?"

"I think we have to be ready to do something. Who knows what is going to happen? The way the talk has been going, he's liable to announce the beginning of the Plan right now."

"He wouldn't!"

"Why not, Lilith?"

"Well, because of us."

"He might decide that's the best way to deal with us."

"I'm not sure that I like the idea of being 'dealt with.'"

"None of us does, Lucifer, but—"

"What I mean is that I'm beginning to agree with Asmodai. We should be ready to do something, if we have to."

"I don't know what you mean."

"Neither do I, to tell you the truth. Asmodai?"

"I think you and I ought to get to work. We still have a couple of days; I'd like to see how much the two of us working together can do."

"What do you mean?"

"I think I know. He means weapons, Lilith. He wants to go there carrying as many as we can, so if we find ourselves in a situation where we wish to arm large numbers of the hosts, then—"

"Rubbish."

"What do you mean, Lilith?"

"You're talking nonsense. Arm the hosts? Large numbers? How?"

"Well, we declare ourselves—"

"Oh, come, Lucifer. Who is going to listen to us?"

"We're archangels and Firstborn. They'll listen—"

"To other angels. We're the ones who've been coming up with these plans, and scheming against them."

"What do you mean?"

"The Plan itself, Asmodai. To the hosts, this is the work of the Firstborn and the archangels."

"*We* haven't been doing it; it's Yaweh and—"

"What is there to separate us from them in the eyes of the hosts? How many have you spoken to? When did you make it clear to the hosts of Heaven that we oppose Yaweh?"

"Well, I. . . ."

"Right. There is only one of us who's done that, and he never set out to."

"Satan."

"Exactly."

"Then without him, we have nothing?"

"Basically, Asmodai, that is exactly what I'm saying."

"He's awfully hard to convince, as I'm sure you recall."

"But that's what we must do, if we're going to do anything.

We either convince Satan to join us, or we wrest from him the leadership of the hosts who fear the Plan. Anything else is a waste of time."

"But the weapons—"

"Forget them, Asmodai. If it comes to a need for weapons, we'll have them because the hosts that Yaweh has already armed will be on our side. If the hosts aren't on our side, then all the weapons you could invent won't make a bit of difference."

"I see what you mean."

"So do I. But Lilith, I'm not sure you're going far enough."

"How do you mean that?"

"I'm not sure that we should be trying to convince Satan at all. I think we should be trying to undo the damage we've done."

"Damage?"

"Damage caused by inaction. We should be showing the hosts that we oppose the plan, and that, if they oppose it as well, they can trust us to lead them."

"How do you propose doing that?"

"In the first place, I think we ought to be at this gathering Yaweh is calling. And when he gives his speech, maybe we can give one of our own."

"Hmmmm. Not a bad idea at all, lover."

"Thank you. Asmodai?"

"Well, I still like the idea of building weapons."

"But?"

"But . . . all right. I'm convinced."

"Good. We have a couple of days. I want to rest."

"And I."

"And I."

"You're back!"

"What's wrong with it, honey?"

"What? Oh. You're jesting."

"Sorry."

She gave forth a laugh that sent the waves reeling. "Don't be. It's been so long since I've heard anyone jest that I was afraid we'd all forgotten how."

"It's all right."

"Well, Harut, how did you fare?"

"Not well, honey, but I'm all right now. Lilith rescued me."

"I'm grateful to her. And to many others."

"Yeah. But don't worry. You'll pay 'em back."

"Maybe. Harut?"

"Yeah, honey?"

"Could you play me a song?"

"I can't. My instrument was lost."

"No!"

"I could sing you one."

"But your cithara!"

"Asmodai will build me another one."

"Then I'll be grateful to him, too."

Harut smiled and shook his head. He seated himself on a rock and began slapping his hand on his knee, his eyes closed. After a moment, he began to sing.

From the four Regencies of Heaven, they came. Tens of thousands of angels, hundreds of archangels, all gathering on the hill beneath Yaweh's palace.

At the top of the hill was a platform with great horns set next to it. These, it was said, would carry Yaweh's voice to everyone who was gathered there.

Some had been there two days, some three, and some were just now arriving, weary and footsore, to cast themselves down on the ground and rest for a time. It was only a matter of hours, now, until he appeared. The restlessness and feelings of expectation spread through the crowd and infected each angel present.

It was curious to note that there was no division or separation between angels and archangels, as if the coming presence of the eldest of the Firstborn was enough to make any other division among them trival.

They looked up the long expanse of greenery and waited, and the tension grew.

Soon, they told themselves, soon.

"Abdiel!"

"Yes, Lord Yaweh?"

"I've just heard from Yahriel."

"Who?"

"Yahriel. Chief of the order of Dominions."

"Oh. Yes, Lord?"

"He says that he needs help. There are more angels out there than his Dominions can cope with. Are all of your Thrones back?"

Abdiel swallowed. "Yes, Lord, but—"

"Is there any reason why they can't help keep things orderly?"

"No, Lord, but will a mere two hundred make a difference?"

"Maybe. We should try, at any rate."

"As you wish, Lord. But am I not needed elsewhere?"

"That's true. Is there someone among your Thrones that you can trust to lead in your place?"

Abdiel breathed a silent sigh of relief. "Yes, Lord. I can find someone."

Zaphkiel walked along the perimeter of the crowd. From time to time an angel would begin shouting at an angel next to him over a place in the grass to sit. Then Zaphkiel would look at one of the Thrones, and indicate with his eyes, and the Throne would go and speak quietly until the trouble was settled.

That each Throne carried a naked sword in his hand may have helped somewhat.

At one point he met Yahriel, who was engaged much the same way. They nodded without speaking. Sometime later he met Michael, who was watching the area beyond the edge of the gathering. Zaphkiel bowed low.

"Who are you?"

"Zaphkiel."

"These seem to be Abdiel's angels."

"They are."

"Yet you seem to be leading them."

"I am."

"Well?"

"He's busy."

"I see. Well, I'm sure you'll be of help to Yahriel."

"I hope so."

Michael cocked his head and studied the other.

"You don't say much, do you?"

"No."

They stood looking at each other. Michael felt uncomfortable. If Zaphkiel felt uncomfortable, he didn't show it. After a moment, Michael moved on.

Zaphkiel continued, his eyes always moving. Suddenly,

there was a low rumbling sound. Zaphkiel identified it as the sounds of thousands upon thousands of angels, all sighing or muttering at the same time. The sound began near the top of the hill and spread backwards.

He looked up at once and saw a distant figure that he identified as Raphael. Next to her he recognized Abdiel. The two of them were walking toward the platform, and there was a continuing rumble from the gathered angels.

Zaphkiel shifted his eyes to the Palace and saw an angel he assumed to be Gabriel leading some dozens of angels toward the platform. Next came twenty angels led by Uriel. In their midst walked Yaweh, barely to be seen. The shouts from the host were nearly deafening.

Yaweh walked up to the platform.

Having seen all there was of interest, Zaphkiel returned to scanning the crowd.

"'Tis strange, milord, that none can see us, yet we are so near."

Satan shrugged. "We can hardly see them. It works out."

"Verily, milord."

They sat within a small grove of trees just over the hill from the platform. They had made their way in the night, and remained still and silent. The trees were thick, but sound carried well, and there were many angels walking nearby.

"The sound of angels yelling, milord."

"Yes?"

"Methinks the time of Yaweh's speech draweth nigh."

"I imagine so."

At that moment, there was sudden silence in the center of Heaven. Yaweh had raised his arms.

"I am Yaweh," he said, and through the trumps at his sides his voice carried to every corner of the hill and valley. "I welcome each of you."

He paused and turned his head to look across their great expanse. He lowered his arms and continued.

"Each of you may be at ease, and be assured that I know you, and love you all. I have gathered you together today, in part, to tell you that. You have come, in part, because you know it already.

"This is as it should be.

"I existed, timeless and eternal, alone in the void, from the beginning. This you know, because the beginning was when I came to be. Before me, there was only flux.

"After me, there will be only flux again."

He stopped to let that have its effect. He wondered about the truth of it, but put it out of his mind. In a certain, poetic sense at least, it was true. That would have to be enough. Unpleasant as it was, he could not fail in his duty to the hosts over a matter of interpretation. And as he looked through the gathering and saw the effects his words were having, he knew that Abdiel was right.

For a time there were murmurs throughout the valley and hillside, mostly consisting of, "Did you hear that?" and, "What did *that* mean?"

Yaweh raised his arms and there was silence again. Then he said, "I did not know I was lonely, at first, because I had never been unalone. But I was alone, and wished for others like myself." This was possible. He wasn't really aware of the very beginning—he couldn't remember when he had become aware of himself as such. He made a note to ask Lucifer about this, then remembered that he couldn't. He shook the mood off and continued.

"I reached into the flux, and I drew forth the Firstborn, as, indeed, they have done for the archangels, and the archangels have done for the angels, and the angels will do for whomever follows.

"This is how it was. This is not how it must be.

"I envisioned a place where there would be safety for those made by the flux, whom the flux wishes to have back. Thus, Heaven came to be. Those who were with me during the time known as the First Wave helped to build and extend it. Those who came later did the same. Thus, Heaven is here for us all, though we must defend it from the flux.

"This, too, need not be.

"I have said that this will end—that we need not live in fear of cacoastrum, that there will be a time of peace.

"This peace is coming. But, as I have opened my heart so that you may be, now I ask that my gift be returned. I ask that each of you think of me with love, so that we may all become one, and together establish a realm of peace, harmony, and love."

• • •

"Milord, what means this?"

"I don't know, Beelzebub. I wish I knew whether he believed all of this himself, or why he's saying it if he doesn't. But don't speak. I want to hear more."

"Aye, milord."

"What is he doing, Asmodai?"

"I don't know, Lucifer. Should we move?"

"I don't think so, yet."

"Why not, Lilith?"

"Because we don't know what he's doing. There has to be a point to all of these claims—"

"These lies!"

"As you wish. There has to be a point, and he hasn't reached it."

"Do we want him to?"

"I think so, Asmodai. If for no other reason, then to know what we're up against."

"Maybe. What do you think, Lucifer?"

"I'm still not certain. But let's wait a bit longer."

"Sith?"

"Yes?"

"Why are you on your knees?"

"I don't know."

"Oh."

"Now you're on your knees too. Why?"

"It's so. . . ."

"I feel terrible about what we said, you know—what we were talking about . . . before."

"Me too."

"What should we do?"

"Let's just listen. Maybe he'll tell us."

"Okay. You know, Kyriel?"

"Yeah?"

"If he asked me to . . . do what we were talking about, before—"

"Yeah."

"I'd do it."

"Me too, Sith."

• • •

As Yaweh stood before them in silence, many fell to their knees.

Yaweh surveyed them for a moment longer, then spoke again.

"We will join together, and make something more than any of us can be alone. Look around you. Your brothers and sisters are all around you. As you love me who created you, and I love you whom I have created, so you love each other, who were created together.

"Now rise, all of you, and join together before me. Come closer now, here in front of me, so you are as one. That is well. Breathe together and think together and be together. Yes. Even closer now, all of you, so you are as one.

"Do you feel how I love you all? Can you return my love for you? Try...."

Abdiel turned to Raphael and whispered, "He speaks well. I'd never have thought it."

Raphael didn't answer.

"I think we should begin," said Abdiel.

"Very well."

"Can you remember what to do?"

"I remember."

Abdiel closed his eyes and felt Raphael next to him. The two became as one, and then Yaweh was there, guiding and leading, and slowly, the angels of Heaven were there, too.

A few at first, and then gradually more and more. Abdiel felt Yaweh begin the working—begin to turn the illiaster into a form that he could use, to create, and bring about his desires.

Still more angels joined. Abdiel felt the force of Yaweh's will commanding the force of the illiaster in nearly all the hosts of Heaven.

Abdiel had never had a notion of Yaweh's tremendous will. Otherwise, he would never have entertained fanciful thoughts of turning this event in a direction of more direct use to himself. But Yaweh was in total command of the energy—his will dominated the three of them; the force of his mind overpowered them.

Some of those in the front began to sway, but they didn't seem to notice.

Yaweh was utterly silent and motionless as he worked, and

nothing came closer and closer to becoming something. Angels near the front began to fall over, and those further in back were wavering.

Abdiel and Raphael felt the lines of tension from Yaweh as surely as they felt the lines of force from the assembled hosts.

Then, taking a deep breath, Yaweh began in earnest.

Ten

And all those souls joined in a holy dance,
and then, like shooting sparks, gone
      instantly,
they disappeared behind the veil of
      distance.

—Dante, *Paradiso*, Canto vii:7-9

Lucifer, Lilith and Asmodai watched in silence as the ceremony continued. They saw those in the front falling, and those behind begin to stagger, but they didn't say anything. After a time, they saw Yaweh close his eyes, bow his head, and begin to work his hands in and out of fists. Lilith said, "What is he doing?" "I don't know," Lucifer answered. "I can tell that he's drawing on his illiaster, but—" "More than that," said Asmodai. "Look closer. He's drawing on the illiaster of every one of those angels."

"You're right!" said Lucifer in wonder. "How can he do that?"

157

"I don't know. But he seems to have them, doesn't he?"

"Yes. I think we missed our chance to do anything."

"I agree. Well, what now?"

"I want to see the rest of this," said Lilith.

"Yes, so do—what's *that?*"

As they watched, Yaweh spread his hands, and a glowing ball appeared in the air before him. The three leaned forward and stared.

Yaweh continued, forcing his will upon the illiaster that had begun to take shape between his hands. Abdiel and Raphael were sweating now, directing the energy toward him.

Yaweh was up to the hard part. It wasn't simply a matter of doing it—he was creating a thing that no angel had ever before attempted, and the level of detail required was more than he had ever had to deal with. In a lucid moment, he found himself suddenly wishing Asmodai were there.

This brought him back to memories of why Asmodai wasn't, and his concentration was almost broken by a sudden spasm of anger directed at Asmodai, Lucifer, Satan, and the rest.

This, too, went into his creation.

"Sith?"

"Eh, what?"

"I . . . something happened. I fell over."

"Me, too. What was it?"

"I don't know, I just felt dizzy, and . . . then I was down here."

"I feel . . . drained."

"Yes. Me, too."

"Can you see what's going on up there?"

"No. There are still some people standing in front of me."

"Oh. Kyriel?"

"Yes, Sith?"

"Would you mind getting off me?"

"What? Oh. Sorry."

"Thanks."

"I think I can get up now."

"Good luck."

"Thanks."

"Well done. Can you help me now?"

"I'll try. My legs feel weak."

"Okay. Ah! There. Wait . . . good. Thank you."

"You're welcome. Let's—Sith!"

"Huh?"

"Look!"

"Where? Oh . . . by the flux! Now who is that?"

He grew from nothing, and stood before Yaweh, tall, strong and powerful. He had a full black beard, a massive chest, and a large head full of black hair. His eyes were set deep, and of a piercing brown.

He stood before them naked, his hands at his sides, the muscles of his chest and legs standing out prominently. He turned and looked fully at Yaweh. Then, before them all, he dropped to his knees and bowed his head, clasping his hands in front of him.

Yaweh walked forward once more to the edge of the platform and he spoke, saying, "This day I have brought forth him whom I declare to be my son. He will be called Yeshuah, for he will save us from our suffering.

"I give him to you, to lead you through the coming days when our hardships will increase tenfold, that our joy may increase a thousand-fold thereafter.

"Yeshuah, created by love before you all, and no other, is rightful king of Heaven, and he who does not accept his law or disobeys him earns my wrath and shall be expelled from Heaven on that day. For this I can do—the Walls of Heaven are not such that they cannot be opened to permit me to return to the flux any who reject the law of Heaven as I declare it to be—for the good of us all. I have lived alone amid only cacoastrum—who among you could do this?"

His eyes had taken on a burning aspect that those in the front could clearly see. Now they softened.

"My people," he said, his voice low, "it grieves me to threaten, and to say you must do this, or you cannot do that. It hurts me. But it hurts me more to see you destroyed by the mindless enemy that lives outside. Destroyed by the hundreds and by the thousands. I will not permit it if I can stop it. Now, I can stop it. Now, no one will keep me from stopping it. And now, he who will lead us in this is here.

"Now, all of you who have seen the birth of him who will save us, pay him homage. I am Yaweh, I have created Heaven and I am father to you all. As you love me, let Yeshuah, my son, begotten before you all, be my arm amongst you."

He stepped back then and made a sign for Yeshuah to rise and stand by his side. Then all the hosts of Heaven before them fell to their knees and bowed their heads.

Yaweh felt the waves of love and adoration directed at him and at his son, and he basked in them. He smiled. He looked out upon those tens of thousands of angels, and he saw that it was good.

"Milord? What means this, what we have seen?"

"I'm not sure, Beelzebub. I had no idea he could do that."

"Do what, milord?"

"What he just did. You saw—he created a being himself, out of illiaster taken from the angels. I'm . . . amazed."

"Aye, milord. Amazed, verily. But what of his speech. What signifies it?"

"I'm not certain. It's obvious that he has some scheme of how to use this, but I don't even know what he wants anymore, much less how he plans to achieve it."

"What he desires, milord? Certes 'tis clear—'tis all for the Plan that—hark!"

"What is it?"

"Can'st thou not hear, milord?"

"Your ears are better than mine, Beelzebub. What is it?"

"Conversation, milord. They speak in whispers, yet 'tis nigh."

"Which way? I'd like to know who it is that also wants to hide. Where are they?"

"This way, milord."

Lucifer looked around quickly. "Did either of you hear something just now?"

The others shook their heads. Lucifer shrugged.

"Well," said Asmodai. "Now we know. What do you think?"

"What do *you* think?" asked Lilith.

"I," said Asmodai, "am disgusted. Look at them out there, groveling to that . . . that . . . *thing*."

"I see what you mean," said Lucifer.

"Don't you feel it?"

"Yes," said Lucifer slowly, "I feel it. But I guess it's different for me."

"What do you mean?"

"Remember, I was with him from the beginning. I know what he was like before, and I see what he's become now. I don't know what he's going to be like in a hundred days—or ten. It's sad. You feel for those who are groveling, and that's good. But I feel for the one who is making them grovel. What's happened to him, Asmodai? You knew him. Did he ever seem to you someone who would fill his palace with angels, armed with swords to prevent anyone from seeing him? Who would tell such a lie as to say that he was responsible for us all? Who would make thousands of angels bow down to him? Is that the Yaweh you knew before?"

"No," said Asmodai slowly, "it isn't."

"So what has happened to him?"

"I don't know."

Lilith cleared her throat. They looked at her.

"Yes, Lilith? What is it?"

She shook her head. "No, I don't have an answer to your question. But I've seen enough. Let us leave, now."

"And go where?"

"Anywhere."

"And do what?"

"Anything. I can't take any more of this."

"All right. I think it's time we found Satan. I'm still not sure what we're going to say to him, but we should at least let him know what has happened. Maybe he can explain it to us."

"I agree," said Asmodai. "It is time to find the Lord Satan, and tell him that the time has come for him to act. If he is the one that the angels will look to, we must have him for—"

"Drop it, Asmodai. You're dreaming. The angels aren't going to look to anyone, now. They've been too thoroughly taken in."

"Are you telling me we've lost? Before we've even begun?"

"Can you look out there and tell me anything different?"

"I can—"

"Please," said Lilith. "Let us leave here."

"All right," said Lucifer. "Let's go back to Asmodai's home and figure out how we're going to find Satan."

"All right," said Asmodai. "For whatever reason."

They stood as one and left the woods.

• • •

"I don't see anyone now."

"Nor do I, milord. Yet their scent doth linger. 'Twas Lucifer, Lilith, and Asmodai."

"Do you think we should try to find them?"

"An thou wouldst. I can follow them."

"Then let's see where they went, if we can."

"Aye, milord."

Harut stiffened and turned his head from side to side, slowly, as if he were looking for something. Then he stood and took the path his feet knew so well, to the ledge by the shore. He wasn't surprised to hear Leviathan already swimming toward him.

"You felt it, too?"

He nodded.

She said, "Any idea what it was?"

"No," he said. "You?"

"It felt like the start of a Wave, but different, somehow."

"You felt the flux?"

"Maybe," she said, her voice sounding confused and hesitant. "I wish I knew what it meant."

"Someone is doing something."

"Yes."

"Yaweh's speech?"

"Maybe."

"Lucifer, do you think?"

"I wish I knew."

"Should I try to find out?"

"I . . . wish you wouldn't. I'd like you to stay here."

"All right," he said softly.

"I wish . . . never mind."

"I know, honey. I do too. But he's gone. He wouldn't want us to dwell on it like this."

"I know. But it still hurts, sometimes. And then sometimes I become so angry when I think about it that I don't trust myself."

"That's not a good way to be."

"I know. But what can I do?"

"Don't dwell on it. Think about other things."

"Such as?"

"I don't know."

"Sing for me, Harut?"

"All right," he said.

And he did so while they waited.

Zaphkiel fell to his knees and bowed his head for what felt like the right length of time, then rose and resumed studying the angels around him.

He decided that there weren't going to be any immediate problems, so he moved toward the top of the hill where he could get a better view. Presently he came across one of his Thrones still kneeling, his head bowed.

Zaphkiel touched him on the shoulder. The figure remained motionless. Zaphkiel struck him sharply in the back.

The angel looked up and focused in on him. "Why did you do that?" he asked.

"What is your name?" asked Zaphkiel.

"Camael."

"Get up, Camael. We have work to do."

"Oh. I was overcome by. . . ." He gestured vaguely toward the top of the hill.

"We haven't time to be overcome."

"All right. What do you want me to do?"

"Go through the host, finding the rest of us, and gather them together here. I'll give further orders then."

"All right."

"And go quickly."

"All right."

Camael gave a slight bow—he wasn't sure why—and began moving through the crowd as quickly as he could, looking for Thrones. Zaphkiel continued standing where he was, waiting.

Michael, alone among them all, had not fallen to his knees. He stood, staring blankly at Yaweh and Yeshuah, and wondered what it all meant.

His puzzlement had begun at Yaweh's speech. Could Yaweh have believed those things? Could they be true? Why was he saying them?

Then, as the rest of the scheme unfolded, even though he had been in on it, he found himself filled with a deep sadness. He had known that Heaven was changing; he hadn't realized how much. He still believed fervently in the Plan; he wondered why these things were necessary for it to work.

Slowly, the angels began to rise. The Virtues began to assemble around him. Without any conscious decision, he found himself beginning to walk, moving around the assembled angels, looking for problems, knowing he wouldn't find any.

His head turned this way and that, without registering anything he saw.

He felt a strange wetness on his cheek, and wondered at it.

Zaphkiel looked over the Thrones, quickly counted them, and nodded to Camael. He began leading them, looking through the host, missing no details, yet seeing nothing that required attention.

After a time, as more and more of the angels began to rise, Camael approached him.

"Zaphkiel?"

"Yes?"

"Do you think there will be problems? Now? After what has happened?"

"No."

"Then why—"

"It is what we are to do."

Camael looked at him, then bowed his head and stepped back. Zaphkiel continued walking, looking and sensing the mood of the angels around him.

On the platform, at the top of the hill, Yaweh and Yeshuah stood next to each other, their hands held up and palms outward. They bowed, and together they left the platform and returned to the Palace, the Cherubim leading and the Seraphim surrounding them. Raphael and Abdiel walked behind them.

The mass of angels began to drift away. Zaphkiel watched closely, looking for any possible trouble, but none came. The angels dispersed quietly and quickly, each seemingly lost in thought or sharing thoughts with one other.

Zaphkiel nodded his satisfaction.

Michael gathered the Virtues, Yahriel gathered the Dominions, and Zaphkiel gathered the Thrones. They met near the bottom of the hill and began the long march back up it toward the Palace.

Michael turned to look at Zaphkiel from time to time, as if he was going to say something, but he never spoke. Zaphkiel, for his part, didn't seem to notice.

Suddenly Zaphkiel stopped. "Bide," he said, and sprinted off into the small woods they were passing. He disappeared from view for several moments, then rejoined the others.

"What was it?" asked Michael.

"There were angels watching from there. I guess they didn't want to be part of the event."

Michael nodded.

From behind them, Camael said, "That grove has been defiled by their presence. We should cut it down."

They made the rest of the journey in silence.

Far to the north, under mountains known for vulcanism, Belial turned in his sleep. One of his great eyes opened, and he looked around the chamber where only he could see, but there was nothing.

He wondered what it was that had disturbed him.

Then he sensed something. A strange feeling, almost as if a Wave were beginning, but different somehow—controlled. He thought about following it to see what it was, but after a time it stopped.

It continued to disturb him, though.

After a few hours, he returned to his sleep, but it was not as deep a sleep—it was as if he expected to be disturbed again.

His great eyes closed, there in the dark, and all was silence.

Eleven

Woe unto them who are wise in their own
eyes,
And prudent in their own sight!

—Isaiah, 5:21

Mephistopheles spotted them going through the woods, and
his eyebrows lifted briefly.

So, he decided, they were watching, eh? That's interesting.
I wonder what they thought of it all.

He debated speaking to them, but didn't. Instead, he listened
to their discussion, or as much of it as he could catch. It was
enough to allow him to conclude safely that there had been
still others in the woods.

After the pair had passed him, he slipped by and set off
after the ones who must be ahead. He hurried, hoping to catch
them soon.

"Do you feel any better now?"

"Yes, Lucifer. Thank you. I couldn't take that."

"It's all right."

They had left the area of the Palace behind them and were

approaching Asmodai's home. They had moved quickly, putting them well ahead of those who had actually been involved in the events, for these latter were walking slowly, as if still in a stupor.

"I'm surprised," remarked Asmodai, "that we haven't been harassed—or even visited."

"Don't expect it to last," said Lucifer.

"I won't."

They walked a little further, and Asmodai's home came into view.

"Where should we begin looking?" asked Lucifer. "He could be anywhere."

"I know. What I'd *like* to do is to get Mephistopheles to find him, but I still don't trust him."

"That's wise," said Lilith. "He's not committed yet—if he ever will be."

"He's committed to Leviathan," said Asmodai.

Lilith shrugged.

"In any case, he isn't here. How do we find Satan? Do you suppose he went to visit Leviathan?"

"He may have," said Lucifer. "He never had a chance to speak to her."

"He may have indeed," said a voice, "but he didn't."

The three of them stopped and spun. Lucifer's hand went to the wand at his side. "How long have you been behind us?"

"This is becoming boring," said Mephistopheles.

"Answer my question!"

Mephistopheles shrugged. "Not too long. I've been trying to catch up to you. You've been walking quickly. I wish you wouldn't do that, by the way. It's tiring."

Lucifer's nostrils flared. "Why were you following us?"

The dark angel shrugged. "To tell you what I've just told you. Satan did not go visit Leviathan."

Lucifer began, "How do you—"

"Where did he go, then?" asked Lilith.

"He came here."

"What do you mean?"

"Do you think you three were the only ones in that small wood, which just happened to be the one place where someone could watch and hear the entire affair without being seen?"

"Are you saying that Satan was there the entire time?"

"Basically, yes."

"How do you know?"

Mephistopheles simply smiled.

"Oh. You were there too, of course."

"Of course."

"So," broke in Asmodai, "Satan was there. Where is he now?"

"I couldn't say for sure, but it looked as if he were following the three of you."

Asmodai turned to Lucifer. "What do you think?"

Lucifer nodded. "It could be."

"Let's go inside," suggested Asmodai.

"All right," said Lucifer.

Lilith nodded.

Asmodai turned toward Mephistopheles and raised his eyebrows.

"No, thank you," said Mephistopheles. "I wouldn't want to inhibit your conversation."

Lucifer cocked his head and studied him. "And you'll find out what we decide anyway, won't you? Whether we choose to tell you or not."

Mephistopheles smiled and didn't answer.

After he had left, Asmodai said, "So, should we set out after him?"

"Why?" said Lilith, shrugging. "As I said before, what will we tell him?"

"I don't know. Lucifer?"

"You know how I feel."

"Oh, yes. You think we've lost already. Well, I think you're wrong."

"Why?"

"You seem to think that, because you see them bowing and scraping to him and his 'son,' they aren't ever going to feel any differently."

"Well?"

"Well, look: I'm your friend, am I not?"

"Of course you are, that isn't the point. I don't doubt that you're sincere, it's just that—"

"Please. That isn't what I'm getting at. Okay, you're my friend. Now, suppose I were to walk up and strike you?"

"Eh? I'd wonder why."

"And suppose I were to do it again? And then again? And then I emerged from my workshop with an exploding rock and threw it at you? And then—"

"Sometime in there," said Lucifer, "I would give you back your gift." He touched the wand at his side.

"But I thought you said you were my friend."

"But—I don't see what you're getting at."

Asmodai shrugged. "After I'm proven your enemy, you wouldn't treat me as a friend, would you? Well, those angels are pretty thoroughly taken in, now. But when Yaweh begins trying to force the Plan on them, we'll have a different story."

This time Lucifer shrugged. "That was a nice tale you concocted, but I'm not convinced. We're talking about the hosts, not an individual."

Asmodai shook his head. "That," he said, "is a very dangerous error. The 'host' you're referring to is nothing more than a collection of individuals. If you see them as an amorphous mass, you'll be dealing with something that doesn't exist."

Lucifer shook his head. Lilith chewed her lower lip for a moment, then said, "I'm not certain who is right, but it doesn't matter."

Lucifer started to say something, but Lilith held her hand up.

"What I mean is this: I have decided to oppose Yaweh's plan. I think he's wrong, and dangerous, and the events of today have proven it. I mean to oppose him. I wish to see him cast down from his Palace, and I wish to see him no longer able to force his will on me, or the hosts of angels who are now under his dominion.

"Since I will oppose him, everything that follows from that I will do. I am not certain whether Asmodai is right or not, but I don't think that the next thing to do is to find Satan in any case."

"It isn't?" asked Asmodai. "Then what is?"

"To expose this plan to as many angels as we can, as soon as we can. To expose it for what it is—a dangerous, frightening gamble with the lives of the hosts. To expose Yeshuah for what he is—a cheap attempt to gain the loyalty of the hosts to prevent just opposition. And to expose Yaweh for what he is—a deranged, sick angel, whom Raphael should be curing rather than aiding."

"I see," said Lucifer slowly.

"How do you think to do this?" asked Asmodai.

"By gathering them together, as many as we can, and simply speaking to them, even as Yaweh did. We won't have any tricks, as he did, but we have the truth. That will have to serve us."

"How do you propose to gather all of these angels together?" asked Asmodai. "And where? And when?"

"How? By telling them. Now! While the hosts are still near the center. We'll spread the word as fast as we can, starting at once. Where? I don't know. And when depends on where, but as soon as everyone can arrive."

"What about Yaweh?"

"What about him? He can come if he wants."

"That's just it. He will. And he'll bring an army. Then what?"

"Then," said Lilith, "we fight. The angels will see what they are dealing with, and we must be prepared to defend ourselves, and help them in defending us."

"I think," said Lucifer, "that I like it. Yes! We'll do it, by the flux!"

She leaned over and kissed him quickly. "Good! Asmodai?"

"I'm not sure. I still want to know where."

Lucifer said, "How about near the shores of the sea? Leviathan, I think, is with us. She certainly will be when she hears what happened today, and it would be good to have her with us if there's trouble."

"Not bad," said Lilith. "Asmodai?"

He nodded. "Yes, that might—"

"No!" said Lucifer suddenly. "I've a better idea!"

"Oh?"

"Yes! We'll solve both of our problems at once. And there's another advantage, now that I think of it. If Asmodai will take a few minutes to work it out with me, maybe we can show them a trick or two after all."

"Just what," said Lilith, "are you proposing?"

Lucifer smiled. "We will call them together in twenty days— at the Southern Hold."

Lilith's eyes widened, then she smiled. Asmodai was silent. After a time, he nodded. "We should begin at once, then."

"No," said Lucifer, "we should wait for Satan, if he is indeed coming here. Especially if we're going to use his home for this."

Lilith shook her head. "He won't agree to it."

"But then—"

"No, we present it as something already done. Then he will choose."

Lucifer snorted. "If we do that, I can guess which way he'll choose—and we won't like it."

Lilith shook her head. "I'm not so certain. And it's what we have to do."

Lucifer opened his mouth, but Asmodai cut in. "She's right," he said. "I don't approve of using him either, but we'll never be able to force him to make a choice any other way. It's the same as I mentioned before. With the hosts believing in the Plan now, he won't be moved by argument; he must see, experience what this is all about. We'll be honest about it— we have to be. But there isn't any other way to convince him."

Lucifer looked at them, then sighed. "All right."

"Good," said Asmodai. "Now, what is this idea of yours?"

"Good day to you."

"Good day to you, my Lord. How may I serve you?"

"What's your name, my friend?"

"I'm called Jetrel, Lord."

"Jetrel. A pleasure. I am Asmodai."

"Asmodai! I've heard of you, Lord."

"Nothing bad, I hope."

"Not at all, Lord. It is said you made the sceptre and the sword and—"

"That was all long ago."

"Yes, Lord."

"I'm building other things now."

"Indeed, Lord?"

"Yes. Do you know where the Southern Hold is?"

"Yes, Lord."

"Good. There is to be a gathering there twenty days hence. Tell everyone you know about it."

"A gathering, Lord?"

"That's right."

"What sort of gathering, Lord?"

"Well, you see, Jetrel, not everyone is completely happy with what's been heard of the Plan."

"Lord!"

"We're going to get together and talk about it. Why don't you try to be there?"

"Lord, I—"

"Think about it, all right?"

"Yes, certainly, Lord, but—"

"And tell everyone you know, okay?"

"I will, Lord, but—"

"Fare well, then, Jetrel."

"Farewell, Lord Asmodai."

"They seem to have left again. Can you pick up their trail?"

"No, milord. The tracks are too numerous."

"Hmm. All right, then."

"Where to, milord?"

"We may as well go home, I suppose."

"Wilt thou not speak to Leviathan, as thou has said thou would'st?"

"Maybe, Beelzebub, later. But not now. I'm . . . tired."

"Aye, milord."

"Twenty days, you say?"

"Yes, Yaweh. That's what I've heard."

"Father?"

He turned. "Yes, Yeshuah?"

"I would like to attend."

"What?"

"Sword in hand, Father, I would like to attend."

Yaweh look at him. "I am pleased by your zeal, my son, but no. Now isn't the time."

"As you wish, Father."

Yaweh signed for Michael and Raphael to leave. When they had done so, he sat back to think. His eyes turned to Yeshuah, who met his glance openly with a smile of affection.

Am I really pleased? he wondered.

"Sith."

"Yes, Kyriel?"

"Have you heard?"

"You're talking about the meeting at the Southern Hold, aren't you?"

"Right."

"What of it?"

"Well, I have to say that I'm surprised that there are some who still oppose the Plan, even after what happened."

"Yes. But I guess there's no understanding some angels."

"I guess not."

"I wonder what Yaweh will do."

"Do? Why should Yaweh do anything?"

"Well, doesn't this threaten the Plan?"

"Nothing can threaten the Plan. Yaweh isn't going to worry about a few hotheads."

"I guess you're right."

Yaweh tried to think above the noise of the workers putting in a second throne next to his. He tried to organize his thoughts, blamed the inability to do so on the noise, and realized that that, too, was a lie.

After a while he looked at Yeshuah, who stood by his side, smiling warmly. As their eyes met, Yeshuah's face became troubled.

"What is it, Father?" he asked.

Yaweh's voice was the smallest whisper. "I don't know what to do, Yeshuah. Now they are conspiring openly against me. They are going to bring together the hosts and undo all the good we did. How can I stop it without doing more hurt? And can I let them do this to the Plan?"

Yeshuah's eyes suddenly moistened, and he dropped to his knees beside the throne. "Father," he said. "You must do the right thing. I know that you love them—Satan, Lucifer, and the rest. I know, because I feel it too. But—to abandon the Plan—that is unthinkable, isn't it?"

Yaweh nodded.

"But wouldn't it be worse to carry it out, but only part way? To try it, and have it fail? To lose thousands of angels in vain?"

Again, Yaweh nodded.

"Then it is no kindness now to show kindness. If you act quickly, decisively, and firmly, we can end this rebelliousness. It may hurt you, Father, and I feel for that, but what choice do you have? If you make a single, strong showing, there may not be any need for any more. If you hesitate, it can only lead to disaster."

Yaweh looked up and searched the other's face.

"I'll think it over," he said at last, his voice still only a whisper. "I'll think it over."

Camael had no idea what he was doing there, but it made him nervous. He had been lounging around the Palace when suddenly Zaphkiel had appeared with Abdiel, pointed directly at him, then left without a word. Abdiel had approached, called him by name, and escorted him to a place just outside the throne room. Then he had left.

For five minutes, Camael stood there, and he had known days that went by faster than those five minutes.

Then the door opened and a Seraph appeared, motioning him in. He was escorted up to the throne, where he was flanked by Abdiel and Michael. Yaweh looked at him.

"You are Camael?"

He bowed deeply. "Yes, Lord. How may I serve you?"

"I asked Zaphkiel for the name of someone who could be chief of a new order of angels that I am now creating, and he gave me your name."

Camael gasped.

"*My* name, Lord?"

"Yes. This new order will be called Powers, for through it, the Power of my will shall be felt throughout Heaven. The order will number five thousand, whom you will select. Swords will be provided. You will take these five thousand angels and you will go to the Southern Hold. In nineteen days, there will be a gathering of miscreant angels there. You will have weapons; they will not. You will attack them as my right arm. Michael will be there with one thousand angels called Virtues, Yahriel with five hundred angels called Dominions, and Abdiel with the two hundred angels called Thrones. What say you?"

None noticed, but Abdiel paled slightly as Yaweh said this.

"My Lord," stammered Camael, "I'm honored. I don't know what to say."

"Do you want it?"

"Yes, my Lord! That is, if you think I can do it."

"I think you can. Very well. It is settled. Go and select the angels of your company."

"Yes, Lord. At once. And, thank you, Lord."

Yaweh smiled. Camael bowed low and departed.

"He'll do, I think," said Yaweh.

"I hope so, Lord," said Abdiel.

Michael said nothing.

Lilith was tired when she got there, but it was nothing compared to when she had run for Belial. She stood by the shore for a moment, gasping, then began walking along it. She studied the rolling waves, looking for a break in them.

After a time, she saw an angel seated against a rock near the shore. She approached and said, "Good day, Harut."

"Why, hello, Lilith. What you doin' here?"

"I have to speak with Leviathan."

He nodded. "She'll show up. You may as well get comfortable, honey. It could be a while."

"All right."

"Well, what do you think? How many will we have?"

"I don't know, Asmodai. I hope a good number."

"Yes. Fourteen more days."

"That's right. And we should step up the pace. We're going to have to take about four days after we get there to set up everything."

"I know. Lucifer? Do you really think we can pull this off?"

"You mean the trick part?"

"Yes."

"It depends on Leviathan's control of her element. I made a study of it shortly after it happened. She has a profound control of that water, and it seems to extend to other bodies of water near her. I think it'll work."

"Hmm. Okay."

"If it doesn't work, it won't matter all that much. The important thing is going to be the speech. I've never given a speech before."

"Just explain the bare facts. That will do a great deal. Satan will do the rest."

"He certainly *can* do the rest—but *will* he?"

Asmodai shrugged. "If not, Lilith will speak to them. She's good with words."

Lucifer smiled. "I know."

"So," said Lilith, "what do you think?"

"I'm with you," said Leviathan. "I don't know if what you're doing is right, but what Yaweh is doing is wrong. It's obvious that he condoned the killing of Ariel, and I can't forgive that. And what you say about this new angel—no. I can't support that, and I can't stand neutral."

"I'm glad," said Lilith. "What about Lucifer's idea?"

"I think I can do my part. Water is water. But I wonder how much good I'll be able to do, if there's trouble?"

"That doesn't matter. We want the effect."

"All right, then." Leviathan looked down at the other angel. "What about you, Harut?"

"If Lilith will guide me, I think I can walk to the Southern Hold in ten days."

"I'll guide you," said Lilith.

"It is good," said Leviathan.

"I," announced Asmodai, "am beat."

"That's too bad," said Lucifer. "We haven't started working yet."

"I know. But we made that trip fast, and I'm not cut out for long walks."

Lucifer shrugged. "We got here ahead of everyone. That's the important thing. Now let's get to work."

"How?"

"Uh. . . ." He looked around the area near the Southern Hold—flat and rock-strewn. "There," he announced, pointing to the northwest. "That will do, I think. I'll mark out the perimeter; you figure out a way to make the hole."

"What about filling it?"

Lucifer looked at the sky. "Soon," he said, "it will begin to rain."

Abdiel marched at the head of two hundred Thrones. "How does this keep happening to me?" he wondered. "Every time I begin to think I'm safe, something comes up."

He sighed. He was well aware that Satan would be looking for him, along with Beelzebub and who knew who else? There had to be a way to get out of this without looking as if he were running from battle. Only four days left, and they would be there. What he wanted to do was to turn command over to Zaphkiel and go back home.

He snapped his fingers. He could . . . but then, of course, he'd be taking other risks. What if they didn't show up on time?

This wasn't very good, he realized, but it seemed to be safer than the other way, while looking even better. And might even do some good.

Yes, he decided, he'd do it.

He turned his head. "Zaphkiel!"

Zaphkiel caught up to him.

"Take over here. I'm going up ahead. I have an idea that ought to help. Make sure you don't delay your attack. Arrive as quickly as you can and keep a watch on things. When the right moment comes, go ahead. All right?"

"Yes," said Zaphkiel.

"Good." Abdiel nodded to him and ran on ahead, up the trail and out of sight.

Zaphkiel continued walking as he had, but now in the front of the line as if it were his right and natural place. The Thrones, marching behind him, hardly noticed the change.

Call it an exodus, if you wish to be dramatic. You wouldn't be far wrong, at that.

They came from the center of Heaven to its southernmost reaches and gathered there before the Southern Hold. There were some who didn't know why they were there, only that friends had told them to be. Others thought to hear more of the Plan revealed; still others hoped only for a good show.

But they came. By the middle of the allotted day, nearly a third part of the angels of heaven had gathered, including all who dwelt in the Southern Regency.

Slowly, from those who dwelt there, rumors began to spread, and the angels began to cluster around the lake, and it was said that this lake had never before been there, and those to whom the sight of the Hold was commonplace wondered at how it had come to be.

Gradually, the space near the lake became more and more crowded, but they feared to touch the water, as if it were cacoastrum itself. They came near to it, and some found stones and threw them in, but nothing unusual occurred.

Soon, they knew, things would begin. By unspoken agreement, they kept their eyes on the water and waited.

Satan was staring out the window at the gathered angels and the new lake when he was told that Lucifer wished to be admitted to the Hold, and to see him. He nodded. When Lucifer arrived, Satan fixed him with a cold stare while motioning him to sit down. When he had done so, Satan took a chair opposite. His eyes never left Lucifer's face.

"Good day, Lord Satan."

"Good day? Is that what you have to say to me? Good day? By the flux? Is this your doing, Lucifer?"

"Yes it is, Satan. I've brought them."

"You say that pretty calmly!"

"Thank you very much."

Satan stood quickly. "I'm not joking, Lucifer. Do you know

what you've done? I don't know what you have planned, but whatever it is will be attributed to me. And what about that lake?"

"Asmodai and I built it."

"Why?"

"We needed it."

"Indeed? You are out of your Regency now, Regent of the East."

Lucifer, still sitting, snorted. "Don't speak to me of Regencies. You saw what Yaweh did. Do you think the idea of a Regency means anything any more?"

"You came here and brought with you I don't know how many angels, and dug up half a square league of my land, and all you can say is that it is because Yaweh needed some flashy nothingness to get Heaven behind him? So what?"

"Is that how you view what Yaweh did? Flashy nothingness? Humbling all of Heaven? Those lies—"

"They weren't lies, Lucifer. Distortions at worst, and not even that, necessarily."

Lucifer brushed it aside. "I see it as a threat to the freedom of every angel in Heaven—that's more than 'flashy nothingness.'"

Satan snorted.

"All right, then—see how he reacts to this gathering, and then tell me that our freedom isn't threatened."

"What do you mean?"

"I think Yaweh will attack us."

"What? Don't be absurd. Why?"

"Because he has no choice. We threaten the Plan. More, we threaten to expose all the lies the Plan is built on. He *has* to stop us."

Satan stood and stared down at Lucifer, green fires in his eyes. "I think that is nonsense, Lucifer. But if you really believe it, how *dare* you subject thousands of helpless angels to an attack?"

Lucifer looked up at him and smiled slightly. "Not helpless," he said. "That makes all the difference. They won't be helpless, because you are going to prepare them."

Satan's eyebrows climbed. "Indeed?"

"Yes. If they are prepared—if they know they are in danger and are ready to face it, the weapons of the others won't matter. Yaweh is sending their own brothers to attack them. If the Thrones, or whatever, see the hosts ready to defend themselves—a united, solid body—few of them will attack. Therefore, we're asking you to speak to them and prepare them."

Satan turned and resumed his seat. For long moments, he sat in silence.

"I think you really believe all this, Lucifer."

"I do."

"What if I say no?"

"Then Lilith will speak to them. Think about it, though. You'd be far more effective."

Again, Satan was silent for a time. "All right," he said at last. "I'll think about it."

Lucifer rose and left the room. Satan wandered back to the window and presently saw Lucifer emerge, pass through the crowd, and be joined by Asmodai. The gathered angels made way for his gold cloak, and he and Asmodai came to the edge of the water.

For a moment they stood there; then the angels around them began to back away. Soon, even from his window, Satan began to feel the power that they were calling upon.

They stood, side by side, hands extended out over the lake. The angels around them continued to move away, and Satan could hardly blame them.

Then there came a faint movement within the water, as if the middle of the lake were boiling. Steam began to escape from it, and waves began to lick at Lucifer's and Asmodai's feet. Then, amid a great cloud of smoke and a boiling of waters and splashing in all directions, a great head appeared, dark and scaled.

Leviathan stood before them in her power and surveyed them all. There were cries and screams from the host of angels, and they scrambled to escape.

But the angels had heard of her, and didn't fear her. As the first shock wore off, and Leviathan remained motionless, silence settled over the assembly, and those who had fallen regained their feet.

Lucifer turned toward them, and in a clear, piercing voice, which carried to each of the thousands of angels there, he said, "We will begin soon. Be patient."

Then he and Asmodai walked through them, and so came to the great doors of the Southern Hold and passed within.

Twelve

"Tis written: 'In the Beginning was the *Word.*'
Here am I balked: who, now, can help
    afford?
The Word?—impossible so high to rate it;
And otherwise must I translate it,
If by the spirit I am truly taught.
Then thus: 'In the Beginning was the
    Thought.'
This first line let me weigh completely,
Lest my impatient pen proceed too fleetly.
Is it the *Thought* which works, creates,
    indeed?
'In the Beginning was the *Power,*' I read.
Yet, as I write, a warning is suggested,
That I the sense may not have fairly tested.
The Spirit aids me: now I see the light!
'In the Beginning was the *act,*' I write."

              —Goethe, *Faust*

"They seem to be returning, milord."

"Yes. They probably want to wait, to let the tension build before they start."

"There's contempt in thy voice, milord."

"Hm. Well, shouldn't there be?"

"Perchance, milord. But wilt thou speak to them?"

"Maybe. We'll see."

"As thou wilt, milord, yet—hark!"

"What do you hear?"

"They come anon, methinks."

There was a knock. "Yes?" said Satan.

Lucifer's voice came from the other side. "I'd like to speak with you again. Lilith and Asmodai are here."

Satan bit his lip, then shrugged. "All right. Come in."

The door opened. "Thanks," said Lucifer.

"Sit down."

They sat.

"Well?"

"What do you think about the Plan?"

"You asked me that once before, Lucifer. At that time, as I recall, you were for it, and were upset that I wouldn't help with it. Now it seems that you're upset that I won't help against it."

"Things have changed," said Asmodai.

"Such as?"

"Ariel."

Satan nodded, slowly. "Yes, there is that. But is that enough to make you decide that a Plan that will benefit all of us is now somehow wrong?"

"Don't you think it's enough?" asked Lilith.

"It didn't change my opinion of the Plan; it changed my opinion of a few people, that's all."

"It's all a matter of people, isn't it?" said Lilith. "Yaweh is a friend, so you won't oppose the Plan, even though you don't like it. You dislike Mephistopheles, so it doesn't matter to you whether he's on our side or the other side. It's all just a matter of personalities, isn't it?"

Satan shifted uncomfortably. "I'm reminded," he said, "of a conversation I had with Mephistopheles recently. But still— what else can we judge by?"

"How about right and wrong?" said Lilith, a touch of irony in her voice.

"Well, that makes it simple, then, doesn't it? But, as I've said before, I'm not sure that the Plan is wrong. How can I be? You know what Yaweh is hoping to gain. Is that something that is wrong?"

"If it were right, would he have to do the things he is doing? I'm not even talking about Ariel, now. I'm talking about what we saw the other day in the woods, where you were watching as we were. Is that an action that comes from a worthwhile plan?"

"How should I know what that proves? How can you claim to know? Because someone performs an evil action, does that mean it can't be for a good cause?"

"Yes, that is exactly what it means," said Lilith.

Satan shrugged. "What do you want from me?"

"Everything you have to offer."

Satan snorted. Lilith continued, "You are known and trusted by many throughout Heaven. You may not know it, but word spread that you opposed the Plan at the same time as word spread of what the Plan was. You are now looked to by all those who mistrust it. Your support of us would mean a lot to them."

Satan shifted in his chair and studied Lilith. Then he turned toward the others. "Is this true? Am I really 'looked to' by angels I've never met?"

"Yes," said Lucifer. Asmodai nodded.

Satan looked from one of them to the other, his brow furrowed. "That's . . . interesting," he said. "Beelzebub, what do you think?"

"'T amazes me not, milord."

"I see."

"So, will you speak, Lord Satan?" asked Lilith, watching him closely. "You've been standing in the middle—showing opposition, but refusing to take a stand. You probably thought to make a decision when you had to. Well, now you have to."

"Because you forced it. That isn't likely to make me feel well disposed toward your position."

"I suppose," said Lilith, "that you could say we forced it on you. I would say that events forced it on us."

"Evasion," said Satan.

"Truth," responded Lilith.

"Satan," said Lucifer suddenly.

"Yes?"

"It was my idea to use the Southern Hold."

"Well?"

"It was the only place we could find that satisfied all the requirements—and that's because it is your home. You have played a role in all this, merely by setting it off, that makes you central—and whether you wanted to be or not is beside the point."

There was a brief silence, then Asmodai said, "They are waiting for us."

Satan nodded. "I'll let you know in two minutes. Leave now."

They stood. "Let's begin," said Lucifer. "If he decides to speak, we'll work him in. If not, we won't."

"I agree," said Lilith. Asmodai nodded.

They bowed their heads to Satan and Beelzebub, then left the room.

Satan turned to Beelzebub.

"Well?"

"'Tis thy decision, milord."

"That isn't much help, old friend."

Beelzebub scratched himself with his right hind leg.

"What will happen, Father?"

Yaweh looked over at Yeshuah and shrugged. "I can't say for sure. But we are sending thousands of armed angels with swords to stop them from organizing a rebellion. I can't imagine our angels failing."

"But what if they do?"

"Then we'll do whatever we have to. We won't hear anything for at least another fifteen days, unless someone thinks to speed up a messenger. There isn't any point in worrying about it.

"Your attitude," he continued, "seems to have changed in the last few days. It was you who urged me to do this, wasn't it?"

Yeshuah nodded. "I know. I gave you reassurance when you needed it. Now I need it myself."

"I understand. But don't fret about it. Things will fall out as they do."

"I wish you had sent me."

"Now isn't your time, Yeshuah. That will come later. Whatever happens at the Southern Hold, it won't decide anything."

"What do you mean?"

"That nothing final will come of it. At worst, it will be a setback. At best, we'll have gained on them. But the leaders are too slippery to catch this way."

"But the whole reason we did it was—"

"I know. But since then, I've come to realize that it is too much to expect of a thing like this. We'll set them back, but we won't stop them."

Yeshuah stared at him. "But if it doesn't stop them, it'll make it worse! If we show what we're willing to do, but don't fully end the resistance, they will see us as tyrants, and that will feed the rebellion."

Yaweh didn't answer at once. When he did, his voice was low and gentle. "See us as tyrants, Yeshuah? We *are* tyrants. That was what was so hard for me to come to terms with. We don't wish to be, but to do what we have to, we must tell, not ask. And to tell the angels to do something, we must be ready to back up our words with force."

Yeshuah's eyes were wide, his lips parted. Yaweh continued, calmly, almost in a monotone. "That is what I had to confront, Yeshuah. I had to either abandon the Plan entirely or become a tyrant. What else could it be? You urged me to attack the rebellious ones, thinking it would end the rebellion. Now I tell you that it won't. But if it did, would that make me any less a tyrant? I am choosing not to allow them to do what they want."

He looked at the floor. "No, this will be only the start, unless we are very lucky. And I don't want you to have any part in it." He looked up, staring directly into Yeshuah's eyes.

"But when it comes time for the final match, I promise you'll be there."

"Thank you, Father," said Yeshuah, his voice barely audible.

"You don't have to thank me; it isn't your happiness I'm thinking of. You are the symbol of the unity of Heaven. As such, it has to be you who delivers the final blow to show that the unity of Heaven is superior to the disunity."

"I see. Father?"

"Yes?"

"I've become worried about Raphael. She seems unhappy about what we're doing."

"I know. But don't worry about Raphael. When it comes time, she'll be with us."

"Will she?"

"Yes. She doesn't like what we're doing, but she is more firmly behind the Plan than anyone else, excepting, perhaps, Abdiel. When a choice must be made, she'll never support Satan."

"I hope you're right, Father."

"Don't worry. I've known her from the beginning."

Yeshuah nodded. Then he said, "I wish we could see what was going on there."

Yaweh shrugged, then he cocked his head to the side. "Perhaps we can, at that," he said.

"What do you mean, Father?"

"I've never tried it this far between Waves, but it's worth the attempt. Watch."

Yaweh closed his eyes, then opened them suddenly. In the air before them, a soft blue glow began. Then it grew until it became a cloudy image. This solidified, and slowly the Southern Hold appeared.

"This is easier than I'd have thought," said Yaweh. "But I don't know if I'll be able to hold it long."

"How are you doing it?"

"My own illiaster. I can't really explain."

"But you can find anyone you want that way!"

"I can't find angels, only places. I suppose it comes from being part of Heaven. But let us watch."

Yeshuah nodded, his eyes fastened eagerly on the angels before him. The scene slowly closed in. They saw someone in a gold cloak standing in a high window of the Southern Hold.

Before the Throne, the Seraphim gasped, and all eyes turned to the scene. Then, faintly at first but with increasing strength, Lucifer's voice came into the room, as if he were speaking from the vision itself.

". . . which is, in fact, the Plan. It is not my intention to claim that the plan is somehow wrong in conception—I approve of its goals as much as anyone. But you should be aware of the cost and decide for yourselves—is it worth it?

"That is why you have been gathered here. When I saw the Lord Yaweh and heard him speak before you and your brethren, I saw that he wished to subjugate you to his will, and this I oppose. It is you who will take the risks of the Plan; it is you who should decide whether or not it will be executed.

"As to what we will do, should you decide that it isn't something you wish for, I don't know. The Lord Satan has thoughts on this that he would share with us. Please listen to him."

Lucifer bowed and left the window. Satan walked forward.

Abdiel stood in the crowd and watched. He decided that Lucifer hadn't impressed him. On the other hand, he noticed, he now read doubt on faces that before hadn't had any. He thought of what would happen to him if the Plan were discredited, and he shuddered.

So, for greater reason than he had had before, he had to do something. When? Not yet, he decided. He'd wait. His chance would come. It always did.

He concentrated on the glowing ball of light in his middle. Yaweh could do it; Lucifer could too; therefore he, Abdiel, could do it. And he would have to, soon.

So that's the way the wind is blowing, Mephistopheles decided. How interesting; they've finally decided to commit themselves. He didn't know whether to be pleased, amused, excited, or worried. It was clear that the situation called for something.

It occurred to him to wonder if Yaweh would do anything about this. Well, if he did, it wouldn't be pleasant.

He looked up at the window and saw Satan emerge. So, he decided, the Lord Satan is committed too. Or is he?

Mephistopheles decided that if there was trouble, the lake would be the safest place to be; he began moving toward it.

Satan stood at the window, his cloak bright at his back, his emerald clearly visible upon his breast. He surveyed the angels before him in their thousands. He tried to guess what they were thinking. He saw that he had their attention, at least. Most of the faces he could see held doubt and confusion. So Lucifer had shaken them some, anyway.

He cleared his throat. The sound seemed to carry for leagues. He licked his lips.

"Brothers," he said, his voice soft and even. "I have been asked what we ought to do. This is difficult for me, because I'm not certain myself.

"I was asked, when the Plan was first being considered, to take on the task of making sure each of you did his job. That is, I was to report to the Lord Yaweh the names of those angels who failed, or were delinquent in their duties, and devise means to remedy their actions.

"At first I accepted this. But as I began to think more and more of what it would be like, I wondered if it were really *right* that such a thing be done. Why should I ask someone to risk himself if he chose not to? Who gave me this right? The more I thought, the less pleased I became. At last, I resolved that it would be someone else who did this, that I could not take this role. If I must have a task, I would work on the Plan as others do.

"I never had the chance to speak with the Lord Yaweh. By the time I decided, things had gone too far, and his rage was too great to allow him to speak to me. Well, so it was.

"But this does not mean that I counsel anyone else to oppose the Plan. I see it as a benefit to all of Heaven, and I see no reason to try to build anger at it. If any of you, however, *do* oppose it, I would say that you should not go forth hostile toward the Lord Yaweh. Rather, speak to him, or to those whose role it is to assign you your task, and explain why you do not favor this Plan. Why should we subject ourselves to threats we create when we live in a world with threats enough from that which is outside of Heaven?

"If this fails, then, if you are prepared for the results of your actions, refuse to engage in helping the Plan. I warn you that the results of this may be severe, but, above all, you must be honest with yourselves.

"Do not go forth from here armed as for war. Remember that even if we do not accept the Lord Yaweh's claims, we all owe him much, as the first of the Firstborn, and I would not see him opposed by force.

"That is all I have to tell you. Thank you for listening to me."

"Stay where you are, coward and villain!"

Abdiel's voice came thundering up from the crowd and was as loud as Satan's own. Satan stood, stunned, and began looking around the crowd for the source.

"I said remain there," the voice continued, "and hear the truth, along with those whom you wish to take in with your lies and your half-truths. Who would have thought to hear such words spoken, and so soon after our Lord has brought us together in the greatest happiness we could have known!"

Satan spotted him at last, and, before them all, gnashed his teeth in rage and frustration. Beelzebub was suddenly next to him, looking down, but too far away to act.

Far off, near the lake, someone else recognized the voice. His eyes narrowed to slits, and his mouth drew up into a grim smile. Mephistopheles began working his way toward the voice.

"Abdiel," he muttered to himself. "Your time has come."

"You have defied Yaweh, from whom our lives flow, and you lead these others to do the same. How dare you! He from whom we are all sprung may yet forgive you and those who have listened to you if you will fall, now, upon your faces, and ask his forgiveness. Pray to him, and it may not be too late. Refuse, and the wrath of Yaweh will descend upon you!"

By this time, Satan had recovered somewhat. He remained where he was and looked at Abdiel. "It is very interesting, Abdiel, that you find life to be so important that you ask these angels to sacrifice theirs to the one who, you claim, created it. If life is so important to you, I challenge you to explain the death of Ariel! Remember, I saw—"

"Don't tell me what you saw, false one! I have seen the Lord Yaweh, and I have seen Yeshuah! I have seen you, trying to stir the minds of the angels against them, and now you wish to turn my arguments into paths of your own choosing, to further confound the faithful. Why do you not speak of why you defy the wishes of your creator?"

"We will speak of that, then. You forget, Abdiel, that I, too, am of the Firstborn. I know what our debt to Yaweh is, and I know what its limits are. Since you force the issue, I will say this: it was no conscious act of Yaweh that brought life to Heaven. It may have been an act of his, without thought or deliberation, and we do owe him a debt, but—"

"Oh, miscreant angel!" cried Abdiel. "I fear you are lost. You will be cast out from Heaven for this treason against your creator. But what of these others? Will you continue to delude them, and so lead them to follow you to your doom?"

"I lead no one," said Satan. "And as for the rest. . . ."

"He's debating with him!" said Lilith.

"So?" said Asmodai. "He has to answer those claims, doesn't he?

She shook her head. "He's making his arguments legitimate merely by discussing them. He's—Lucifer? What are you doing?"

"My own form of debate," said Lucifer. In his hand, his wand was glowing bright red. He was walking toward the window.

"No!" said Lilith. "If you destroy him, you give his arguments that much more weight."

"Wait," said Asmodai. "You don't want to debate, and you won't let us kill him. What *do* you want?"

"He must be silenced, but not killed. He must be cut off, so he can't be listened to. If Satan won't do it, I—I'll show you what I'll do!"

She walked toward the window. Lucifer walked behind her, still holding his wand.

"If you fail," he said, "I won't."

"Harut!"

"Yeah, honey?"

"Do you know how they're doing that trick of talking so loud?"

"No idea. Why?"

"Then you'll have to go for me. Can you find the Southern Hold if I point you at it?"

"Sure."

"Good. Get there and warn Satan. There are angels marching toward us—armed angels. They'll be here in minutes."

"I'll hurry."

Mephistopheles slipped through the angels as if he were water, sliding in and out, all but unnoticed. Closer and closer, but not quite there. He had no weapon, but needed none. His hands itched for Abdiel's throat. At every step, an image of Ariel appeared before his eyes.

The sound of Abdiel's voice came to him as from a great

distance, though he was nearly to him now. He saw a ring of angels and knew that they were watching Abdiel. He moved past them.

Lilith stepped up beside Satan and opened her mouth, at the same time moving to push him aside. Behind her, Lucifer raised his wand and took aim at Abdiel. Asmodai held his hand on Lucifer's shoulder.

Suddenly he tightened his grip. "No!" he said, whispering.

Lucifer turned. "What—? Oh!"

Then Lilith saw it. Then Satan, in mid-sentence, stopped and looked.

Over a small hill, angels were running, swords flashing in their arms.

The four of them stood in stunned silence, then Lilith turned to Lucifer and cried, "Get him! Quickly!"

Lucifer turned back, then he howled with rage. Abdiel was nowhere to be seen.

Zaphkiel calmly led his Thrones into the angels nearest him. His sword swung, almost slowly, and the angel in front of him cried as it cut into his side, and a sickly orange glow came from the wound. Without slowing, Zaphkiel swung again, and another angel fell, holding his head and screaming. Behind him, two hundred Thrones entered the fray, and the sound of screams spread in an ever-growing circle around them.

Michael started swinging his great sword well before he reached the angels in front of him. They fell back from the goldenhued blade and ran. They tripped over each other, and many lay sprawled on the ground.

Behind him, the Virtues came, likewise swinging swords in wide arcs. Angels on the ground were trampled beneath their feet. As panic spread, the moans of the injured filled the ears of those nearby, with distant screams for accompaniment.

"Father! Do you see? They are being put to flight!"

"Yes, I see. But remember, this is only a beginning. I—wait."

"Yes, Father?"

Yaweh frowned for a moment, looking around at the shocked faces of the Seraphim, then said, "All of you, get out! Return in an hour. You have no need to see this."

They bowed as one and left the room, except for Uriel. "May I stay, Lord?"

Yaweh looked at his face, filled with zeal and flushed with excitement as his eyes feasted on the battle.

"Yes," said Yaweh, feeling suddenly sickened, "you may stay."

"Kyriel?"

"Yes, Sith?"

"We were wrong. We were right before. Remember, we said that Yaweh wouldn't do anything to them, that they were just listening?"

"I remember."

"I want no part of this. I may be changing my mind too much, I don't know. But I know my own stomach, and it rebels at what I just saw."

"Well, Sith, I'm unhappy too, but—"

"You first convinced me that we could take ourselves away from this."

"But that was before we saw with our own eyes how—"

"I don't care! I won't be a part of this. It would be like throwing myself out into the flux. Maybe Yaweh will do that to me, but he'll have to catch me first. And he *won't* catch me helping to throw my brothers out there."

"But you are of the Seraphim, now. You can't—"

"Just watch me!"

"Sith, I—"

"I'm leaving, Kyriel. Are you coming or staying?"

"Sith, I can't . . . I don't know."

"Decide. Now."

"But I . . . all right. I'll come."

"Good. What are you doing?"

"I'm putting down my sword. I'm not going to need it, am I?"

"Aren't you?"

"Do you think to—are you going to *fight* him, Sith?"

"If he tries to throw me into the flux, I'm not going to lie down and let him."

"But—all right. I'll keep it."

"Let's go."

Thirteen

Set out running but I take my time,
A friend of the Devil is a friend of mine.
If I get home before daylight,
I just might get some sleep tonight.

—Robert Hunter, "Friend of the Devil"

Michael looked about him.

All of the angels before him had run; only angels of Yaweh remained in sight. He nodded his satisfaction, then stopped. His eyes narrowed as he looked at the lake and saw Leviathan towering above it. Her eyes locked with his.

He licked his lips and tightened his grip on the sword. He marched toward her. She remained unmoving, staring at him. When he was close, she said, "Must you, friend Michael?"

He stopped. "Will you swear eternal allegiance to the Lord Yaweh and the Lord Yeshuah, newly anointed king of Heaven? Loyalty and obedience in all things, unquestioning?"

"Of course not," she said. "Don't be foolish. Do you really believe all that?"

He shrugged. "No, not in the way you mean. But today you acted in concert with those who threaten Lord Yaweh, whom I swore to protect long before we knew what oaths were. I can't let you hurt him; I won't let you interfere with the Plan. So what choice do I have?"

"Anyone else in your group, Michael, I would destroy."

"Which means?"

"You've won, for now."

Her head disappeared beneath the water, followed by the length of her body. Her tail showed in the air for a moment, then it, too, vanished.

Michael knew, somehow, that she had gone, though he didn't know how she had done so. He suddenly felt lighter, as if he had been carrying a burden that was now removed.

Without another look, he turned and headed toward the Hold.

Zaphkiel and Camael stood together as their forces assembled. They surveyed the scene, clean and empty except for the Thrones, Dominions, Virtues, and Powers. They saw Michael walking back from the lake, but he didn't appear to see them.

Camael turned toward the Southern Hold. "Might they still be in there?"

"Doubtful," said Zaphkiel. "I'll check, though."

"No need," said Camael.

"Oh?"

"If anyone is left, we'll find him."

"As you will."

"As the Lord will have it."

Zaphkiel shrugged. Camael motioned toward several of the Powers who stood nearby. "Kindle fire," he said as they approached him.

They hastened to obey. If Zaphkiel noticed the strange lights burning in Camael's eyes, he gave no sign.

The fires were soon lit.

Abdiel spotted Zaphkiel and quickly approached him. "Well done," he said.

Zaphkiel nodded.

"Your timing was quite adequate. I think we got all the effect we could. I'm going to get us back together now, and—

what in Heaven?!" Abdiel turned as he spoke, in response to a cracking sound from behind him. He saw smoke, then flame welling from the near wall of the Hold, then a blast of hot air struck him and flames appeared from the windows near the top. He spun back to Zaphkiel. "What's going on?" he asked.

"Camael."

Abdiel turned back to watch the blaze. Slowly, he nodded. Michael came up to them. "Who did you say?"

"Camael."

Michael studied the blaze. "Why?"

Zaphkiel shrugged.

Camael motioned the last of the Powers out of the area and remained behind, a flaming brand still in his hand. He spat, then, into the fires and walked slowly out. Behind him, a portion of the ceiling fell in. Below him, out of his sight, the flames licked the barrels of lamp oil and worked their way closer to the refinery.

Satan held himself still, crouched behind a rock formation about three leagues distant from his home.

"They're still there," he said.

"They will leave anon, milord."

"I just can't believe it."

"Can'st not, milord? That is passing strange. Thou hast struck the Lord Yaweh; he hath returned thy blow. It amazes me not."

"But how can you say I struck him? I never intended— what is that?"

"What, milord? Thine eyes are better—"

"Smoke! There's smoke coming from . . . *NO!*"

He lunged forward, but Beelzebub was the quicker. His teeth fastened on to Satan's leg, tripping him. Satan fell, rolling over onto his back, and Beelzebub landed on his chest.

"Thou shalt not, milord! 'Tis foolish. They will slay thee ere thou canst call out."

Satan pushed him off and started to get up, but Beelzebub jumped again, catching Satan as he was starting to rise, and he fell over once more.

"Beelzebub, let me—"

"No, milord."

Satan lay there glaring, then he suddenly turned and looked back. He slowly got to his knees and stared at the red tongues that began appearing in the distance near the top of the Hold. Beelzebub watched him, ready to spring again.

"There's naught thou canst do, milord."

Satan shook his head.

"Why would they do that, Beelzebub? My home! It went back to the Second Wave, a part of the foundations of Heaven. Why? What does it gain?"

"Perchance some overzealous archangel, milord. Thou hast no way to know 'tis Lord Yaweh's doing."

Satan watched for a moment longer. "He will pay dearly for inspiring such zealousness, then."

"What wilt thou, Lord?"

Satan stood quickly and turned his back to the Southern Hold. "Come," he said. "I wish to see the mighty Lord Yaweh. I will have words for him that he has never heard in all the ages of Heaven."

He began walking. Beelzebub paused to urinate against the stone where they had stood, then hurried to catch up.

Like a prophecy, Harut stood amidst inferno. Like a prophet, he heard, and felt, and smelt, and tasted—but could not see what was before him.

He had heard the sounds of feet below while he was on the stairs to deliver his message, and so he ducked into the nearest room, guessing who it was. The sounds had come and gone, and then came the smell of smoke, and the incredible heat. He breathed it in and felt it scorching his lungs. He touched a wall and nearly screamed from the pain.

He stumbled out of the room and tried to get down the stairs, but he tripped and fell, choking and gasping on his way. The fumes were musky and thick, and he became aware of pain in his nose. His eyes watered, and he tasted the coarse, harsh grittiness of ash. His cheek touched the floor, which was amazingly cool.

He used his arms to begin rolling, and almost screamed again when his hand touched a burning spot on the floor.

From long experience in the dark, he didn't lose his sense of direction, so he knew which way the door was. He continued rolling, feeling the flames lick at his clothing and skin.

He wondered as he rolled if the angels who had started the fires would be waiting outside, but he couldn't stop.

His head cracked into the door. He felt the sudden dull pain almost as a relief, and for an instant he nearly lost consciousness, but he pulled himself together and crawled out the door on his knees, his arms stretched out in front.

Then something hit him in the back, at the same time as a cracking sound came from behind him. He felt himself picked up and hurled forward, his legs screaming from the flames that had caught there. "So close," he muttered, and then he knew no more.

By unspoken consent among the Chiefs of the Orders of Angels, they moved away from the smoking ruins of what had been the Southern Hold and continued their march for the center as quickly as, that same day, they had been marching away from it.

Michael hurried because he needed activity to keep his mind from what he had seen and done and nearly done.

Abdiel knew he would feel safer once he had returned to the protection of the Palace. Even here, among his Thrones, he feared what, or who, could be behind each stone or tree they passed.

Camael knew that more tasks awaited him at the Palace for Yaweh's greater glory, and he longed to smite His enemies once more.

They stopped only rarely during the day, and briefly at night. None of the Chiefs of the Orders spoke to each other. If they had, they would have had to ask each other why, after a battle where the enemy made not even a token resistance, each of the Orders had barely half as many angels as it had when they set out.

"Lord Yaweh."
"What is it, Uriel?"
"Lord. . . ."
"Yes? Speak up?"
"I . . . don't know how to say this, Lord."
"Well?"
"My Seraphim, Lord. They—"
"Yes?"

"Some of them are gone, Lord."

"Gone? What has happened to them?"

"I don't know, Lord. I think they left."

"I'm not surprised, Uriel. I should have expected it."

"Father—"

"Yes, Yeshuah?"

"I don't understand."

"Why they left? Because they were in here when we watched the battle at the Southern Hold. They saw what I commanded other Orders to do and saw themselves in it. In all of our history, we have looked on each other as brothers. Now they have found that I have had them kill each other. Of course, they no longer wish to serve."

"And yet, Father, when they joined the Orders, didn't they understand that this could happen?"

"Understanding it is one thing, Yeshuah. They've had to nearly live it, now. And I expect it will be worse for those who were actually involved."

"But—what shall we do?"

"We—a moment. Uriel, you may leave."

"Yes, Lord."

"Now. We ignore this problem."

"Ignore it?"

"As much as we can. Yeshuah, we are not going to win by keeping angels ready to fight. If we are to win, it will be by fighting the right battle at the right time and place. And I still have no idea when and where that will be. But in the meantime, they desert. That hasn't hurt us. We must keep enough to protect us should Satan or Lucifer try to destroy me—or you. But we will find angels to fight for us as we need them."

"I don't understand, Father."

"All right, think of it this way: whoever takes any action against the other is lessened in the sight of those around them. We took an action; we were seen by many as in the wrong. Now it is their turn. They will act, and the tide will shift the other way."

"So now we wait for them?"

"Maybe. It is also possible that we can end it quickly, if we have an opportunity to take their leaders—just as they could end it quickly by getting to you and me."

"How are we to do that?"

"I don't know. I'm thinking about it."

"Father?"

"Yes?"

"There's something—I don't know. You've changed, somehow."

"I know. I feel it, too."

"Why? What is it?"

"Yeshuah, I never mentioned it before, but I sent an archangel named Raziel to learn things. I wanted to make sure that I wasn't misunderstanding, that Satan really did want to stop the Plan and would do anything to achieve this. He was skilled, too. He would have learned whatever there was to learn.

"Well, Yeshuah, the last I knew of him, he was at the battle near the sea. Of all the angels, only he was destroyed. I cannot count that to chance. I have to conclude that the rebels destroyed him.

"You say I've changed, Yeshuah? Well, yes, I have. I no longer have any hope."

Lucifer looked into the distance, his eyes straining against the growing darkness. Lilith came up and stood at his side.

"What is it, my love?"

He put his arm around her waist. "You haven't called me that in a long time."

She leaned her head against his shoulder. "What are you looking at?"

"Nothing, I think. But for a moment, I thought I'd seen—there it is again!"

"What?" she asked, looking now in the direction he gazed. Asmodai joined them, also staring into the distance.

"A flash of gold, way up ahead."

"Gold? What could it be?"

"Only two things come to mind. Michael's sword—"

"But he went up the road at the head of his legions," said Asmodai.

Lucifer nodded. "Michael's sword," he repeated, "or the cloak of a Firstborn."

"Do you think—?"

"Maybe. Should we find out?"

"Yes!"

They changed their direction slightly and increased their speed.

• • •

Michael entered, dusty and grimy. He still held his sword in his hand as he approached the throne.

"Yes, Yaweh? You wanted to see me?"

"I have another task for you, old friend. If you'll accept it."

Michael shrugged. "What is it? I can report on—"

"You don't need to. I—"

"Don't interrupt me."

Their eyes locked for a moment. Yeshuah stirred uncomfortably. Then Yaweh nodded. "Sorry, old friend."

"It's all right."

"But call me Lord. Just for form's sake."

Michael's nostrils flared and his eyes narrowed. For a moment he seemed to balance between walking out of the room and attacking Yaweh. The Seraphim shifted on their feet.

Then Michael smiled wanly. "All right, *Lord,* if it will help you sleep nights. As I was saying, I can report on the last expedition."

"Thank you, Michael, but it isn't necessary. As I said, I have another task for you. Take your Virtues, and I'll instruct Camael and Yahriel to go with you and find Satan. Wherever he is. I hope that by tomorrow when you set out, I'll know where to look for him."

Michael nodded. "All right, Ya—Lord. I'll be pleased to find Satan for you. I may not be able to bring him back, however."

"What do you mean?"

"I mean that he will be easier to destroy than to capture, and I'm not in a mood to work harder than I must."

Yaweh sighed and studied the back of his hand. Then he shook his head.

"That will be as it will be. You may refresh yourself now, if you wish."

"Thank you, Lord, I will."

Michael gave him a nod that could almost have been a bow and took his leave. Yaweh sat back thinking.

"Raphael, wait!"

She stopped on her way out of the Palace and looked back. She didn't answer him; she simply waited.

"Will you spare me a moment? Please?"

She stood for another second, then sighed. "All right, Yeshuah."

"Is there someplace where we can talk?"

She looked around the hallway, then said, "We could walk outside, if that would be all right."

He nodded and came up beside her. They left the Palace and walked down the long steps. They didn't speak at first, but let their feet carry them along. They found themselves going around the castle until they came to the hill where Yeshuah had been created, but continued past it into the woods. There they stopped and seated themselves under the trees.

"You don't like me, do you?" Yeshuah began.

"What do you mean?"

"What I said. I have the feeling that you don't like me. Am I wrong?"

Raphael cocked her head, then pulled up a long blade of grass and began chewing it.

"No, I guess you're not wrong."

"Why?"

"Why don't I like you?"

"Yes."

She shrugged. "One can't like everyone."

"Why not?"

"Are you serious?"

"Raphael, I *love* everyone."

She stared at him. "Don't make me laugh, Yeshuah. I heard you talking of Satan and Lucifer. Don't tell me you love everyone. I wonder if you love *anyone.*"

He looked away, then: "But I do, Raphael. I love them: Satan, Lucifer, Asmodai, Lilith. I can't help it. I was born knowing and loving them. I was created by love. You saw; you helped."

"Don't remind me!"

He shook his head. "You don't understand. I love them—yet I feel great rage at them. Those things are part of each other for me. If I didn't love so much, I couldn't feel such anger."

"You're right," said Raphael. "I don't understand."

Yeshuah nodded, then buried his face in his hands. Raphael sat there unmoving, her face etched in stone. Then he lifted his head up and spoke softly, almost whispering.

"I am Heaven. I am a product of my father, and of all those who gave their love so that I might live. I feel this rage, because what they are trying to do is destructive to all I love—even them."

Raphael shook her head. "Do you believe that? About all of those angels 'giving their love'? It was a trick, and you know it, to draw the hosts together and crush those who oppose us. What's destructive to Satan and those around him is the force that your 'father' is sending against them—to find Satan, did I hear? And if they find him, and he is destroyed, that's 'so it will be'? This is the love you're speaking of? If I didn't believe in the Plan with all my heart, I would have joined them long ago."

"No," said Yeshuah, "it wasn't a trick. It was suggested as a trick, and sometimes my Father thinks it was a trick, but it wasn't. It was love. I know, because it created me. Do you know what that means? I'm different from the rest of you, but you don't understand *how* I'm different. The rest of you were created by acts of violence. I was created by an act of love.

"Please, Raphael, don't turn from me. I know why you want to. You think of me as a fraud, because I can't help my rage and because you have more love in you than anyone else I know, and hate sickens you. But try to forgive me—I can't help it.

"I guess that's all I can say."

Raphael sat with her head bowed. Then she looked at him as if trying to see through his eyes.

"I'll try," she said at last. "I'll think about it. That's all I can do."

She rose and walked away.

"Raphael?"

She stopped and without looking back said, "Yes?"

"*I* forgive *you*," said Yeshuah.

She clasped her elbows and hugged herself, then relaxed. She left.

Yeshuah put his face into his hands and sobbed.

Mephistopheles made his way back south, moving as quickly as he could. Speed was vital now, because he had no idea how much of a lead they had. He knew they had a lead, because he was still following their trail.

In a little while, he would risk certainty of their destination—in a little while, but not yet. To err, to pass them up and go to the wrong place would be disaster. He had to stay with them until he was sure he knew where they were going, then get ahead of them and arrive at their destination with enough of a lead to give the necessary warning.

It would certainly be close. And it would be tiring—he had days ahead of him, and there would be precious little time to rest, if he could judge by how they were traveling now.

Well, it could be worse—he could have no chance of giving warning. But that, of course, hadn't been an accident. Mephistopheles had known full well he might find out something useful when he had followed Yeshuah and Raphael into the woods.

"Did you see them, Sith?"

"Yes, Kyriel. What of it?"

"I have an idea of where they're going."

"So?"

"Uh, Sith, you haven't seemed interested in much since—well, since we left. Are you regretting it?"

"No . . . no, I'm not regretting it. It's more that I don't know what to do."

"I know. That's why I mentioned that army that Michael was leading. I'll bet they're going after Satan. We could follow and join Satan if we wanted to."

"So what? Satan isn't doing anything. You heard him talking as well as I did. What is he doing about anything? He just stood there while they—it doesn't matter."

"Sith, he's all we have."

"Well if he's—oh, I don't know. All right, I guess we can follow them. Why not?"

"There's something else we could do."

"What?"

"Well, we could go find Bath Kol. I'll bet that'd cheer you up."

"No, I'm afraid we can't."

"Oh?"

"She was at the Southern Hold. I saw her. She didn't live through it."

. . .

Finally, after nearly four days, they caught up with him in a narrow valley, and they yelled. He heard the echoes, stopped, and looked back.

They ran up to him, nearly exhausted.

"We've been following you," gasped Lucifer, "since you left the—since you set out."

Satan didn't reply. Beelzebub studied the three of them closely. There was silence while they recovered their breath.

"I hope," said Lilith, "that you're proud of that speech. You managed to—"

"Shut up, Lilith," said Satan.

Lucifer took a step forward. Beelzebub growled. Satan ignored them both.

"I don't care to discuss it."

"Then," said Asmodai, "why don't we discuss what we're going to do now? And I mean *we*. You're with us whether you want to be or not. We aim to oppose Yaweh. If you won't take a side in this, you'll be crushed. That is just how it is. Will you discuss *that?*"

"Yes," said Satan slowly. "Yes, I'll discuss that. I'll discuss it to say that I am not now or ever going to join you, and if you are counting on me to, you will be disappointed." His voice remained low, but began to grow in intensity. His words were clipped, as if he were working to control his rage.

"I'm not joining you," he repeated. "However, *you* may join *me*, if you wish. I'll offer you that for what you've done. I'll forgive you for setting off a chain of events that led to the destruction of my home. I'll place the blame on Yaweh's shoulders, and I'll allow you to join me. That is what I can do."

The three of them looked at each other. Satan continued.

"I will take twenty days, then, to gather me an army. And then that army will march for another twenty days until we are at the Palace of Yaweh, and I will treat his home as he has caused mine to be treated, and I will treat him as he wished to treat me.

"You asked me, Lilith, what I think of what I said before? I think that I willingly chose to bend my knee to Yaweh, and I'll not do so again."

"And the Plan?" said Lilith. "What of it?"

"I'll decide that afterwards. But if I find I must commit this evil to prevent greater evil, I'll at least not pretend it's a good.

"Well? Will you join me?"

"I," said Lilith, "will gladly join you, Lord Satan."

"And I," said Lucifer.

"I also," said Asmodai.

"Good. Then the Lord Yaweh and his 'King Anointed' may begin counting their days."

Lucifer smiled. "May he enjoy his reign. It will last forty days and forty nights."

"Methinks that hath a pleasant sound," said Beelzebub.

Fourteen

'O father, what intends thy hand,' she cried,
'Against thy only son? What fury, O son,
Possesses thee to bend that mortal dart
Against thy father's head? And know'st for
　　　whom?
For Him who sits above, and laughs the
　　　while
At thee, ordained his drudge to execute
Whate'er his wrath, which He calls justice,
　　　bids—
His wrath, which one day will destroy ye
　　　both!'

　　　　　　—Milton, *Paradise Lost,* II:727-734

"What are you doing here?"
"Oh. Good evening, Lilith. I'm just out walking. I needed to think. What about you?"
The campfire was a ways off, and the darkness of Heaven's

night was almost complete, but Satan could see her teeth as she said, "I guess I wanted to keep you from thinking."

He chuckled. "That may not be a bad idea."

"What were you thinking about?"

"Oddly enough," he said, "you."

He heard her coming closer. "What about me?"

"Lilith," he said slowly, "do you know what it did to me when you left?"

"No, and I don't want to."

"All right."

They stood near each other for a while longer, then he began to walk further from the fire.

"Satan. . . ."

He stopped. "Yes?"

"What *did* it do to you when I left?"

He turned and came back. When he was close, he said, "You were right not to want to know. I shouldn't have brought it up. You did what you had to, and it's over now, anyway."

This time it was Lilith who chuckled. "I've never heard anyone say that before, but it still sounds trite."

"How long have you and Lucifer been together?"

"I don't know. A thousand days? Two thousand?"

"A long time."

"Yes."

"I barely lasted three hundred."

"Satan, I—it was different."

"I know. I pushed you. I shouldn't have. I didn't think it through."

"And so now you spend all of your time thinking, instead of making up your mind—"

"No, not anymore. That's over. Now I get an idea and I act on it, just like before."

"Good. I think—"

Before she could say anything more, his arms were around her, and his mouth had covered hers.

A long time later she said, "I think there are advantages to both systems. I'd like to sleep now."

"All right."

He moved a little so she could rest her head on his chest, his arm around her shoulders. It was a tossup which one fell asleep first.

• • •

"Lilith?"

"Methinks she is well, Lord Lucifer."

He continued looking around the camp in the dawn light, but didn't see her.

"Where is she, then?"

"The Lord Satan did leave the camp late last night, and Lilith did follow some time later."

"And they haven't been back?"

"No, Lord."

"Hmmm. All right."

After a moment, he added, "I hope they enjoyed themselves. They can both use it."

"Thou art wise, Lord Lucifer," said Beelzebub.

They heard the sounds of heavy boots on hard ground and looked up. Satan reached into the pile of his clothing and found his emerald. Lilith found a rock that fit neatly into the palm of her hand, tested it, and waited.

Mephistopheles appeared before them. He looked Lilith up and down, not appearing to notice the rock in her hand, and the corners of his mouth rose a bit.

Satan said, "You wanted something, dark one?"

Mephistopheles nodded, still smiling slightly and still studying Lilith. "I came before Michael—and a few thousand angels."

"What?" Satan was on his feet, staring and leaning forward.

"As I said. It seems Yaweh wants you, and he didn't waste time going after you."

"How far behind you are they?" asked Lilith.

"Two or three days."

"By the flux!" said Satan. He put the emerald around his neck and found his pants. Lilith tossed her rock aside, found her gown, and shook it off.

"We'll have to gather our forces as we go," she said.

"Yes." He turned back to Mephistopheles. "How many does he have?"

"A few thousand. Not as many as he'd like."

"Oh?"

"Yes. After the attack at the Southern Hold there were desertions."

"Desertions?" Satan finished with his pants and found his jerkin.

"Yes. He is down to four of the Seraphim, eight of the Cherubim, a little more than a hundred Thrones, and—" Mephistopheles shrugged.

"I don't recognize those names."

"He's created orders, as he calls them, each with a Chief. I don't really know why."

"All right." Satan shook out his cloak, then fastened it on. "Let's speak to the others."

Lilith and Mephistopheles followed him to the camp.

Harut woke to pain. There was a burning in his legs, on his back, and on his hands. There was a pressing sensation against his cheek as if tiny knives were being pushed in and out.

He felt a sudden churning in his stomach, then vomited with great wracking heaves that sent jolts of agony up his chest.

He forced himself to turn his head, tried to breathe, and coughed, doubling up and dragging his face through the vomit on the ground.

He forced himself to breathe again, slowly and deeply, and managed not to cough. He repeated the process, then repeated it again.

Then, because he knew how things worked, he forced his aching hands over his body, checking for damage.

His face and neck were fine. His shoulders were okay, too. He avoided contact with his chest.

He carefully touched his hands, each with the other, and noted that all of his fingers were there. His hips were in the right shape, and his legs seemed to be—he stopped.

His legs, both of them, ended just above the knee.

He lay back in his pain and sickness and squeezed his useless eyes tightly shut, and took a few more deep breaths. "I'm alive," he told himself. "Whatever else, I'm alive."

He felt some heat then from the direction his head was pointing, which meant that the ruins of the Southern Hold lay in that direction. That meant that the lake was over *there*.

With palms that seemed to blaze with their own fires each time they touched the ground, he began inching his way toward the water.

Satan surveyed them. He stood before the newly lit fire while they sat on the ground before him. His eyes took in

Lucifer, Lilith, and Asmodai in turn to make sure they understood, then he continued.

"So it is clear that we must move. We will gather what
forces we can as we go. We should leave—at once. We'll
have to circle Michael, so we'll need time. And as we meet
angels, we will tell them what we are about, and they may join
us if they wish. Any questions?"

"Yes," said Lilith. "What if they say 'no'?"

He shrugged. "What if they do?"

Lilith nodded as if that had been enough of an answer.

"Any other questions?"

There were none. Satan stood before the fire and touched
his emerald. The flames died. The others stood, and Satan led
them away from the camp.

"Sith?"

"Yes?"

"Why are we here?"

"Where else would you want to be?"

"That isn't the point. When they hailed us, I thought you
were going to run, and then all of a sudden you were going to
join them. I don't understand why."

"Huh? Sure you do. I wanted to run when I thought these
were angels of Lord Yaweh. When I found out—"

"I think you're here because of Bath Kol."

"Have it your own way. We're both here, and we're going
to fight—unless you leave."

"No, I'm not going to do that."

"Then that'll have to be good enough."

"I guess it will, then."

Yeshuah turned to Yaweh. "Father, *please* allow me
to—"

"No, my son. Not yet."

"But if Michael finds him—"

"Our problems will end. Michael will destroy him. We will
be pleased. We will put all of our will power into being pleased.
In any reasonable way of looking at it, that is the best thing
that could happen. If Michael does not find him, you will lead
the hosts into the final battle."

"But I wish to be the one—"

"No! You are King here, after me. When you make decisions that affect the fate of your subjects, do you think your own pride should be what drives you, or should you concern yourself with the good of all of Heaven?"

"Of course, Father, I should think of the good of Heaven, but—"

"Then stamp out that pride wherever you find it in yourself! You cannot make decisions based on your own needs for self-satisfaction and also assure the safety of Heaven. Pride is a disease. Cure yourself."

"Yes, Father. Father?"

"Yes, my son?"

"Could we look upon Satan? To see if he knows, yet?"

"Well, it is some effort . . . but why not? I'm curious too."

Yaweh's brows furrowed, and his hands worked in and out of fists. For nearly an hour, scenes appeared and vanished before them. Finally they found him amid a body of angels. Yaweh's eyes opened wide, and he leaned forward.

Yeshuah gasped. "He's marching!"

"Yes, and with nearly a hundred angels."

"Where is he?"

"Nine days' march from here, and heading toward us." Yaweh's voice remained even.

"Where is Michael?"

The scene shifted several times before coming to rest on the host of angels led by Michael. "Following them as fast as they can. Michael is about three days behind, as near as I can tell. Satan must have discovered Michael before Michael discovered him and gone around."

"By the flux!"

"Don't swear, Yeshuah."

"But you have only twelve defenders, Father! What are we going to do?"

For answer, Yaweh turned to the Seraph nearest him and motioned him over. The Seraph bowed.

"You are Nisroc, aren't you?"

"Yes, Lord."

"Do you love me, Nisroc?"

Nisroc, a short, dark angel with black hair and a full black beard, dropped to his knees. "Yes, Lord!"

"And do you love my son?"

"I do, Lord!"

"Good. Then rise, Nisroc. Go forth and find as many angels as you can, and give them swords. Hold yourself ready. When Satan is close, I will send you against him, to take or destroy him. Do you understand?"

"Yes, Lord! I will do it!"

"Good, Nisroc. Now, go!"

"Hail, Lord Yaweh," said Nisroc, and departed. Yeshuah bit his lip.

"Well, friend Satan, what do you think?"

"To tell you the truth, Lucifer, I'm amazed."

"At the support we've been getting?"

"Yes. I'd hoped for some, but this! How many angels do we have?"

"I'm not sure. Three, three and a half thousand?"

"And getting more all the time." Satan shook his head. Their army was a full day's march from the palace. Every moment it seemed more angels had shown up to join them.

This close to the center, they were out of the rocky areas and into grassland, occasionally spotted with trees randomly thrown up by Lucifer during the Third Wave when his powers got out of control. Under such a tree they rested now, for a while.

"You see," said Lucifer, "they've been ready for some time, waiting for someone to lead them."

Satan raised an eyebrow. "Are you about to lecture me, old friend?"

Lucifer chuckled. "No. I should, because you need it, but I know better than to try."

Satan nodded. "I think," he said, "that we'll split up."

"What do you mean?"

"This evening you'll take a fourth, Asmodai will take a fourth, Lilith will take a fourth, and I'll take a fourth, and we'll plan on coming at the Palace from each side. We'll have to come up with some way to use messengers to stay in touch with each other to coordinate the attack. What do you think?"

"I don't understand why you want to divide."

"Yaweh. I want him. Alive. I don't want him to escape."

"But why not wait until we get there?"

"We're talking about Yaweh, remember? Remember what he can do?"

"Oh . . . I'd forgotten."

"Yes. We never used to use our powers between Waves, but we've all started to, as much as we can, and Yaweh might, too."

"You're right. He could have been watching us all along."

"Yes. But he wouldn't run before we get close. And by the time we get close, I don't want him able to."

"Good idea."

"What of Michael?" asked Lilith.

"He's still a day and a half behind us, according to Mephistopheles."

"Hmmm. Isn't that strange?"

"What?"

"Mephistopheles. I'd just about given up on him ever commiting himself to anything. I guess I was wrong."

"It just goes to show," said Satan.

Beelzebub rolled over and looked up at him, then returned to his nap.

Leviathan lolled in the water near the spot where Harut liked to stand. Where was he? She had sent him to the Southern Hold herself, but she shied away from that line of thought. She couldn't accept that she might have done to him what she had done to Ariel.

But where was he? He would have returned, if he could. Was he taken, then? For the first time in aeons, she gnashed her teeth at her body's restrictions.

He could be in chains by now, brought to Yaweh and humiliated or even harmed. Or he could have not escaped—no! She wouldn't think of that.

But there was nothing she could—what was that? Something? His voice? Where? She looked around, but saw only the rocky shore with its small cleft, and nothing but ocean around her.

She listened again, and realized that the voice was coming from within her mind. In that instant, she realized where Harut was and what she must do.

"Well, there it is, Lord Satan."

"We've made it, Mephistopheles, unhindered. How many are we now?"

"Our group has about four thousand angels, Lord. The last

reports indicate that the others are about the same."

"Good! Could you tell how far behind Michael is?"

"I saw the dust cloud from that last hill. He's a long way off still, but moving fast. He knows where we are. I think they'll be here in another day."

"Hmmmm. They outnumber us, too."

"About three to one, Lord Satan. But by the time they get here they'll be nearly exhausted from the run, the way he must be pushing them."

"That's something, then. We'll have to move quickly, though."

"I agree, Lord Satan."

"Good. Beelzebub, have you looked over the area near the Palace?"

"Aye, milord. There are scarce two hundred angels to defend it."

"That's fine. Are you up to running another series of errands?"

"Aye, milord."

"Good. Tell Lucifer, Lilith, and Asmodai to meet me here, right away. We're going to plan the attack."

"Aye, milord. It shall be done."

Beelzebub ran off.

"How many days has it been, Mephistopheles?"

"Since we left camp? Eighteen."

"Not bad, eh?"

"No, Lord Satan. Not bad."

He turned his eyes toward the Palace below him. "If you're watching, Yaweh, know that your time has come. And remember that you brought it on yourself; it was no doing of mine."

Michael, Yahriel, Zaphkiel, and Camael walked into the dusk of Heaven, nearly running. Behind them, thousands of angels matched their speed, for they were all committed to the Lord, and they knew that he was in danger.

Michael knew nothing but anger. In part, he was angry with Satan and all of his crew, who threatened Yaweh's life. But mostly he was angry with himself for having allowed Satan to slip past him. He could tell by the footprints they passed that Satan now had hundreds, maybe even thousands of allies. It should never have gotten this far. He pushed on.

Yahriel was an archangel of medium height, somewhat thin, with stringy brown hair. He looked young. He had a mind able to deal well with the abstract problems of how to move this many angels to here, or where to cut off distances, but he had never given any thought to why the fight was being waged. When he had heard of the Plan, it had fascinated him, but it had never seemed real. He had followed Yaweh because Yaweh had been there. Now he followed Michael because Michael was there. Michael said that they had to move quickly, so Yahriel worked on how to go faster. The moral problems he left to others.

Camael led the Powers, and they were all infected with his love of Yaweh and his adoration of Yeshuah.

Camael had no time to be critical of himself or Michael for Satan having gotten past them, nor was he worried about it. He knew that if this happened, it was as the Lord had willed it, for was not all of Heaven his to command? No, this was as it should be, and it meant that he must hurry, for the Lord wished to test his servants to see if their zeal was all it ought to be. That was the only reason Camael could see for this, and he was determined that, for his part, the Lord would have no cause for complaint.

Zaphkiel understood what had happened. He had suggested, exactly once, that Michael send scouts to the sides, but his suggestion hadn't been listened to. This, he knew, had to do with Michael's dislike of him.

But that was the past, and his future was ahead of him. He had seen Satan and spoken to him. He had seen and spoken to Yaweh. He knew what the possibilities were and understood them, and the only two questions were: which would happen, and where would he fit in?

Zaphkiel was created during the Third Wave, near the border of Leviathan and Belial's regency. He was created early, so he had actually been aware of what was going on as he fought. From time to time he had seen, in the distance, one angel coming to the aid of another, but he was too far away. There was no one to help him. He had learned to fight alone and survive alone, and he knew that anything he got, he would get alone. He trusted no one and depended on no one.

Zaphkiel had no need to agonize over plans and decisions.

The proper action was obvious, and would come as close to insuring his success as anything could. It depended, however, on his being at the right place at the right time.

So he sent his own scouts ahead to determine exactly how many angels had gathered and how Satan had deployed them, and he hurried.

For Zaphkiel, for Camael, for Yahriel, and for Michael, speed was everything.

"You must ask to parley, Lord."

"Don't be stupid, Abdiel. Why would he parley? Would I, if I were in his position?"

Abdiel shrugged. "I don't know, Lord. But Nisroc was only able to gather nine or ten score of angels. They have thousands. We have to delay them."

Yeshuah was silent. Yaweh turned to Raphael. "What do you think?"

"He's right, but I don't see any way to do it. As you said, why will Satan stop to parley? He knows that Michael will attack soon."

Abdiel shook his head. "Promise him that you'll tell Michael to hold back, from a good distance. He'll believe you."

Yaweh shrugged. "But why will he parley in the first place?"

"I know him," said Abdiel. "He'd rather talk than fight. Tell him that you'll negotiate. That you're willing to discuss the Plan and how to do it and if to do it, and—"

"No!" cried Yeshuah. "We will *not* give up the Plan!"

"I," said Yaweh, "am of the same mind as Yeshuah on this."

Abdiel shrugged. "All right, don't give it up, then. Just speak to him about it. What else is there to do?"

The others looked at each other. "He has something, at that," Yaweh admitted.

"We can at least speak to him," said Yeshuah.

"Yes," said Raphael. "He will speak to us."

"But," added Yeshuah, "we will not give up the Plan. Agreed?"

"Yes." Yaweh motioned to one of the Seraphim. "Sarga," he said.

The Seraph came forward. "Yes, Lord?"

"Find Michael, quickly. Make sure you skirt around Satan,

and tell the Lord Michael to stop where he is and come forward no farther until he is told to."

"Yes, Lord," said Sarga, bowed, and departed.

Abdiel sighed. "I would like to retire now, Lord."

Yaweh nodded. "You may go, Abdiel."

"Thank you, Lord," said Abdiel. Yaweh sat back in his throne.

Abdiel left the room. As soon as he was out, he caught up to Sarga in the hall. Abdiel took him to the side and spoke to him in low tones for several minutes.

They sat on top of the hill, in plain sight of the Palace. Lilith and Lucifer held each other close, not having seen each other in some days. Asmodai sat next to Beelzebub, who was next to Satan, who was next to Lilith, so completing the circle.

"Things have changed," began Satan, "since I called you together."

The others looked at each other.

"Changed?" said Lucifer. "How?"

"I have received a message from Yaweh, saying that he has ordered Michael to hold his position and he wishes to talk."

"Talk!" cried Asmodai. *"Now* he wants to talk? He can do his talking to the flux!"

"That is my reaction, too," said Lilith.

"And mine," said Lucifer.

"He is willing," continued Satan, "to discuss the Plan itself. He says that he will consider modifying the Plan, or making us all full partners in it."

"I have no wish to discuss anything with him," said Lucifer.

"I'll talk to him. Or rather," Satan added with a grim smile, "messengers will talk for me. Yaweh said that he doesn't wish to see me personally—that he doesn't feel safe with me, so he suggested messengers."

Lucifer snorted. Lilith turned away. Asmodai shook his head.

"And the loss of life," said Satan, "means nothing to you? If we can get what we want peacefully, will you reject it?"

There was silence for a moment, then Lucifer said, "I guess it can't do any harm to see what he has to say."

Lilith nodded. "Listening to him, yes. But I will not be talked out of a victory that we have nearly achieved."

Satan looked at her. Then he said, "All right; I'll make no decision until morning. I have to think this over. This council has ended."

He rose and walked back into the darkness.

Abdiel stood in the darkness outside the Palace. The air was chilly, but he found it, somehow, pleasing. There had to be a way out, he knew. First Ariel, then Raziel, and now one step further.

He shook his head. Could he really do it?

Could he *not* do it? When Yaweh found out that Michael had attacked, they would question the messenger. Abdiel couldn't allow that. And who was that Seraph, anyway? A nothing, a nobody. It wasn't for himself, Abdiel decided. If nothing was done, Yaweh would either abandon the Plan, despite all his promises, or Satan would attack and destroy them.

No, it was unfortunate that *he* had to be the one able to recognize what had to be done—but it still had to be done, and all the debates he could hold with himself wouldn't change that.

He took a deep breath and set off into the night, holding a sword tight so it wouldn't hit the ground.

Fifteen

Forwards! the doubt, my strength
      benumbing,
I won't encourage foolishly;
For were the witches not forthcoming,
Why, who the devil would Devil be!

—Goethe, *Faust*

"Well, now, who in Heaven are you?"

Mephistopheles, half smiling, looked at the angel who barred his way.

"I am Nisroc. You cannot enter here."

Mephistopheles raised an eyebrow and looked at the angels who were clustered before the doors to the Palace.

"That may be," he said. "But if you find someone to tell the Lord Yaweh that the emissary from the Lord Satan is here, I expect you'll find you're wrong."

Nisroc's eyes widened a bit, then he turned his head and told an angel behind him to relay the message. He faced Mephistopheles again and said, "We'll wait."

221

The dark angel smiled, folded his arms, and began whistling between his teeth.

Soon Uriel came from the door. He saw Mephistopheles and stopped. "You!"

"You were expecting Leviathan?"

"I ought to have guessed," he said, "that you would—"

"Dump it out, Uriel. We can exchange compliments later."

"As you will. Follow me."

"Right. Take me to your leader."

They went through the halls, where Mephistopheles grinned and nodded at the Cherubim, to the throne room. He noticed the second throne set to Yaweh's right and remarked, "You've been remodeling."

"What says the Lord Satan?" Yaweh asked.

Mephistopheles approached the throne until he was stopped by a pair of Seraphim.

"He is willing to discuss it," he said.

"Good."

"Have you a chair?" asked Mephistopheles. "My feet are tired."

Zaphkiel considered the situation. Why hadn't Satan attacked? The only thing that might delay him was if he was negotiating with Yaweh. And if he was, why hadn't they received a message telling them to hold off? It was strange that—

"Lord Zaphkiel?"

"What is it?"

"This angel claims to have a message from the Lord Yaweh."

Zaphkiel looked at him. "Bring him to Michael."

"Yes, Lord."

"Wait. You. Come here."

"Yes, Lord?"

"What's your name?"

"Sarga, Lord."

"Are you a Seraph or a Cherub, Sarga?"

"A Seraph, Lord."

"Is it an order to delay the attack?"

"I can't tell, Lord. I'm sorry."

"It doesn't matter. You just did. Don't try to hide things; you haven't the face for it." Zaphkiel mused for a moment. "How odd," he muttered to himself. Then to Sarga, "Did a messenger from Satan arrive there before you left?"

"I can't—"

"Answer!"

"No, Lord."

"Very odd. You must have been in the room where the idea to attack was decided upon, weren't you?"

"My lord, I—"

"Just say yes or no."

"Yes, Lord."

"Fine. Who suggested it?"

"I don't know, Lord."

"Rubbish. I know you Seraphim. You spend all your time on duty watching and listening to Yaweh's conversations. Now, whose idea was it? Abdiel's? I'd believe that."

"No, Lord." Sarga got a strange, confused look on his face. "Abdiel wasn't there when it was discussed, Lord."

"What? Wasn't there?"

"No, Lord. I . . . don't remember seeing him at all."

"Well, where was he then?"

"I don't know, Lord."

Zaphkiel leaned forward and looked closely into the Seraph's eyes. Then he nodded. "I see."

He turned to the Throne who was waiting. "That's all. Take him to see the Lord Michael. Then tell all sentries to pull in and get some rest. We don't need to worry about spies tonight, but we'll be moving soon."

"Yes, Lord."

Zaphkiel stared off into the distance.

As the acting head of the highest ranking Order present, Zaphkiel should have taken charge of the final arrangements. But he was only acting head, he had no interest in it anyway, and Michael had been given the mission. In any case, Michael would not have allowed it, and Michael was a Firstborn—as well as simply being Michael.

All of which is to say that the Orders of angels and the rankings therefrom had not yet caught on, so to speak, as well as they might.

So it was Michael who stood while Yahriel, Camael and Zaphkiel sat. He cleared his throat. "As you can see, we are on time. For some reason, Satan has chosen not to attack. We

are near his lines now and could advance at once. I had thought
to wait and receive instructions from the Lord Yaweh, but he
sent a message answering my question before I had asked it."

"Of course," said Camael. "He would."

Michael ignored him. "A Seraph has come from the Lord
Yaweh. We are to attack as soon as possible. If necessary, we
may take the evening to rest."

"No!" cried Camael. "At once!"

Zaphkiel said, "I am of like mind. We have had several
hours' rest. It should do. We want to maintain our advantage
of surprise, and we risk losing it by waiting."

Michael said, "All right. When?"

"Now!" said Camael.

"Why not?" said Zaphkiel.

"All right," said Michael, nodding. "Ten minutes to get to
your positions, fifteen minutes to arrange for battle, then we'll
go."

"I have the smallest unit," said Zaphkiel. "I would like the
honor of being in the middle, if I may have it."

Michael nodded. "If you wish."

Camael glowered at him for a moment, obviously wishing
that he'd thought to ask first.

Zaphkiel had been telling the truth about wanting his unit
to take the middle, but he had lied a bit about the reason. The
arriving Seraph had allowed him to reach a few conclusions,
bringing together things he had heard or seen but hadn't been
able to make sense of before.

Raziel had spoken to him, and from the questions he asked,
Zaphkiel had realized that there was something unusual in some
of the movements on the day Michael and Raphael had gone
to bring back Satan. Zaphkiel had been following the activities
of Lucifer, Lilith, Asmodai, and Satan, as well as those of
Yaweh, as closely as he could. He, like Yaweh, saw a mystery
there—they were not acting as he would have expected them
to.

He had noticed the disappearance of Raziel, as Yaweh had,
but had left it a question mark, to be resolved later.

Unlike Yaweh, who had had confidence in the angels around
him until recent events had damaged it, Zaphkiel had never
had confidence in anything except his own judgment. So when

things didn't add up right, he was slow to brush them aside.

He still couldn't solve anything, but one close look into the eyes of the Seraph delivering the message had allowed him to make several deductions.

He felt no sense of outrage and didn't stop to consider whether anything that had been done was right or wrong, but he did see opportunity when it presented itself.

Therefore he made sure that his Order was in the middle of the attacking angels. He expected that, before long, it would be his Order in name, as well as in fact.

The first Satan heard of it were the shouts from the other end of the camp. He stood to see what was going on, but others had the same idea and he couldn't see past them.

It was night, but swords reflected well in the light from the campfires. And when the shouts turned to screams, possibility became certainty.

For long moments he stood there in shock, unwilling to believe that Yaweh had betrayed him. Then as angels from his army began flying past him, yelling, and many limping or wounded, he moved forward.

An angel appeared before him, shouting wildly with sword cleaving air. Satan touched the emerald at his breast. It had worked well enough with the campfire; now he would see. . . .

There was no ripping, tearing effect of illiaster exploding around him, but the angel before him stopped, made a gurgling noise in his throat, and dissolved into nothingness.

Satan picked up the sword the other had dropped, his face devoid of expression, and swung it experimentally a few times. Another angel suddenly appeared before him, but before Satan could move, Beelzebub had him by the throat. The angel dropped his sword and clutched at Beelzebub, cried out once, and was silent. Then he was gone. Beelzebub turned to him. "One apiece, milord."

Satan didn't answer.

Another came in front of him. Satan swung clumsily and missed, but so did the other. Then Satan brought his sword up over his head and sent it crashing down on the other's blade. The angel fell, holding his shoulder and looking up at Satan fearfully.

But the Regent of the South ignored him. He took another

step forward while more and more of his army streamed by, running from the unexpected assault.

Another came before Satan, but his blade was held low and pointed to the side. Beelzebub crouched but didn't spring.

Satan looked at the other angel. "Greetings, Zaphkiel," he said calmly.

"Greetings, Lord Satan. Would you mind coming with me?"

"As it happens, Zaphkiel, I would. I have never had less of a mind to see Yaweh than right now."

"Then you are a fool," said Zaphkiel.

Satan shrugged. "I'm obviously a fool, or I wouldn't have believed that Yaweh dealt in good faith."

"Yaweh *did* deal in good faith."

Satan snorted.

"I'm telling the truth," said Zaphkiel in a matter-of-fact tone of voice. "When Yaweh learns of this, he will be furious. As will Michael. There is one angel to blame for this betrayal, and, I suspect, a great deal more. The way to deal with him is to expose him.

"You may not know it, but Yaweh has never heard your side of many events that have happened in the last few hundred days. I think, if you come with me, you will be pleased that you have done so. But I think you should move quickly. It took some doing to arrange these moments by ourselves in the midst of a battle, and I doubt that Camael or Michael will think so highly of my idea."

Satan cocked his head. "Why are you doing this?"

"Reasons of my own, of course, that I have no wish to discuss. But, as I say, we have little time."

Satan looked down at Beelzebub. "What do you think?"

"I believe him, milord."

Satan nodded. "All right, Beelzebub, find Lucifer. Tell him to take command and to bring the armies to Leviathan. If I don't return, he is on his own. And may he make better decisions than I!"

"Aye, milord," said Beelzebub, and he was gone.

Satan threw his sword to the ground. "I'm at your disposal."

"Good," said Zaphkiel.

"Maybe," said Satan. "But how do we get there through the middle of a battle?"

"My scouts have explored this terrain. I know paths to the Palace that won't be used. Follow me."

• • •

"That does it, Sith."

"What does what, Kyriel?"

"This is absurd. The way they hit us back there. Why didn't we get any warning? You know, one of them almost had me!"

"We didn't have any sentries posted, that's why."

"And why didn't we?"

"Because Yaweh had promised—"

"So what? After all this, they believe Yaweh? Hnuh! *He's* no fool. He knew he could sucker Satan in any time he wanted to. We had 'em, and we let 'em go. Is that how you win a war?"

"That isn't my job, Kyriel. I'm just here to fight."

"Then you're as big an idiot as Satan is. Why are you just standing there looking at me? Do you *like* being in a war where everyone making decisions on your side is a fool, or worse?"

"No. But I'm on the right side, and it's all we have."

"The right side is the one that wins, Sith."

"Maybe. If you think so, and if you think we aren't going to win, why are you staying?"

"Staying with what? Where's the army now?"

"I saw a few angels heading west, so I imagine that's where we're going to gather. That's why we're walking this way."

"Yeah? Well then, I'm going to walk east."

"Michael is that way, Kyriel."

"So I'll join Michael. Maybe I'll be on the winning side for a change."

"If that's what you feel you must do."

"By the flux, Sith! What's got into you? You walk around like you're asleep, and you talk like you don't care about anything anymore."

"I care, Kyriel. But if you want to leave, I won't stop you."

"By Heaven itself, I will, then!"

"Fare well, Kyriel."

"Farewell, and good riddance!"

Beelzebub caught up to Satan and Zaphkiel half a league from the Palace.

"I'm glad you decided to join me, old friend, but it was unwise."

"Thy orders were given, milord."

"Good."

"Meseemeth the lord Lucifer to think ill of thy doings here, milord. He thinks thou wilt be killed."

"Maybe I will," said Satan. "But not alone," he added, touching his emerald.

Zaphkiel appeared not to notice. He took them the long way around the Palace, passing through the woods at the top of the hill. Beelzebub led them through this, pointing out trees and roots and stones in a whisper so that Satan and Zaphkiel would not trip in the darkness.

As they left the woods, the lights from the Palace set up enough illumination so that they could see their path somewhat. Zaphkiel held up his hand for them to wait.

Soon they saw a pair of angels with swords walking by. As they disappeared around the other side of the Palace, Zaphkiel motioned them forward.

They ran, as quietly and as quickly as they could, to a small door. Zaphkiel opened it and they stepped inside, shutting it softly.

They found themselves in a poorly lit hallway. This they followed for several turnings until they came to another door.

"Now," said Zaphkiel, "act confident."

They nodded.

He opened the door, and they stepped out into a large hall filled with angels, many of whom were sleeping. Zaphkiel strode forward, nodding to them, and went for the door into the throne room.

A Cherub moved to bar the way and started to speak, but Zaphkiel snapped, "Out of the way, idiot." Before the other could decide what to do, they were past.

"Wonderful guards," muttered Satan.

Then things happened quickly. As soon as they were inside, Zaphkiel slammed the door shut and drove his sword under it as a wedge. There were cries, and the two Seraphim who were awake leapt at them while the other, Uriel, woke up.

There was a flurry of movement, and one of them was on the floor, Beelzebub's teeth at his throat. The other was against a wall, gritting his teeth while Zaphkiel cooly held his arm pinned behind his back.

Uriel, awake now, rushed forward. Satan touched his emerald and a portion of the floor vanished as Uriel set his foot there. Uriel gave a cry and fell over. Satan walked up to him and hit him in the back of the head. Uriel stopped moving.

Satan walked forward, past Uriel, and looked at the two figures on the thrones. He addressed the stranger first.

"You must be Yeshuah," he said. "I've heard much about you."

"And I," said Yeshuah, his eyes blazing, "have heard much of you. How did you manage to seduce that one?" He indicated Zaphkiel.

"It's pleasing to know, Zaphkiel, that you didn't trick me. That is a real pleasure, since it seems that everyone else has."

Yaweh spoke then, holding his sceptre high. "If you've come to destroy me, you'll not find it easy, I think."

"Likewise," said Satan.

There were cries from the other side of the door and sounds of it beginning to give way.

"As it happens, I'm only here to talk. Zaphkiel tells me that you didn't order the attack on us this evening."

Yaweh's eyes widened. "Attack! There was no attack."

"There are several score of angels who would argue with that, if they could."

Zaphkiel turned. "Including the Seraph you sent with the message to Michael, I think."

Yaweh sat down heavily. "Michael attacked you?"

Satan nodded. "Yes. And I'm convinced now that it wasn't by your orders. That is what Zaphkiel tried to tell me. He also said that many things we've been accusing each other of weren't done by us. He said I should speak to you about it."

Yaweh seemed to be in shock. Yeshuah said, "Should we speak with them then, Father? If so, we should do something about those who are about to break down our door."

Yaweh nodded dumbly. Yeshuah went up to the door and yelled. "Stand back! All is well. I'm opening the door now."

The noise from the other side ceased. Yeshuah removed the sword that was holding it closed and opened it. "All is well," he said. "Wait out here, though, until you are needed."

There were sounds of agreement from the other side. Yeshuah returned as Zaphkiel and Beelzebub released the Seraphim they were holding. These rose and helped Uriel stand up. He seemed to be recovering.

"Well," said Satan, "where should we begin? How about with Ariel? That's what bothers me the most, I think."

Yaweh looked puzzled. "I don't know anything about Ariel. But why did you refuse my first invitation?"

"I never received an invitation."

Yaweh shook his head. "I don't—Uriel, bring Gabriel in here."

Uriel hastened to comply.

Mephistopheles was in an upstairs hallway awaiting Yaweh's reply when he heard the commotion below. He walked down and discovered that the door was sealed from the inside and that some one or ones had sneaked past. Since the Cherubim had decided not to say anything at all beyond that, it took him several minutes to find out that Zaphkiel had brought Satan and Beelzebub in to see Yaweh, and that they had been in there for some time now with Yaweh's approval.

It took him several more minutes to figure out what must be happening, and it was only confirmed when a Seraph left the room and returned a few moments later with Abdiel walking behind him.

As the door closed, Mephistopheles remarked, "It might not be a bad idea to guard this door well."

One of the Cherubim looked at him, then looked away. Mephistopheles shrugged. "There is a chance that someone will come flying out of that room in a moment, and if you stop him, you won't have to—"

The door flung open. Abdiel came dashing out, down the hall, and was gone.

"Catch him!" cried Yeshuah, appearing at the door.

Mephistopheles sighed. "I'm so smart I almost can't stand it," he remarked to no one in particular.

As the Cherubim started off, Yaweh appeared at the door. "Let him go," he said. "He's done his damage; we can catch him later."

The door closed. One of the Cherubim turned to make some remark to Mephistopheles, but Mephistopheles was nowhere to be seen.

"I don't quite know how to take all this, Satan."

The Regent shook his head. "I don't either. I feel that we've been fighting for no reason—and yet, have we?"

"I don't know. But it seems that neither of us want to fight, and our reasons for fighting never existed."

Satan nodded.

"Well then," Yaweh continued, "how do we end the war?"

"I'll return to my army and tell them . . . hmmmm."

"Exactly. Tell them what? That you are now willing to cooperate with the Plan? That I no longer am? Though one thing I'll do now." He turned to Zaphkiel. "You are now Chief of the Order of Thrones. Return to the field and tell Michael to cease hostilities until further notice. Also tell him to inform everyone that Abdiel is to be found."

"Yes," said Zaphkiel, and left.

"In any case," said Yaweh, "we're going to have to find a way to cease hostilities permanently. And remember, I will not abandon the Plan."

Satan shrugged. "Are you willing to be honest about it?"

Yaweh furrowed his brow. "What does that mean?"

"It means, are you willing to explain to everyone what dangers there are? How many may be destroyed, and try to convince them that it is the right thing? If you'll do that—"

"Father."

Yaweh turned to him. "Yes?"

"It won't work."

"What do you mean?"

"In the minds of the hosts, those on both sides, you are committed to destroying Satan. Do you think you can announce that it was all a misunderstanding? You'll be laughed out into the flux—both of you."

Satan narrowed his eyes and studied him.

"What are you saying?" asked Yaweh.

"There must be a surrender. Complete and full. And an apology."

"I don't see why," said Yaweh.

"Because you have claimed to be the father of us all—the creator of Heaven, practically omnipotent. He has opposed you. There must be an apology and then forgiveness, or our credibility is destroyed forever—and the Plan with it."

Yaweh shook his head. "Wouldn't it be just as bad if I claimed to forgive him?"

Yeshuah nodded. "Yes, Father. After all of this, you can't forgive him. But I can." He turned his head and looked fully at Satan. "I do," he said.

Yaweh nodded slowly. "You're right," he said. He turned to Satan. "Will you do it?"

"Just what," said Satan, "are you asking?"

"That you publicly say that you were wrong to oppose me. To call on those who trust you to serve me. To back up my claim to being supreme Lord of Heaven. To bow down to Yeshuah as King Anointed after me, the supreme being of Heaven. To—"

"Lie through my teeth? No!"

"What do you mean?"

Satan's eyes blazed with green fire. "I'll see myself thrown into the flux first!"

Yaweh's eyes opened wide. "I don't understand."

"Every decision you have made, as far as I know, has been right. Every decision I have made, from what I can see, has been wrong. But there is one thing: I have never lied about who I was, what I was doing, or why I was doing it. You have done all of these."

Yaweh started to speak, but Satan cut him off.

"I know why you did it now, and I understand. But I will not support you in these lies and half-truths. All I have left from this mayhem is that I know I was always honest and did the best I could. I will not throw that out.

"No! There has been too much. I will not admit to something I think is wrong. Had you gone before all the hosts and simply told them the truth instead of creating a false image of yourself as some sort of god, and creating this, this *thing* here as some sort of demigod, this wouldn't have happened."

Yaweh's face twisted for a moment, but he got the better of his anger and said, "If you object to my claiming godship because it is a lie, my only choice is to make it truth. I have said that any who oppose my son will be cast out from Heaven. I will prove my godhood by doing so. Is that what you want?"

"No. But I prefer it to being part of a lie."

Yaweh turned to Yeshuah. "You see, my son, why I said that pride is dangerous in a ruler."

A low growling sound came from Beelzebub. The Seraphim were suddenly alert. Satan held his hand out before Beelzebub as if to hold him back.

"You," he told Yaweh, "have destroyed my home—or your overzealous minions did. You have lied about me and forced me to kill an angel. Now you want me to be part of continuing a lie, and imply that I deserved all that happened to me. No. I will not. Now what?"

Yaweh was silent for a moment. Then, his face hard and cold, he said. "Zaphkiel brought you here with the understanding that you would be safe. I hold myself bound by this, though it was not my doing, because he was acting as I would have had him act. Therefore, you may leave in safety."

Satan nodded. "For this, I thank you. Zaphkiel knows that we are gathering our host near Leviathan's regency. I will await you there."

He bowed his head and left, Beelzebub at his side.

When he had gone, Yaweh looked at Yeshuah. "For a moment," he said, "I had hope. . . ."

Yeshuah remained silent.

Sixteen

They come from a far country, from the end
of heaven, even the Lord, and the weapons
        of
his indignation, to destroy the whole land.

Howl; for the day of the Lord is at hand;
it shall come as a destruction from the
        Almighty.

—Isaiah, 13:5-6

Word spread quickly of what had happened between Yaweh
and Satan. One of the first to hear was Raphael.

She thought about confronting Yaweh, asking him just what
he had in mind by driving Satan away, ready for war instead
of prepared to reconcile, but she could have asked Satan the
same thing.

She wasn't surprised at what had happened between them,
merely saddened. Nor was she angry at Abdiel. No doubt he
had had reasons for what he did.

She found that she had no interest in the war, and very little in the Plan. If the Plan was used, she would be pleased. If it was not, she would be disappointed. But, to her, it had already cost far too much.

So, without being aware of a decision, she found herself leaving the Palace and the center, and heading away from it all.

It was a mere accident, if such is possible, that led her to walk west toward the sea, where Leviathan waited with the gathering army of Satan.

Lucifer looked up as Asmodai approached. "Well?"

"Well what? No word from the Palace, if that's what you mean."

"No. I mean the state of your forces."

"We're all here, and we're all ready."

"Morale?"

"Not very good, of course, but as good as we can hope for."

"All right. Find Lilith for me."

Asmodai left to do so, and returned with her shortly.

"We are ready," she said.

"Good. How about stragglers from Satan's host?"

"Maybe a thousand. Not more."

"Lucifer?"

"A hundred at most. We were the farthest away when Michael attacked."

"Yes. We've gotten eight or nine hundred so far. And we're three days' march from the shore, and Michael is a day behind us."

"So," said Asmodai, "you're going to do as Satan said?"

"Yes," said Lucifer.

"Why?"

"Asmodai, if you are trying to start an argument, I'll have to disappoint you. I'm not going to say, 'Because he told us to,' so you can say, 'So what?' We're going there, if for no other reason, because it makes sense. Right now our most powerful allies are Leviathan and Belial. Belial is more than fifteen days away, even marching quickly. Leviathan is three. She can't come to us; therefore we go to her. Okay?"

Asmodai nodded.

"Lilith?"

"I never disagreed."

"Good. Then we move—all together—in an hour. What else is there to discuss?"

"Should we try to find out what has happened to Satan?" asked Lilith.

"I think not," said Lucifer. "We assume he is dead or captured, and if we're wrong, all the better. I don't want to waste any energy worrying about him. We go on as we can."

"All right," said Lilith. Asmodai nodded.

"Anything else?"

There wasn't.

"Then let's get busy," said Lucifer.

"A message, Father?"

"Yes. From Michael. He says that they are ready for battle and are preparing to set out after Satan's host. He also says that the enemy is moving west, so Satan was telling the truth."

"What about numbers?"

"Michael picked up a few hundred who deserted Satan after the last battle, and there were more who simply ran away. All in all, they still have more than we do, but not by much."

"So Michael is going to attack anyway?"

"Yes. He is deciding now on his exact strategy, but we are going to end this. He will be approaching from three sides with the sea before them, so the rebels will have nowhere to run."

"But if they outnumber us—"

"We have an advantage."

"What is that?"

"You, my son. You will lead this attack. You will take with you all the Seraphim and the Cherubim; these will be your personal guard. You will lead our hosts against the enemy, and you will drive him into the sea. This will be your hour. What do you say?"

"Father! I'm ready!"

"Then go at once. You should be with them as soon as possible."

"I'm on my way, Father."

"Farewell. And, Yeshuah—"

"Yes, Father?"

"You have my blessing."

• • •

Michael looked up from the maps. "Zaphkiel, how far behind are we?"

"Half a day."

"Where will Satan be now?"

"If he's joined up with the army—"

"That's what I meant."

"—he has nearly reached the shore."

"Good. We will take our time traveling the rest of the way so we can arrive rested, and then attack as soon as we arrive."

Zaphkiel nodded. "I saw something interesting a few hours ago."

"Oh?"

"Raphael. Walking westward, alone."

"That *is* interesting. Do you suppose she's joined with Satan? I can't believe it."

Zaphkiel shrugged.

"Well, nothing to be done about it—Yeshuah!"

Zaphkiel turned, and it was, indeed, Yeshuah who stood before them. About his waist was a belt of gold, and in his hands was a sword as long as Michael's. A circlet, also of gold, was set upon his head.

"I am here," he said, "by the wishes of the Lord Yaweh. I am to lead the battle against the enemy. These are my father's wishes. What say you?"

Zaphkiel nodded. Michael said, "You can have them! Here are the maps of the sea area, such as we have, and Zaphkiel can give you the information about our personnel. I'm going to get some sleep."

He bowed to each of the others and strode away. Yeshuah turned to Zaphkiel. "Let us begin, then."

"Good day, Leviathan. How are—*by the death of Cherubiel! What happened?*"

Leviathan didn't answer. Raphael stared down at the legless form of Harut, lying burned and scarred before her. Raphael swallowed hard; then old training took over. She knelt at his side while taking her six-pointed star in one hand. She ran the fingers of her other hand over the top of his head, down each side of his face, around his neck, and over his chest.

"What happened?" she repeated.

"I don't know," said Leviathan, "he hasn't spoken. He was in the battle at the Southern Hold, but I don't know what may have happened there."

Lilith touched his chest and nodded. "These could be burn marks, then. He may have been near the Hold itself when it burned down."

"Burned down?"

"You didn't know? They set fire to it. Burned it to the ground."

"That's it, then," said Leviathan. "I'd sent him there with a message." She turned her great head away and swam out of sight.

Raphael turned back to Harut and tried to summon what power she could.

Mephistopheles went slower and slower as the hours went by. The ground was harder here, and the trail more difficult to pick out. Also, it was apparent that Abdiel had no destination in mind, but was simply running wherever his feet took him. This meant that Mephistopheles had to be sure of every step.

Still, he decided, he wasn't losing much ground. Abdiel was obviously running until exhausted and then resting, which was not the way to cover long distances in a hurry.

More and more often, he would find signs of Abdiel's having collapsed. At the same time, the signs began to get fresher, and the ground began to get softer and grassier.

For a while, Abdiel was actually on the road to the South, which required Mephistopheles to cover all the ground on both sides to see where he stepped off. This didn't last long, however.

By the evening of the third day, Mephistopheles felt that he was only a few hours behind. Of course, Abdiel wouldn't be stopping for the night, but he wouldn't be going very far, either.

Mephistopheles was content to wait the night. Tomorrow, he felt, would see things settled.

"Stop! Who are—Lord Lucifer? No! Who are you?"

Satan looked at the angel whose sword was leveled at his breast and said, "Who else around here wears a gold cloak?"

The angel held his torch a little closer and cried, "Lord

Satan! You're safe! We had heard—"

"I don't doubt it. Bring me to Lucifer, please."

"At once, Lord!"

He called for someone to take his place and set off toward the middle of the camp, Satan striding behind him, Beelzebub padding along complacently.

They reached the central area, lit with enormous fires, and they heard the sounds of a hammer on metal. They followed these sounds to a makeshift forge set up on the shore of the sea, and saw Lucifer, Asmodai, and Lilith speaking together while Asmodai struck something with a hammer in the midst of the coals.

Satan thanked the angel who had brought them and dismissed him with a nod. He approached the trio from behind and coughed gently. Lucifer turned around, and—"Satan!"

"Yes."

"And Beelzebub! He let you go!"

"Yes."

By this time Asmodai had dropped his hammer and was standing next to Lucifer, staring intently. Lilith was also studying Satan, as if to see if he had changed.

"Where can we talk?" Satan asked. "There are a lot of things that need explaining."

Lucifer nodded and led them off to the rocks by the sea. Satan at once noticed a large shape in the water.

"Leviathan?"

She approached. "Yes, old friend. We didn't have a chance to speak last time."

"I know. Now, however, I can answer some of the questions you would have had to ask of me."

"How is Harut?" Lilith interjected.

"He will live," said Leviathan.

"Good."

"What is this?" asked Satan. "What happened to Harut?"

"As near as we can tell," said Lucifer, "he was inside the Southern Hold when it was torched. He managed to get out and somehow got to the lake. Leviathan brought him back."

Satan shook his head. "But he'll be all right?"

"He will live," repeated Leviathan.

"Excuse me," said Lilith. "But why don't we start at the beginning? And that, I think, means hearing from Lord Satan first."

Satan nodded. "All right." He seated himself. "You may as well get comfortable. This is going to take a while."

What Abdiel noticed, after becoming aware that he was close to the sea, was what he had tripped over. There was a large, jagged hole in the ground several feet to his right, and cracks went off from it in various directions. He had tripped in one of these, which was as wide as his foot and nearly the depth of his arm from elbow to wrist.

He approached the hole, and noticed, in the growing light, that it was blackened in the middle and around the edges, and deep enough that he could hide himself in it entirely. It was a moment later that he realized what it was: the spot where Michael's sword had struck the ground instead of striking Satan.

He studied it a little more carefully.

As he approached it, a dizzying sensation came over him, followed closely by near-panic. He felt a drifting dissolution creep over him and realized that he was about to fall apart— to return to the raw illiaster from which he had come.

He dived away from the hole and instinctively commanded his body to retain its form.

He succeeded effortlessly. This, in itself, was nearly as surprising as the sudden threat had been.

He approached the hole again, more cautiously this time, and studied it. As he did so, a sudden gleam came into his eyes, and a smile stole across his lips.

He moved back after a while and composed his mind for the effort.

Harut stood up. He was supported on either side by Lucifer and Lilith. Asmodai stood a ways back and studied his legs.

"Can you stand alone?" he asked.

"I don't know," said Harut. Lucifer and Lilith stepped back. Harut wobbled, and held out his arms for balance, but didn't fall.

"I guess so," he remarked, grinning broadly.

Leviathan smiled. "I wouldn't have believed it," she said.

"Me neither," said Harut, still smiling.

"Thank you, Raphael," said Leviathan. And, "Raphael? What's wrong?"

Raphael, who had been carefully ignoring everyone except Harut, didn't look pleased. When Leviathan spoke, she still didn't meet her eyes, but said, "I'm surprised at how easy it was."

"You're unhappy about that?" asked Leviathan.

"Not unhappy. Surprised."

Lucifer studied Leviathan closely, a worried expression coming over his features as if to match hers. Lilith noticed and said, "What is it?"

"I'm not sure," said Lucifer. "But—Raphael, how hard was it to grow new legs for him?"

She shrugged. "I didn't have to call on my powers as much as I'd thought I would, but it was hard." She pondered, looking at Lucifer closely. "Still, not as hard as I would have thought."

"You've answered my question, I think. Why wouldn't it take as much effort to use your illiaster? Could it be that we've been wrong about how hard it is to use it between Waves? That all it takes is practice?"

"I haven't practiced. If it was always this easy between battles, I could have saved his eyesight before."

"Then something is going on that I don't understand," said Lucifer. "And whatever it is, I want to know about it."

"Raphael?"

"Yes, Asmodai?"

"What you said, about if it was always this easy. . . ."

Raphael nodded. "I've been thinking about that. Come with me, Harut, if you will. I'd like to try something."

Mephistopheles awoke, made a hasty meal, and continued following the trail. He noticed that they were getting close to the sea and wondered if something, unknown to Abdiel, was drawing Abdiel there.

Everyone else was gathering there, and Michael would be attacking at any time now, and the real issues would be settled soon. It was clear that Abdiel had no real knowledge of where he was going; it was a bit of coincidence that he'd ended up so close to everyone else.

The trail got fresher and fresher as Mephistopheles went along, and the signs of Abdiel's falling more and more frequent. Another hour or two, he decided. And then—they'd see.

Then Mephistopheles noticed that the trees before him had taken rather unusual shapes that he couldn't remember them having before. Branches were bent back around the trunk, some leaves were shaped differently than others. Even the trunks had unusual bends in them. Odd. What could cause that?

He noted landmarks, and signs of the flood that had washed over this land. Could the waters have done that? Unlikely, he decided.

As he walked, he saw that the oddly twisted trees were becoming even more oddly twisted.

"Whatever it is," he told himself, "I'm walking right into it. But then, of course, so is Abdiel."

He hurried on.

Yaweh had left the Palace shortly after Yeshuah.

There had been no one there to see him off, but that was fine; he didn't want knowledge of his leaving to escape anyway.

He had no intention of leading this fight—it had to be Yeshuah's. And yet—he couldn't stay out of it because it was his.

He had been right, he knew, in his lecture on pride, but he didn't make any claims to perfection. If he fell, so be it. Yeshuah would make a good leader if they won, and it wouldn't matter if they lost.

He had also been correct in allowing Abdiel to escape; it would be a grave error to let anyone be distracted from the important issues by a personal consideration. But Yaweh had nothing left but personal considerations, and now he knew where to lay the blame for losing the friendship of angels he had loved since the beginning of time, and, pride or no pride, he would settle this.

An understanding of hate had been a long time in coming to him, but it had come at last. And with it, he understood more fully than he ever had before the love he still felt for Satan, for Lucifer, for Leviathan, and the others.

He had begun with dissatisfaction, gone from there to hope, and graduated to hopelessness. Now, no matter how things fell out, he knew that he had lost.

"Am I going after Abdiel hoping he'll destroy me?" he wondered. "No. Not him. If I fall, let it be by Satan's hand, or Lucifer's, but not by Abdiel's."

It was surprisingly easy for him to hold the image of Abdiel before his eyes and to follow the image. His hand held the sceptre, which could be a weapon of destruction if need be.

What, he wondered, was Abdiel doing at that hole? It certainly looked significant, but what *was* it? Well, he'd find out before he destroyed him, if possible. If not, amen to that, too.

Far to the north under mountains known for vulcanism, the angel who most feared and hated the cacoastrum awoke fully. Something that had been disturbing him, little by little, had finally crystalized. A slowly growing unease which went back many days became solid—and hideously frightening.

His great eyes opened to the darkness, and he felt it with every nerve in his massive body. Fear shot through him, paralyzing him for long moments. He didn't know why it was happening, since it felt so different from the other times, but he knew fully what it was.

Could he actually fly right into it to stop it? No. Could he resist doing so? Also, no. How long could he stay like this, not doing anything, afraid to do nothing? That would have to be seen.

Lucifer nodded. "I will admit," he said, "that this makes many things clear that weren't before."

Asmodai and Lilith nodded. "However," said Lilith, "it doesn't change anything."

"I agree," said Satan. "We do what we must."

They sat in silence, none of them wishing to address the next question. The silence became uncomfortable. It continued, and became intolerable.

Finally, Lucifer said, "All right, I may as well ask it: Who is going to lead our forces?"

Beelzebub nodded, but was silent. Satan cleared his throat.

"It is clear," he said, "that I have been wrong every time I made a decision—except, perhaps, the decision to see Yaweh. I am no longer capable of—"

"Crap," said Lilith.

Lucifer looked at her. "Huh?"

"It seems to me," said Asmodai, "that you, Lilith, are the only one of us who understood from the beginning what this was about. It is obvious—"

"Crap to you, too," she said. "Lord Satan, it is unfortunate that you are the one the angels look to, but that is just how it is. It is also unfortunate that you won't be content to let others lead in your name, but I know you. You won't."

Satan nodded, watching her closely.

"Well, since you won't, we're stuck with you. If you had had the courage—the courage of mind, I mean—to lead us before, we would have won long ago. If I had had the courage of mind to challenge you openly and campaign among the angels to win their allegiance, we would be in a position to win now.

"But none of those things happened. The angels still look to you for leadership. Therefore, you will lead us. But listen to me, Satan: It is only because we are so much stronger than Yaweh that we have survived all of your hesitations so far. We have, still, a chance of winning. That is despite you, not because of you. If you err once more, we will lose, and be cast out of Heaven or destroyed.

"So be careful. Dealing with enemies who are angels is no different than dealing with the flux. You do what you must, when you must. Remember that, as we go into this. Do you understand?"

Satan looked at her a long time. Then he nodded, once.

Abdiel worked hard and fast, but carefully. He had to hold tight control over himself to keep from being destroyed by the powers he was using.

The seepage he had detected allowed him to expand the area of the hole, which he did before trying to deepen it. After half an hour or so, it was as deep as his height, and as wide.

Slowly, then, he began to work his way down further. As he did so, he felt the cacoastrum grow stronger, and he had to use more and more of his energy to prevent its affecting him. But, at the same time, he had to use less and less to do the actual work.

The top of the hole was well above his head now, and the deepening would soon begin to happen on its own. When that began, he would leave and get as far from there as he could—using the illiaster to transport himself.

Then he would watch, laughing, while the angels busied themselves trying to fight the Wave. Of course, he might die himself, but if he didn't, there was at least some chance that all of those who were after him would die.

And if not, well, he would make them remember him, anyway!

He chuckled to himself. "The angel who started the Fourth

Wave." Not a bad name to be remembered by, he mused. And they would certainly regret having listened to those who—

"Good morning, Abdiel."

Abdiel looked up and saw Mephistopheles standing at the edge of the pit, looking down at him, the corners of his lips turned up into a half smile.

"Hard at work, I see. Mind if I interrupt?"

Seventeen

God would not permit such a crime.

—Alexander Dumas

Yeshuah stood on a large stone and surveyed his army. Thousands of angels, swords gleaming in the morning light, looked at him. He smiled and nodded, then turned the other way.

He could hear the sound of the surf just a league or two distant. He could smell the salt in the air. And he could see Satan's army lined up in their thousands across shore.

To Satan, the sea would be a place to stand, to hold from. To Yeshuah, it was a place to drive the enemy into.

Yeshuah reflected that it was odd, but not surprising, that Satan was on the defensive despite his larger numbers. All of the recreant angels who served him knew deep in their hearts that their foe was the Lord God, omnipotent, immortal, timeless, and eternal. How they must be quaking!

Yeshuah raised his sword high and brought it down again. He leapt forward off the rock and ahead of the angels in front.

The Seraphim marched with him, two on either side, because he would have no one first. The Cherubim came behind, the eight of them clustered as close as they could. Uriel was at Yeshuah's right hand; Gabriel was directly behind him.

Even with the rearmost of the eight Cherubim came Zaphkiel, off to the right flank with his Thrones numbering twenty. On the other side was Yahriel with a hundred Dominions.

This was the vanguard. Behind them came five hundred Virtues led by Michael, whose sword shone so brightly that none could look directly upon it. And next came Camael, who led two thousand Powers, and Nisroc after him with ten thousand angels formed into a new Order created for the battle and called Principalities, for they fought for Yeshuah, the Prince of Heaven, and they cried his name as they came.

Behind them, Barachiel, his beard black and his eyes bright, led the Archangels who stood for Yaweh, and the rest of the angels who had chosen Yaweh came behind, and their Chief was called Adnachiel. The army followed in Yeshuah's wake. Knowing the terrain from Zaphkiel's reports, he took them through a path such that four could walk abreast. Then it expanded.

It took a long time for them all to go through. When they did, they saw a cleft. It was three leagues deep and two leagues wide. Those in the vanguard moved forward so the others could file in behind them and form ranks. This also took a long time.

But when it was done, they began to march forward. Those on the right flank looked to the small path on the other side, but nothing was there. Yeshuah, in front, moved toward the far edge of the cleft where the waves crashed against the rocks.

Opposite them was Satan, who still wore the gold cloak of the Firstborn. The emerald still shone upon his breast, and his green eyes were narrow and grim.

His right hand held a sword, the point of which rested on the ground. His left hand was held out to the side, telling those behind him to wait. He seemed made of stone.

At his right side was Beelzebub, also still and unmoving, his eyes fastened on the oncoming army. His weapons were his teeth.

A pace behind him to the right stood Lucifer. He held a short rod of scarlet light with a golden hilt in his right hand.

He, also, wore the gold cloak of the Firstborn. Lilith stood to
Satan's left, and she held a spear—a gift from Asmodai. It
seemed to jump in her hand as she rested its butt against the
ground.

Behind these four came the might of the angels in rebellion,
their faces grim, their hands holding blades, spread out before
the cliff some fifty paces in front of it.

Behind them were a few large shapes that the oncoming
army couldn't quite see, but gave little notice. And behind
these, just barely, they could make out the awesome shape of
the head of Leviathan, eyes blazing, maw just slightly open.

The distance between the two lines diminished to a league—
half a league—a quarter.

Satan lowered his hand.

Raphael and Harut went to a high place, over the sea and
above the battle. Raphael watched the lines get closer and closer
together, then she went beneath the tree where Harut waited
and leaned against it.

"You don't want to watch?" said Harut.

"No. Would you like me to report what happens?"

"No."

"Tell me something, Harut: Why is this happening? I can't
blame Satan, and I can't blame Yaweh. I can't blame Lucifer,
or Asmodai, or Lilith, and I can't even blame Yeshuah. Who,
then? Is it really all Abdiel's fault?"

Harut shook his head. "It doesn't matter, honey. It is, that's
all."

"That isn't good enough."

"No, it sure isn't, honey. But it's what we've got."

Raphael nodded. "Lie down, Harut. I want to take another
look at your eyes."

Without another word, he complied.

Yeshuah was faster than the Seraphim around him. With a
great cry, he sprang forward to meet Satan. The Regent of the
South held his sword aloft, but before he could swing, Lilith
cooly stepped in front of him and impaled Yeshuah on her
spear.

He gave a cry and went down clutching his side as Lilith
withdrew her spear for another attack. Uriel caught up then,

and, screaming with rage, cut at Lilith's head. She stepped back and thrust with the spear. Uriel twisted out of the way and swung at her head. She ducked the blade, her face expressionless, and thrust at him again. Once more he twisted and cut; once more she ducked and thrust.

Another Seraph tried to come at her from the side, but Satan moved to block him. The Seraph cut downwards, and Satan's sword fell from his hand. The angel lifted his blade again, but Beelzebub leapt at his throat and then they were on the ground, rolling and tearing at each other. Satan picked up his sword and turned back to help Lilith, but saw Uriel on the ground, writhing and clutching at his thigh.

Lucifer behaved oddly. As the Cherubim came up to him, he raised his rod into the air, and it emitted a bright red flash.

From behind the lines, three great machines grunted as ropes were cut, and soon, deep within the ranks of the angels of the Lord, there were explosions of fire and cries of the wounded.

Asmodai, standing behind the lines next to one of the catapults, nodded his satisfaction. "Load them again," he said, "and this time stagger the firing. As you load, you others change the aim a bit."

Zaphkiel turned at the sound of the explosions. His eyes narrowed, and he traced the smoky lines in the air until he saw the three large objects behind the lines of the enemy. He nodded then and calmly directed the Thrones into a spear formation, and led them directly at the line of angels, toward the three machines.

Michael moved toward a side and began to clear it. His sword cut through the blades of his foes as if they weren't there, and one after another fell. Only rarely were they wounded; more often they would cry, fall, and then melt away to illiaster.

Staying close behind him, the Virtues cleaned up anything he missed. Soon the line began to waver, and angels began to break before him rather than face the golden sword whose touch was the final end.

The Thrones, unlike any other of the orders, had taken the time to practice with their weapons. The twenty of them swept through the line easily, and before anyone was aware of it they were back among the engines now regularly heaving gouts of destruction out into the lines.

Asmodai saw them and stepped forward to meet Zaphkiel, rope swinging in his left hand, sword raised in his right. The next in line among the Thrones leapt at the nearest machine—and cried out. Leviathan's head came crashing down on him. His chest crushed, he fell from the machine and dissipated.

The angels who tended the catapults continued frantically loading and firing them as Thrones smashed at them and fell to Leviathan.

Zaphkiel stepped back, made a quick judgment of Leviathan's speed and how many Thrones there were and how long it would take to disable the machines. "Work quickly," he said. Then he stepped back up to meet Asmodai.

"Good afternoon, Lord Satan. Your four-legged companion doesn't seem to be around."

"He's busy, Lord Michael."

"Ah! Then it's just the two of us."

"As much as it can be, in this mayhem. If you don't mind, let's get on with it. I have things to do here, and I'm sure you do also."

"All right, try this, then!"

"Not bad. I see you've learned to aim so that you won't hit the—eek—ground if you miss."

"You can't keep retreating forever, you know."

"I suppose not. Tell me, Michael, will your—eh—will your sword save you from my emerald?"

"Find out, if you dare!"

"I will, if you'll give me a moment to—uh—here we go, then. There. Ah. I see your sword helped a bit, anyway, or you wouldn't still be alive. I'll be going, now."

"I'll . . . get . . . you."

"No doubt, Michael, no doubt."

Zaphkiel realized immediately that he couldn't get past Asmodai's guard, for each time his blade crossed the path of the rope a burning sensation went up his arm and the blade lost a finger-joint's length of point. Therefore, he contented himself with keeping Asmodai busy and protecting himself.

When the catapults were destroyed, he pulled back and yelled for the others to do so. Their retreat was as fast as their advance, so the rebels had no time to stop them before they were safely away. Zaphkiel noticed with some satisfaction that there were still twelve Thrones left.

He looked around and saw where Yeshuah lay wounded with Gabriel fighting over his body. He directed the Thrones that way, stepping over the wounded as they went.

Camael's sword didn't have the characteristics of Michael's, but Camael did everything he could to make up for the lack. When he wasn't laying about him at everything in sight, he was screaming at the Powers to follow, to hack, to rend, to destroy.

With zeal and with the fire of belief, Camael led the angels against the strongest points he could find, which soon became the weakest.

His rage and his joy blended, he cried aloud as he led the angels in the wounding of the healthy and the killing of the wounded.

He saw Lucifer, who was dealing death to any who came near him, and charged, crying, "You're mine!"

Lucifer turned to him. "You're nuts," he said, and calmly destroyed him.

Nisroc was a loyal servant of the Lord, but he didn't let it blind him. He had closely watched each of the preceding battles and he had learned from them. It was for this reason that Zaphkiel had recommended him for Chief of the Order of Principalities.

Nisroc had responded by assigning subranks, each with a Chief, with the implication that they should do likewise as needed. And he had worked out careful plans for how he would communicate with these Chiefs during the battle, with the implication that they should do likewise as needed. It was for these reasons that the Principalities were efficient in battle.

"Nanael! Daniel!"

They approached him. "Yes, Lord?"

"Attack the center, near Yeshuah. Tell Vehuel and Cerviel to guard your flanks."

"Yes, Lord." They rushed off to order their divisions.

Presently, a messenger stood before him. "Lord, Daniel says that Lucifer has arrived and is creating much havoc."

Nisroc nodded. "Tell him to pull back to reserve."

"Yes, Lord."

Nisroc found another messenger nearby. "Have Vehuel move in to replace him." The messenger ran off.

Nisroc turned.

"Imamiah!"

Nothing happened. "Zuriel! Where is Imamiah?"

"I don't know, Lord."

"Very well. Take over for Vehuel's division, and guard his flank."

"Yes, Lord."

Nisroc continued watching. Soon, another messenger approached.

"Lord, Nanael says their lines are wavering."

Nisroc nodded. "Good. Press the attack."

Lilith was beginning to wear down. She broke off her battle with Gabriel, who was standing over Yeshuah, and backed up hoping to rest for a moment.

Suddenly, with no idea of how it had happened, she was cut off. Twelve of the enemy were before her. The foremost was Zaphkiel, who was studying her cagily.

"There is something about her spear," he told those around him. "Go slowly, and be sure."

She backed up. The Thrones followed her until, with a few quick movements, they were all around her. She turned in a slow circle. The Thrones began to close in.

Zaphkiel looked around, then, "Take your time," he directed. "There's no one near."

They slowly came toward her. She tasted sour vomit, and held her spear steady.

His eyesight was keen, but he didn't need it. He could feel the source of his fear and could have found it with his eyes closed.

But he didn't want to. He was flying toward it, but he would rather have been flying away. He knew, as well as he knew anything, that once it started it couldn't be escaped. As he came closer, the desire for flight grew, as did the need to attack the cacoastrum. But—what could he do?

Then he noticed something strange in the air. It looked greyish black, and the smell was—smoke!

Grateful for the excuse to come no closer to the source of

his fears, he went to investigate.

He flew in great circles over what he saw, trying to understand. He had seen something like it once, recently, but hadn't understood it then, either. He began inspecting details and quickly found someone he recognized—a new friend with a gentle voice and firm, warm hands.

He looked closer, trying to understand what was happening; he didn't want to make a mistake. He studied the matter closely and realized that, if he was right, he couldn't waste any time.

Glad for the chance to help a friend without coming any closer to *that,* he moved.

It was mesmerizing, in a way. They had circled closer and closer until now they were well within spear range, and she had done nothing to them.

She became aware of it and decided that she would attack and hope to get one or two of them, at least. Or, she decided, perhaps she would throw the spear at Zaphkiel.

No, she might miss, and then she'd have nothing for her trouble. She took a deep breath and—

The three of them directly in front of her vanished in a burst of flame from above. Her reflexes acted for her, and she dived forward, rolling, just missing a stroke from a Throne who was behind her.

She looked up and saw Belial turn for another sweep.

"Scatter," said Zaphkiel with complete coolness. "Reform forty paces to the right of Yeshuah." He turned and ran, the others doing the same, but none of them coming near her.

Belial landed carefully behind her. Lilith quickly looked around and saw the line beginning to bend under the assault led by Nisroc.

She approached Belial and climbed onto his neck. "Thank you, true friend; I can't say how grateful I am. But if you'd do more for me, take us up and I'll show you where to burn."

"Belial . . . help," was the reply, and they were airborne.

"I wanted to talk to you about Ariel. Do you have a few minutes?"

Abdiel didn't answer. He looked around, as if hoping to see some kind of weapon in the pit with him. Mephistopheles waited, then stepped forward and landed in the pit, his knees bending. Abdiel could see him working to hold himself together against the flux that issued from the weakened floor beneath their feet.

"If now isn't convenient," Mephistopheles continued, "I can wait. It isn't urgent. I've been waiting a long time anyway. I can wait more."

As he spoke, he moved closer to Abdiel, and his hands began to reach out for Abdiel's throat.

"Just let me know what a good time to talk is, Abdiel. We'll set up an appointment. We can—"

"It was an accident!"

"Yes, I know. You were going for Beelzebub, weren't you?"

"I only wanted to hurt him to make him chase me. I wasn't trying to kill him!"

"I understand that. That is why I'm not angry with you. Really. Trust me, Abdiel. As Yaweh and Gabriel trusted you. As the messenger to Michael trusted you. Trust me—"

"Please!"

The dark angel's hands found Abdiel's throat, and cut off anything else Abdiel had to say.

Abdiel, who always had a plan, always had a scheme, always knew how to do or say the thing that would make everything work for him, felt empty as the fingers closed.

Helplessness, frustration, and bitterness—and then a growing veil of blackness that came down from above as if to cover all traces of what he was. There was a final, searing burst of pain from his chest, and then the blackness was complete.

Mephistopheles watched as Abdiel's body dissolved. Then he climbed out of the pit, dusted himself off, and walked back toward the shore to see if matters were completed there, as well.

Harut opened his eyes.

"You're beautiful," he said. He looked at the blue above him, and at the ground beside him. He looked at his hands, and his arms, and—

"Raphael!"

"Yes? What is it?"

"Over there!"

"I don't—oh. Harut, I must—"

"I understand, Raphael. I'll stay here and look at things."

"Fare well, Harut."

"So long, Raphael."

Yaweh looked into the empty pit and felt the emanations from it. So *that* was what Abdiel had been doing! Yaweh decided that he had no quarrel with Mephistopheles for taking the execution on himself—Abdiel had had to be stopped.

He checked the damage carefully and decided that, bad as it was, it could wait until after the war was resolved. He concentrated briefly on the battle, and the scene unfolded itself before him.

Yeshuah, wounded, was being helped by Gabriel and a Seraph, both of whom were also wounded, as they backed away from the conflict. Michael, also wounded, was crawling as best he could. Nisroc was keeping control of the retreat, trying to make it orderly.

Lucifer stood stock still, dealing out death as casually as he had discoursed on light sources and plant growth. Satan was moving all across the lines, directing the advance and shouting encouragement.

Belial had cut off their retreat; whether by chance or design could not be determined. His burnings, however, had also blasted the sides of the other path, widening it, and the retreating hosts were taking that. That would bring them. . . .

He looked up and saw, with ordinary eyesight, angels begin to run toward him. He waited patiently. When they began to get close, he held his sceptre aloft and sent a thunderclap into the air.

The angels, who were now within a league, saw the lone figure, then saw the gold cloak on his shoulders. They began running toward him.

As they came, he motioned them to stand behind him, well clear of the pit, so he could watch the developing battle.

The last of them emerged, the healthy helping to bear the wounded. And behind them came another figure wearing the gold of the Firsborn. They took up lines a full league away near the mouth of what had been a path through a small gorge and was now a valley strewn with rubble.

Yaweh identified Satan, with Beelzebub next to him. Lucifer stood to the side. Overhead, Belial turned in great circles. The angels behind Satan stood tall and grim.

Yaweh looked behind him. Michael lay on the ground moaning. Yeshuah still clutched his side. Raphael was nowhere to be seen. The eyes of the angels reflected only fear, hopelessness, and exhaustion.

Yaweh swallowed hard. After all of this, he had lost. Completely. Finally.

What to do now? Go to him and surrender? It wouldn't be easy, but it would save lives. Could he lead a counterattack? No, too late. What else? Nothing.

After all the murder, destruction, and hatred, there wasn't going to be anything to show for it. The cacoastrum would still come past in Waves and take the lives of thousands of angels. Their safe, secure haven from the flux would be a place of war and death, from within and without. It would—

"No!" he shouted to the skies. *"I won't allow it to be! It will not happen that way! It will not!"*

Then he looked down into the pit and suddenly knew what he must do. He remembered telling them, ages ago, it seemed, that when he ended, Heaven would end. Now he would prove it. As he had started it, so, now that it was hopelessly marred, he would end it. With a feeling of sorrow, perhaps not unmingled with pride and a sense of ultimate triumph, Yaweh stepped forward into the pit to complete Abdiel's work.

"To the Palace, my friend," said Satan. "This time we take it."

"Verily, milord," said Beelzebub. "And with an whole mind, methinks."

Satan's brow furrowed. "You know," he said, glancing behind him at the thousands of angels who followed, "It isn't as if Yaweh was wrong."

"Milord?"

"In essence, he was right. If a leader can't lead, can't make decisions to protect the group he's leading, he isn't a leader. If only he'd—What's that?"

They stopped. Approaching them was an army—yet not an army of angels; an army of colors, of patternless shapes and shapeless patterns exploding from an epicenter before the lines of the opposing hosts.

"That, milord," quoth Beelzebub, "is a poor loser."

• • •

Once more she rode the winds. Lilith had long since forgotten the charging/retreating/winning/losing forms of the angels below her and existed with and upon the breezes, with and upon Belial.

The essence of sundering met the essence of unity, and transformation occurred, as it always does. The oneness of Belial/Lilith became the disjunction of a falling Lilith and a screaming, raging Belial.

The Fourth Wave, she thought in wonder, as the ground rushed up at her. It came much too fast, of course, for the hand of cacoastrum, the ultimate prestidigitator, is quicker even than the eye of the Firstborn.

Cacoastrum exploded around him, and for a brief moment, it was almost peaceful. Here was the old enemy again. Here was the enemy he could hate. It was right that it should claim him again—he had cheated it for a long, long time. Now let it—he realized that he was fighting it.

No, that wasn't what he wanted. He tried to make himself stop, but he couldn't. Yaweh had been created out of the flux with the need to fight it—and fight it he would—it went beyond desire or will.

He howled with rage. Above him, the archangels recognized what was occurring and prepared to defend themselves as they had before.

Yeshuah felt gentle hands upon him, and his strength returned. He opened his eyes, realizing that they'd been closed, and saw Raphael above him, looking worried and harried. "What happened, Raphael?"

"I don't know. It's like another Wave, only different—smaller. I don't understand it. It seems to be coming from that pit. When it started, it was hardly longer than your height."

"What about the battle?"

"You were losing. It's lucky for you the Wave started when it did; your army was in a panic."

"Was? What's happening now?"

"Everyone is dealing with the Wave, of course. There. You're fixed. I owed you that much for—never mind. I have to go now."

She did. Yeshuah got to his feet and looked around. He

suddenly understood why they called it a Wave. From in front of him there was a spreading of colors that were not of Heaven, and a jumble of shapes, a swirling filigree of conception that left nothing in its wake but itself.

He looked more closely and saw Yaweh standing somewhat back from the edge of flux the angels were struggling to contain. He saw Michael standing. And through the flux itself, he could make out more angels, fighting the flux—and, very faintly, he thought he could see a gold cloak.

He realised then that all of the angels on the west and south sides of the emanation were of Satan's army, and those on the east and north were of Yaweh's. Further, those who were not directly involved, as not all of the angels had room to confront the Wave, were divided similarly.

This, of course, was too good a chance to pass up.

Michael, somewhat healed by Raphael, came limping up to Yeshuah.

"Don't do it," he said.

"What?"

"You are about to have our host attack Satan while they fight the flux. Don't."

"Why not?"

"Two reasons. First, because you will be hated forever in Heaven if you do. Second, because I'll destroy you if you try."

Yeshuah smiled. "As to the second, you can't. You have no idea of the kind of power I have, created as I was. You couldn't do it, my father couldn't—"

"Lilith nearly did the job."

Yeshuah shrugged. "I have no intention of letting you get close enough to use physical means, which is the mistake I made then. As to the first point you raised, do you really think so?"

Michael looked surprised, for Yeshuah seemed actually to be considering it. "Yes, I do," he said. "They are working in defense of Heaven itself. If you use that opportunity to attack, you'll be despised wherever you go."

Yeshuah looked thoughtful. Then he nodded, as if to himself. "Come with me," he said. He walked past the waiting lines of angels and came out in front of them.

Then he began to lift his arms as if to signal an attack.

Michael made a growling noise and brought his sword sweeping down at Yeshuah—who, expecting it, stepped nimbly to the side.

The sword struck the ground.

Michael was hurled into the air by the explosion, back toward the line of angels. Yeshuah, however, had braced himself for the shock. When it came, he fixed all his concentration on the spot where the sword had struck. He took one last breath, and briefly wished that he had time for a fast look at Heaven. Then he threw himself at the eruption.

The cacoastrum flowing from the explosion seized him and began ripping into him. Before it could complete its work, however, Yeshuah had a moment—an unmeasurably small instant of time in which to work. Using all the skill he had taken from the minds of those who created him, he directed the cacoastrum where he wished it to go.

He had the fleeting sensation that it had worked; then the flux tore into him, and he was no more.

A great crack appeared in the floor of Heaven. The flux fed back along this weakness quicker than any angel could see it. In the drawing of a breath, the crack had spread in both directions across the floor on which the sea rested until it came to the far wall. There, halfway up, the cracks came together, and the cacoastrum found the weakness even as it appeared.

With a trembling that knocked every angel off his feet, a great, massive block of Heaven's floor and part of the distant western wall split off.

In the drawing of another breath, the flux had found it, open on five of six sides, and these had broken down into nothing.

Belial was beyond panic. His fear had transformed itself into rage, and the cacoastrum fell back wherever he found it. He sought out the flux and destroyed it, mindlessly, unaware of its source or its cause.

In his blindness, he felt that it was because of what he was doing that he was able to search it out, rather than be surrounded by it. He was, therefore, not very surprised when suddenly he *was* surrounded by it. Then he began to twist, turn, dive, and spin, merely to keep himself alive. He had no understanding of the significance of this, but he had no need to understand either.

• • •

It was almost more than he could stand. The death of Yeshuah had been to Yaweh as if a part of him had been forcibly ripped out. And now, seeing the huge hole in the wall of Heaven, it was as if another part of him had been taken. He felt his knees giving way, and his face struck the ground.

At that moment, he felt two pairs of hands on him. One pair was warm and gentle, the other hard and strong.

"Yaweh," said Raphael. "There is nothing you can do to help him, but there is much that can be done for Heaven, and you must do it."

"Leave me alone," he whispered.

"The Plan, Yaweh," said Michael. "You must do it, now, or his death—everything—will have been for nothing."

"Please," said Raphael. Her hands began to massage his shoulders. The star at her side glowed, and Yaweh felt a strange peace come over him. "Please," she repeated.

He got to his knees. With Michael's assistance, he rose to his feet then. He reached into his robes and drew out the papers on which the details of the Plan were inscribed.

He looked out at the angels of the Third Wave fighting and dying to hold back the Wave. He saw that there were still many who were doing nothing but waiting for others to fall, to take their turn.

He looked back at the papers, then at Michael, then at Raphael.

"All right," he said at last. "Michael, here is what you must do. . . ."

Leviathan was frustrated at being out of the battle, except for that small part near the beginning, but pleased that it was going so well. She craned her neck to get a better view and occasionally got glimpses of this or that portion.

When the influx began, she was aware of it at once. This was confirmed by the sight of Belial flying around and attacking it. She wondered why it was so well confined to the inside of Heaven.

"It won't stay that way," she decided. Therefore she, too, was unsurprised to find herself surrounded by the flux and fighting for her life once more.

• • •

Harut felt the effects more keenly than any angel save Belial. While he had been blind, the flux had given him perceptions that other angels lacked. Some of them remained.

He knew what had happened. As he sat on the safe side of the break, he waited for the Wave to find him. And as he waited, he saw what Michael and Yeshuah did. He became aware of the beginnings of the Plan, of the angels thrown out into the flux to create a safe area to work in and of those going out to begin the work.

Heaven, he realized, was shrinking. In order for the Plan to function, most of Heaven had to be given back to the cacoastrum from which it had sprung—there simply were not enough angels to defend it.

He sighed as he thought of the forests of Lucifer, and the shore by the sea where he had visited with Leviathan.

He noticed that the cliff on which he was sitting was soon to be abandoned by those who were defending against the Wave. He thought over the possibilities of retreating to safety and of staying behind. He thought over who was remaining in Heaven, and who had fallen from it.

Then he pitched himself forward into the chasm.

Asmodai saw Lilith fall to the ground near him as he, himself, fell. Then he saw the ground breaking apart around him. Quickly he engulfed both of them in a web of safety that would keep the flux out—for a little while.

Then, hoping it would be enough, he began to build walls. He discovered, to his surprise, that he was enjoying it.

Lucifer had been rallying angels against the flux when it hit, and he was thrown to the ground. Then the ground fell apart and he cried Lilith's name.

Once more he was battling the cacoastrum. He spun and fought, his wand flashing and cutting. He became aware of Asmodai, Belial, and Leviathan, and began helping them.

Three times they erected a wall with two sides, and three times it was torn apart before the third could be added. The fourth time it stayed.

The emerald around Satan's neck spat in all directions as he forced his way forward through the flux. He came at last upon a line of angels working to create a new wall to Heaven, and forced his way through.

Then he was upon the ground again. Behind was an abyss with cacoastrum howling and angels fighting against it. He looked around, but ignored those behind him.

He strode forward to where a group of angels were receiving instructions from Yaweh. As he came near, one of them saw him and moved to interpose himself.

"Who are you?" asked Satan.

"I'm called Kyriel."

"Then move, Kyriel. I'm here to destroy him who you think of as God. If you get in my way, I'll destroy you, too."

Kyriel shook his head. "My best friend has already been destroyed by serving you. You may as well take me, too."

By this time several of the others were moving forward. Satan noticed this and nodded.

"Very well, then," he said. There was a flash from his breast, and Kyriel was no more. Satan took another step and found his way blocked, this time by an angel with a massive golden-hued sword, who wore the gold cloak of the Firstborn.

"A rematch, Michael? All right."

But before he could act, something hit him from behind and he fell. He saw Michael's sword overhead, and then Michael fell back as a four-legged shape crashed into his chest. "Milord," called Beelzebub, "get thee behind me." Teeth flashed, and Michael cried out as his right arm was ravaged.

"Beelzebub!" cried Satan. "Get away!"

But Beelzebub was taken by Zaphkiel, who came from behind and pinned him. Beelzebub looked up at Michael, who was holding his arm and moaning.

"Thou dost see," he said, "that thy sword is not faster than my teeth."

Gabriel appeared, holding a sword over Beelzebub's breast. But he was stopped by a form in black that struck him from behind and sent him sprawling.

Mephistopheles, without stopping, picked up the fallen sword and held it at Michael's breast.

All was still then, for a moment. Mephistopheles coughed. "I'd really hate to have to hurt the poor fellow," he said.

Yaweh nodded. "Take them past the lines and cast them into the void. Let them fend for themselves." He spoke then to Mephistopheles. "Will that do?"

"Quite," said the other.

Satan and Beelzebub were raised up and brought to the brink of the line of angels.

Satan twisted around and looked at Yaweh. "I think you'll be hearing from me again," he said.

Yaweh nodded, but didn't speak.

They threw Satan over, and Beelzebub after him. Then Mephistopheles forced Michael to his feet and the two of them went to the brink together.

"If you plan to take me with you," said Michael in as strong a voice as he could manage, "I don't think you'll like the results."

"Don't worry about it," said Mephistopheles. "Wherever we're going, I wouldn't pollute the place with you."

He looked directly at Yaweh. "It's been swell," he remarked.

Then he threw Michael to the ground, saluted them with his blade, and leapt into the abyss.

Epilogue

Whom reason hath equalled, force hath
made supreme. . . .

—Milton, *Paradise Lost*, I:248

"We cannot stay here," says the one.

"You are correct," says another. "The walls we have built are flimsy things."

"Do you think we should try to regain Heaven?" asks a third.

The fourth one snorts, but makes no other answer.

"Well then," says the third, "what about this place they are building?"

"What about it?" asks the first.

"It will be filled with angels created during its building, will it not? Why couldn't we hide there?"

"This would work," says the second, "until we are discovered. But there are still more of them than there are of us.

They would destroy us."

"Let us think about it," says the third.

"They seem secure there, Lord Yaweh."

"Who?"

"Satan and his angels. They have built themselves a Heaven of their own."

"Oh. Does this bother you, Michael?"

"Some."

"Don't let it. We will be leaving here soon, anyway. Leave them to their Waves, their agonies."

"They won't be content, Yaweh. They'll want what we've built. I know it."

"If only Yeshuah were here. . . ."

"Yaweh . . . ?

"Yes?"

"Well . . . we could, I don't know if you're going to like this, but, well, we could create him again."

"I know."

"Well?"

"I couldn't take it, Michael. Seeing him again, I—I don't know. He wouldn't *really* be the same. Maybe someday."

In six days, the Earth was formed. And the stars, and the planets, and the peoples who dwelt on them.

Millions of angels were created during the building. Some were ruined, and took the form of lower beings. The others were the weakest yet among the angels, and few, if any, could control their illiaster.

Yet, in that world, there was little need for it.

"What is *that?*" said one.

"Beats me," said another.

Yet another said, "Runs pretty well."

"Yeah," another added. "There sure are lots of 'em."

"The angels who live there will be able to ride them, I think," the first remarked.

"No! Really?"

"Why not? They'd get around faster, that way."

The third one put in, "But they won't be able to live everywhere—just in a few places."

"Why is that?" asked the fourth.

"Because what they eat won't grow everywhere."

"For instance, where?" said the first, who was becoming fond of the things.

"Well, that place with all the sand and no water."

"I bet I could build something like it that would work there."

"How?"

"I'll make it able to eat things that grow there."

The third snorted. "Sure. But what about water? They need water too, idiot."

"And," the fourth put in, "their feet aren't really designed for running over sand anyway."

"Well," said the second, "why don't we work on it?"

For Satan, life was "if only."

He remembered deciding not to visit Yaweh. If only. And how Lucifer and Lilith and Asmodai and Michael had urged him to oppose the Plan openly, if he was going to oppose it. If only. And of the first battle, where he had refused to prepare the hosts for a fight. If only.

And so on, and on.

Well, he decided, that wouldn't happen again. He was probably going to be leader of the angels who had fallen from Heaven, whether he wanted to or not. This time he would *be* a leader, for good or for ill.

He looked at the newly formed globe and nodded. Yes, his people would be safe there. But, of course, they had been right: Yaweh would not allow them peaceful access to that place.

So, by that reasoning, why should Satan allow them peaceful access to it either? The new angels who lived there wouldn't know Satan from Yaweh. They would just as soon harbor one as the other. Yaweh, of course, would want them to reject Satan—why shouldn't Satan be equally polite?

He nodded to himself. Another war, that's what it would be. This time, the battlefield would be the minds of the weak, new angels.

Yaweh, of course, would lie, and his minions would scheme—Satan would rely on the truth. Yaweh would want to be worshiped. Satan would be content with being accepted.

He knew that, sooner or later, it would become a physical match once more, and they would line themselves up and settle things for good. It might not be soon, but it would happen.

He looked out at the blue-green battlefield and felt pity for the angels over whom they would fight. This time, however, he would not let that stop him. Yaweh had been a good teacher, Heaven a good school. Satan had learned.

Angels and mortals
Sometimes have to pay....

—Mark Henley,
"November Song"